BEYOND THE ROTTEN PLAINS

PLAINS

BY NICHOLAS PRUD'HOMME

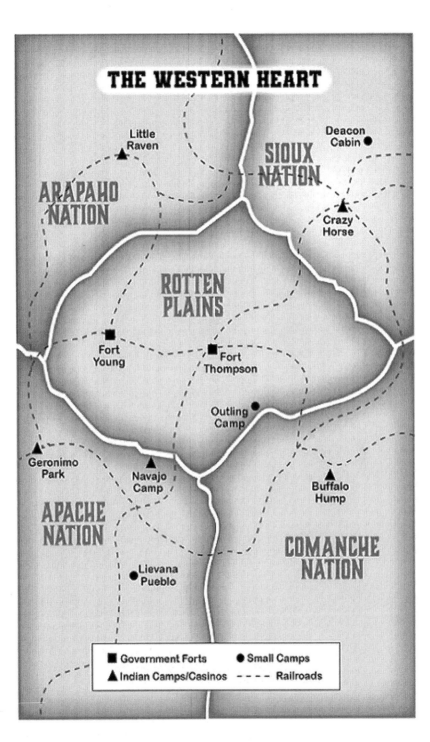

THE WESTERN HEART

The boy followed behind the Marshal as they strolled through the vacant hallway. They entered the room at the end of the hall and sat down at the large table in its center. The marshal unrolled a large map and flattened it out on the table. The boy adjusted his seat so he could get a better view.

"Now pay attention, boy," said the marshal, "I don't like to repeat myself."

The boy nodded and made sure not to miss a beat. "Where do we start, Bill?" he asked.

"The Western Heart," Bill started, "its split into five parts. The Comanche in the Southeast, the Sioux in the Northeast, the Arapaho in the Northwest, and the Apache in the Southwest."

"That's only four," the boy corrected.

The Marshal pointed at the center of the map. "And in the center is a land that's virtually uninhabited---The Rotten Plains."

"Why's it called that?"

"You see, Wyatt, The Western Heart wasn't always controlled by the Natives. It wasn't until the fall of the Government that the tribes were able to take back their land. The Rotten Plains used to be where the Government stored their weapons---weapons powerful enough to wipe out entire continents. Well, at one point they commissioned the local citizens to work on dismantling the weapons---believing they had reached a point where the arsenal was no longer necessary. But the citizens weren't trained properly, and the entire project went awry. The contents of the weapons were toxic, and they ended up poisoning the entirety of the land we now call the Rotten Plains. The plants and animals either died or mutated until they were unrecognizable, as did the people."

"What happened to them?" Wyatt asked.

"They changed. To this day they still roam the Plains. The Natives say they're cursed. I'd say it's a pretty accurate view," Bill explained.

Wyatt scratched his head as he examined the map. "You said the Government collapsed, but don't you work for them?"

"Well, when the Government fell they didn't go away completely. You see, the continent used to look quite different. The rising sea levels washed away the coasts by a good 30 to 50 miles on each side. The Government had tried to stop this from happening---they implemented strict environmental laws, but it couldn't be stopped."

"What kind of laws exactly?" Wyatt asked.

Bill chuckled. "They had so many of 'em it would take me a century to list them all. Most notably, they banned the use of all the certain energies they deemed harmful to the environment. You see, there used to be a multitude of different ways for people to travel---by land, sea, and even through the sky. When they did away with those fuels, the only way left for folks to move around was by train. One thing to know about the Government is that they were afraid."

"Afraid?"

"That's right, afraid that the people they controlled would one day revolt---which they eventually did. They tried everything they could to prevent it. They confiscated the people's books and guns, stuck them on the trains and kept them on the move so they wouldn't get back into the people's hands. Guns and knowledge, Wyatt, the two biggest enemies of anyone with power."

"Guns and knowledge," the boy repeated. He glanced at Bill with a look of confusion on his face. "So, what do the marshals have to do with the Government?"

"There's only a miniscule connection. When the Natives took over the Western Heart, the Government was desperate to keep any influence over the region. They brokered a deal, in exchange for protecting the tracks for the Natives, they would allow Government shipments to freely move through the Heart. The Natives agreed and so the Marshal Service was formed. We're a branch of the Government, but we really work for the Natives."

"So we protect the Natives?" Wyatt questioned.

Bill grabbed the boy's shoulder and looked deep into his eyes. "The world we live in is flawed, but it's beautiful. The only way to protect that beauty is by keeping order. That's what the marshals protect... order."

Chapter 1

THE THIRD CAR

Felina gazed into the mirror as she brushed her long black hair. There wasn't a blemish upon her youthful face, except for the tears that fell from her black eyes and glimmered off her beige cheeks. They were tears of blind optimism that shielded her sadness. It had been four years since she met the man that she loved. He promised her he would come back one day, but said that he didn't know when. She held onto that promise every day from the time she was just 14 years old, and each day she went on believing that he would return to her.

She heard footsteps approaching her room, then a heavy fist knocked against her door. The knocking was so hard that dirt spouted from the corners of the adobe room. "Come in!" Felina called.

Her father, Roberto, poked his head inside and smiled at Felina. His eyes filled with tears as he gazed at her. "Felina," he said, "You look just like your mother did when we first met. Such a beauty you are! I cannot believe my little girl is 18." He spoke with a faint Mexican accent, although he rarely used his mother tongue. He brushed her hair away from her forehead and kissed it. "Feliz cumpleaños, Mija."

"Thank you, Papa," she said. They hugged and she looked down the empty hall behind her father. "Papa… where is Juan?"

Roberto looked over his shoulder and scratched his

head. "He went out this morning. I assumed he would be back by now."

Juan sat and admired the desert horizon. He was a free-spirited young man at the ripe age of 16, he had onyx hair and eyes that matched his sister's, but skin that was far tanner and more aged by the desert sun. He had a strong nose, thick eyebrows, and an adolescent mustache sprouting on his full upper lip. The morning sun ignited the red dirt of the canyons and plateaus in the distance. This was his favorite spot, not only for the scenery, but for the trains that rode through. The winding terrain forced the locomotives to reduce their speed to traverse it, making it easy for him to hop aboard. The morning was young as the sun crept past the eastern horizon, and he hoped that soon a train would appear. He had become quite nifty at snagging supplies and goodies off the back cars, and today he hoped to grab something special for his sister, Felina---perhaps a bracelet or a brooch, something shiny and fit for a woman.

As he thought through all the possibilities, the ground began to shake. He saw a giant freighter zooming toward him as he looked down the tracks. He hopped out of the dirt and ran to a large rock formation he liked to hide behind. It was right by the first narrow turn in the tracks, and the perfect spot for him to wait for the train to pass. He made sure to cover his ears before the brakes started to screech. The first time he heard them, they were so loud he passed out and woke up with a crisp sunburn and chapped lips.

With his ears covered he watched the sparks fly from the small wheels rolling on the tracks. The engine raced past the rock and the cars followed one after the other. The trains typically had a hundred or so cars attached to them, they were about a mile long from front to back, sometimes longer. He counted down the cars as the caboose drew closer. When there were two cars to go, he took off from behind the rock and ran alongside the train. It moved slightly faster than Juan's jog, the perfect pace for him to leap onto the back railing as the last car passed. He felt the end of the train approaching so he started to sprint, and when the back railing caught his peripheral, he jumped.

Pulling himself onto the platform, he crept up to the back door. He took off his tattered shawl, using it to wipe off the window, then looked into the back car. No one was ever in the back, but he checked anyway just to be sure. The room was clear, he slicked back his sweaty black hair, draped his shawl back over his shoulders and entered the car. The doors made a tremendously irritating squeak when they opened, but the trains were so loud that no one would hear it besides Juan. There were boxes piled along the sides of the car, and bags hanging from the top racks. He went through the boxes but found nothing close to what he was looking for. He turned his gaze down the hall and stared at the door to the next car.

After all the time he had spent looting the Apache trains, he developed an in-depth system of do's and don'ts. His most important rule was to never go any further than the third car from the back. The back car was safe; no one was ever all the way back. The second car was mostly safe and worth investigating---the findings were usually far more precious. He had only ever gone into the third car once, and it was the only time he ever thought he would be caught. In the third car he could begin to hear voices and see Apache guards surveying the cargo. If there was one tribe Juan didn't want to be caught by, it was the Apache. He had heard stories of Apache guards scalping thieves, and Juan planned on keeping his scalp right where it was.

He walked into the second car and gently closed the squealing door. He started to rummage through one of the boxes, but became distracted when the train began to shake. The behemoth came to an abrupt stop that sent Juan and the boxes tumbling to the ground. Moments later the train began to move and Juan steadied himself back on his feet. He looked at the mess all around him and started kicking the contents out of his way.

After a few kicks something caught his eye, something shiny and white glimmering through the rubbish. He dug through the junk until he was able to grab a hold of it. He grasped it firmly and yanked it out of the pile. It was a revolver, a gorgeous revolver. He stared at it dumbfounded--- its spotless chrome barrel and refined ivory handle made it the most precious tool he had ever seen. Digging deeper into the pile he pulled out a thick leather belt with a holster attached. There were little loops around the outside with bullets slotted in them. It wasn't what he had in mind for Felina, but it certainly wasn't something he would pass up for himself. For years he searched the trains for a gun and never came across one, so he knew today must be his lucky day. And not only had he found a pistol, but he found the most beautiful pistol in the Southwest.

He fashioned the belt around his waist so the holster hung down by his right thigh. He loaded six bullets into the revolver and slotted it away. The added weight by his side gave Juan an extra boost of confidence. It was an important day for his sister, and he was determined to get her the gift she deserved. He looked toward the door to the third car and found the large slab of steel staring back at him. He moved his hand down the grip of the pistol and rubbed his tawny thumb over the pearly ivory. The next thing he knew that same tan hand was gripped around the handle of the third car's door. He peered through the small window, and saw a vanity table, much like the one Felina had in her room. It had a large lighted mirror and small wooden boxes on the tabletop. He couldn't see anyone else in the car, so he advanced.

He crept low through the doorway so his head could not be seen, then sat down in a small chair by the table and began opening the little boxes. One had little splotches of chalky paint and fluffy brushes. Another, little tubes of different colored sticks of paint. He had never seen boxes like these ones, but they were not what he was looking for. The last box was larger than the others, and it was made from a darker wood and had a glossy finish. Juan brushed the dust off the top and opened it. It was lined with a dark green velvet and contained the most beautiful jewelry he had ever found on any train. There were bracelets and necklaces and brooches and rings. He had just begun to rummage through to find the right piece when he heard a voice approaching the car.

He slipped behind a pile of boxes beside the vanity table. He wanted to grab any piece of jewelry from box, but decided he should stay put. The voice grew louder; as he heard the footsteps just outside the door, he wished to still be in the second car. Then he heard the wretched creaking of the rusty steel door. He peeked through the slit in the boxes and watched as a giant Apache guard marched into the room. Juan began to shake. He hid his head between his knees hoping to make himself as small as possible. But then he heard a voice that did not at all match the body of the guard, and he couldn't help but look again. Right as he raised his head, a body went crashing into the vanity table.

"Now get yourself cleaned up!" the guard shouted. "You need to look nice for work tonight."

As the guard left the room he slammed the door behind him. Juan pushed the boxes away and crawled over to the table. A young girl lay on the floor. Drops of blood ran from the corners of her mouth down to her chin. Juan pulled her up and sat her in the chair. Then with his shawl, he wiped the blood away from her mouth. She looked exhausted as she tried to open her eyes. Shaking his canteen, he heard some water still inside, so pressed it to her mouth and poured a little out---just enough to wet her lips.

The girl's tongue poked out and scooped up the droplets. He tapped her cheek until her eyes fully opened. He had never seen eyes quite like hers, bright blue like the sky on a hot desert day. He hadn't seen hair like hers before either. It was the same color as the red southwest plateaus. And her skin was as white as the snow on the distant mountains in winter. He felt the soft skin on her hands; she may have been even younger than him, 14 or 15 years old perhaps.

"Are you alri-"

As he asked, he heard the door creaking open once again. He turned, and saw the guard staring him in the eyes. The room was dark, but the guard's eyes lit up like a puma stalking its prey at night. He had reddish brown skin and a long black a ponytail that fell past his tailbone. He wore a tan leather vest with no shirt underneath, which exposed a giant scar that ran across the length of his chest.

Juan and the guard stared in silence for a few moments, neither of them moved or even breathed. The guard lifted his foot, but before he finished his step Juan sprung to his feet and bolted for the back of the train.

"Stop!" the guard yelled.

Juan pushed open the door to the second car and ran through. He could feel the guard breathing down his neck, so he slammed the door as hard as he could and hurried for the next car. The man was close so Juan didn't bother to look behind him. He knew as soon as he turned the man would already have a hold of him. He pushed open the door to the first car, and as he tried to slam it behind him the guard lowered his shoulder and crashed into the car. They both fell to the floor. As Juan tried to scramble to his feet the guard grabbed him by the boot, and pulled him back down. Juan tried to jerk his leg free from the man's grasp. He kicked him in the top of the head, digging the heel of his boot into the guard's scalp. The guard's grip loosened. Juan pushed himself back up then sprinted to the last door.

He didn't bother closing the final door. He planned on jumping right off the back of the train, but when he made it outside he realized they were well past the winding tracks. The train had already resumed its normal speed; if he were to jump now his legs would surely shatter---assuming he would even survive. His hesitation got the better of him. He felt the guard's giant hand clamp onto his slim arm. The guard turned Juan around and punched him in the stomach.

"Where do you think you're going, thief?"

Juan grabbed him by his vest. He threw a punch as hard as he could right into his jaw, but the guard didn't budge. The guard grabbed Juan's face, and squeezed it with such force he felt like his teeth would be uprooted.

"You must be the one who's been stealing from us!" said the guard.

Juan tried to answer, but his mouth was being pinched so tightly he couldn't even wiggle his tongue. He braced himself against the rusty railing behind him---in case the guard tried to toss him off the train. Then he felt the ivory handle of the pistol digging into the back of his hand. Juan let go of the railing, and gripped the revolver. He drew it from its holster and stuck the barrel into the guard's gut. Then he pulled the trigger. The sound was deafening. Juan heard echoing bang rattle around in his skull. The guard released Juan's face and felt the hole where the bullet had entered. He pulled his hand away from his belly and found his palm covered in blood much redder than his skin. He lunged at Juan once again, but before he could grab him Juan swung the pistol and struck the man in the face. The strike was not enough to stop the guard's momentum. He fell forward and grabbed onto Juan, and the two went tumbling off the back of the speeding train.

The freighter rattled on toward the horizon, while Juan and the guard lay still on the tracks. As time passed the hot sun scorched the back of Juan's neck. Bullets of sweat poured down his face and slipped into his mouth. The bitter saline moisture on his tongue helped him regain his consciousness, and his eyes flickered open. He wiped his shawl across his face, replacing the sweat with the dirt and blood that covered his clothes. He tried pushing himself to his feet, but as his hands pressed down he felt that he was not on the ground. He looked down and realized he was lying on top of the Apache guard, who himself was lying on top of the tracks. Juan brushed himself off and stared at the man who broke his fall.

Blood leaked out of the guard's ears and from the bullet hole in his gut. His head had struck the metal railing of the tracks when they fell, leaving a deep indent in the back of his skull. As he inspected the body, Juan noticed the man's fancy necklace. He opened his vest to get a better look at the pendant. It was a flat golden oval with a turquoise stone in the middle carved into the shape of an ancient Apache warrior. He had seen the symbol before; when the tribal leaders would come around their home---usually to take any livestock or crops he and his father had managed to produce. He had seen a pendant like this one before; it belonged to the sons of Chief Lipan.

Juan dropped the pendant and started scanning the area. He wasn't quite sure where he was, the train had traveled far beyond familiar territory. And he didn't know how long he had been passed out---there could be Apache scouts on their way for him right now. Killing a lowly guard was one thing, but killing one of the chief's sons was a far more extreme matter. He took a deep breath, got a sense of where he was, then headed back toward his home.

Roberto sat in his old, weathered rocking chair and played a soothing Hispanic tune on his guitar. On the other end of the porch Felina sat watching the wind blow the red sand through the air. She wore an airy white dress; its shoulders large and round with layers of fabric that had red trim on the edges. As the breeze blew through the porch it lifted the bottom of her dress up and exposed her bare feet, and the grains of sand hopping over each of her toes.

"Felina, do not worry about your hermano. Juan will be home soon. You know how he can be late," Roberto said as he continued to pluck at the strings of the old out-of-tune guitar.

"It's not that, Papa," Felina said.

"Perhaps you worry for the other man? The one you have been waiting on since that day?"

Felina looked at her father. His eyes were closed as he spoke and played his tune, and a faint smile flickered beneath his thick mustache. "You think I am crazy don't you, Papa?" Felina said. Roberto didn't answer, he just continued to play and bob his head with the melody. "He will come back... he promised me he would!" Felina snapped.

"Of course, Mija... but I wouldn't get anxious if I were you. Take it from your hermano, sometimes men are late." He played a few more notes then smacked his hand against the instrument's wooden frame with a loud *thump!* He opened his eyes and smiled at Felina. "But I am sure he will find his way back."

It was not his response, but his infantile gaze that managed to bring the slightest grin to Felina's face. Roberto stood out of his rocking chair and reached his hand out to Felina.

"Come, Mija. Let me play for you and show me how you dance!" Roberto said, "It is your birthday, a day that calls for dancing!"

Felina let out a chuckle and grabbed his hand. She walked with him into the small dirt patch in front of their house. He readied his guitar and began to strum it rapidly. Felina threw her hands in the air and spun around in the dirt. As she twirled, her dress flared out to the sides, resembling the small dirt cyclones that twisted around outside of their house. Roberto couldn't help but to move along with her. He left long trails in the red dirt as he took great big steps around Felina and dragged his foot behind him. She continued to spin, and she watched as the horizon whirled around her. She could feel the world moving round and round, and each time she spun she saw a spot on the horizon. As she continued to spin the spot grew larger and larger, until it became so large that she stopped spinning. Roberto continued to play his guitar and dance and sing. He was so enthusiastic that he didn't notice Felina had stopped dancing. She was dizzy and tried to catch her balance, but she could tell that the spot in the distance had split into two, and that they were getting closer.

Perhaps it's Juan returning from his morning run on the trains, she thought, or perhaps it was him, the man she had been waiting for since that day. Better yet, perhaps it was the both of them, coming to wish her happy birthday together. Tears fell from her eyes once again, but this time they were tears of joy. She ran in the direction of the two approaching figures and she called out to Roberto, "Look, Papa!"

Roberto heard her call and stopped playing. He tried to see who was coming, but the wind had picked up and his usually poor vision was further impaired by a large cloud of dust. "Felina!" he shouted, "Felina, who is it?"

She continued running, and another massive gust blew through. It stirred up a great wall of dust that washed out the two figures from her sight. She squinted to try and see where they had gone but couldn't see a thing. She knew they were close, and could hear them getting closer. She heard the *clip-clopping* hurrying toward her. Whoever approached was on horseback, and this concerned her. They had no horses at the house so she knew one of them was not Juan. And the man she was waiting for only had one horse.

"Felina!" Roberto shouted. "Come back to the house, Mija!"

Frantically, she looked around to figure out which direction she came from. She tried to follow her father's voice, but the sound of hooves grew louder, and she could feel their strides shaking the ground beneath her. She still heard her father calling her, but it was not the only voice now. Along with the drumming strides of the horses she heard two high-pitched screams. They sounded like the howling wild dogs, but these screams were much louder and far more terrifying.

"Papa!" Felina cried. The screams grew louder. Their feverish pitch made her tremble. "Papa, where are you?" Then a hand grabbed her from within the cloud of dust and pulled her up onto the horse.

The man wrapped a rag around Felina's mouth to stop her from screaming. They rode up to the house; the second man jumped off his horse while it was still running and tackled Roberto. Felina watched her father struggle, and she too struggled to get free. The man got off the horse and tied Felina's hands together with a piece of rope. He said, "Stay quiet and don't move."

They were Apache. She could tell from their umber skin and long black hair. Apache men had faces that were sharp and muscular, with defined cheeks and tight jaw lines. They did not look as friendly as her father or brother, who had softer features and rounder faces.

The scout who tackled Roberto held a knife to his neck. The blade dug into his skin but did not quite pierce it. "There is a boy who lives here, where is he?" the scout asked.

"I don't know!" Roberto said as he tried moving his neck away from the knife.

"He is your son, is he not?"

"Si! Si!"

The first scout knelt beside Roberto and grabbed him by the cheeks. He said, "One of Lipan's sons was shot and tossed off the back of a train today. The girl who witnessed it said it was a Mexican boy who killed him. The body was found only a few miles from here."

Tears began rolling down Roberto's cheeks. "No, no, no, it can't be," he cried.

The scout tightened his grip around Roberto's face and continued, "Your son is going to have the whole Apache nation after him now, old man." He looked back at Felina, and an evil grin ran across his face. "Lucky for you, you have quite the pretty daughter, so we will just take her instead of killing you. This way when your boy comes home you can make the search a bit easier for us."

Both scouts nodded their heads, then pushed Roberto to the ground and walked back to their horses. Felina tried to scream but all that she could manage was a pathetic muffled cry. Roberto pushed himself off the ground as the two men mounted their horses.

"No!" He shouted, "You stop right there! I would rather die than see you take away my Felina!"

The scouts laughed. The one who had tackled Roberto jumped back off his horse. "You would rather die?" the scout asked. He drew a pistol out of the back of his belt and fired two shots. One burrowed into Roberto's chest and the other into his belly.

Roberto fell to the ground and tried to crawl back to the porch. The scout jumped back onto his horse and the two burst out in laughter. As they rode off Felina looked back at her father. She hollered and cried as loud as she could, but she could hardly make a sound. There was no way to undo what had happened. The horses galloped through the red dirt, kicking it up into the air, and soon her father disappeared behind the thick cloud of dust.

Hours had passed since Juan fled from the tracks. The dusty winds made it hard to know how close he was to home, but from the amount of time that had passed he knew he must be close. The sun had just passed noon, and the day was getting hotter. He wrapped his shawl around his face as the dust began to thicken. Between swirling sands and scorching heat, Juan could hardly breathe. As he trudged closer to home he heard the faint sounds of voices creeping through the wailing winds. Although they were muffled, he recognized one of the voices as his father's. Increasing his pace from a walk to a run, he followed the echoes. He desperately wished to see his family, especially now knowing they were close. His father's voice grew louder, but still Juan could not make out what he was saying. Suddenly his father's voice was replaced by the booming sound of two gunshots. He was close---only a stone's throw away, but the dust was blinding. He heard a pair of men laughing, followed by horses riding off into the distance. Juan sprinted through the impregnable wall of dust until he saw the outline of his house.

"Papa!" Juan yelled, following the trail of blood that led to his father's body. He slid through the dirt and carefully felt around Roberto's torso to find where he had been shot. The wound in his gut was bleeding badly, and the shot in his chest appeared to just miss his heart. The boy pulled off his shawl and tied it around his father's stomach. He lifted Roberto off the ground and carried him inside. Juan was a slim young man but he was strong, and Roberto was even smaller, so carrying him in was no issue.

Juan placed Roberto on the bed, then ran out back to fetch a pail of water. He stuck his canteen into the pail and filled it up. As he poured some water on his father's face he made sure some spilled into his mouth. Roberto's eyes fluttered open, and he took deep breaths as he started to come to. He looked at Juan and grabbed his hand.

"Juanito," he said, "what have you gotten yourself into?"

"What has happened?" Juan asked nervously.

"Felina, they took Felina. They said that you killed the chief's son. That they are going to come after you, that all the Apache will be looking for you, Mijo," Roberto said, coughing after each phrase. Blood rushed out of his wounds with every hack.

"I need to clean your wounds, Papa." Juan said. He ran into Felina's room and grabbed the sewing case their mother left to her. From the kitchen he grabbed a cloth and a bottle of tequila. He set down the supplies and pulled a small knife out of his belt, cut through his father's shirt, and peeled it off him.

He tried to be gentle, but the sultry blood adhered the shirt to his wounds. He dipped the cloth into the water and wiped the blood from the cavity in his chest. Rolling him over on his side, Juan checked Roberto's back. The bullet had gone straight through, leaving an even larger hole out the other end. Juan picked out a needle and dipped it in the tequila to sterilize it. He pressed the bottle to Roberto's lips and watched the liquor spill into his mouth.

"Drink up, Papa. It will help," Juan assured him.

Roberto took a few large gulps then immediately coughed them back up. Juan moved the bottle away from his father's lips and poured the tequila onto his open wound. Roberto winced in pain, but he didn't scream or cry. The pain he felt from the liquor boiling his skin was nothing compared to watching Felina be taken away.

Juan stitched up the chest wound as well as he could, but Roberto's stomach was far more worrisome. Even with his shawl tightly tied around his belly, blood continued to seep out, staining the garment a deep scarlet red. Juan started to untie the shawl---hoping to get a better look, but Roberto stopped him.

He grabbed a hold of Juan; his hand was cold and trembling. "It is no use, Mijo," said Roberto. "Not even a Navajo shaman could save me now. You must leave. They will be back looking for you soon, and you cannot be anywhere near when they return. Go! Leave the Apache land and be safe."

Tears fell from Juan's eyes, forming little puddles on his father's hand. "Papa," Juan cried, "this is all my fault."

"What's done is done, Juanito. What's important is that you get out of danger for now. But por favor, promise me you won't let those people take Felina. Promise me you will get her back, Mijo."

"Si, Papa, I promise." The tears flowing down Juan's face carved a clean path through his dirty cheeks. As he rose to his feet, Roberto's grip tightened.

"Juanito," he said.

"Si?"

"The men that took Felina were Apache scouts. Surely Geronimo Park is where they're taking her. Lady Kai, of the Navajo, she can help get you to safety. Find her, Mijo."

Juan nodded and squeezed his father's hand. He went into his room, packed a small bag of supplies then returned to his father's bedside. He kissed his cheek, and Roberto rolled onto his side to face his son. His brittle fingers pinched Juan's cheeks as he caressed his face.

"I love you, Mijo," Roberto said. His dry fingers were moistened by Juan's tears pouring from his eyes. Juan sat by his father's side for a few minutes more, letting his hands rest upon his cheeks. As the life left his father's body, his touch still felt as warm and loving as it always had.

Chapter 2

GIN

Marshal Wyatt Cole was not an old man by any means, but his face was weathered. Beneath his dirty blonde scruff of a beard was suntanned skin resembling aged leather. His lips were thin and constantly chapped. The marshal business was cruel, and it afforded no downtime, so the young man of only 26 appeared closer to 40. He wore a tattered brown suede hat and a matching brown poncho that fell to his knees. The marshal was a tall, muscular man and his horse was fitting for him to ride. Peaches was a pale mare, a giant bald horse the size of an Alaskan moose. She was strong, with muscles that were large and deeply defined. They looked ready to burst right through her light pink skin. They said he found her abandoned within the Rotten Plains and raised her until she was strong enough to ride. He covered her body in a thick blanket so her skin would not be burned by the sun. He spoke to her constantly so she knew where to go---she was born with a thick film covering her eyes that rendered her blind.

He was riding south from the Little Raven Camp, in the Arapaho nation, after his meeting with their chief, Cheyanne. As a marshal his duty was to patrol the tracks within the Western Heart, and to keep order amongst the various native tribes. That was rather easy in the Arapaho lands, they were a peaceful people. They honored the ways of their ancestors, living off the land and valuing all her fruits.

Other areas were not as easy, however. The Apache, for example, were violent. They ruled their lands with an iron fist, oppressive over the smaller tribes, and combative to those not of the same blood.

Wyatt was raised in the Apache lands, which left him with a certain sense of loyalty to the region, but even so he didn't care to spend much time there. It had been nearly three years since he had been summoned to Geronimo Park, the headquarters of the Apache tribe, and the largest casino west of the Rotten Plains. During his stay at Little Raven, Wyatt received word that his presence was needed at Geronimo Park as soon as possible. Although there was a train depot just outside of Little Raven, Wyatt thought it best to ride Peaches the first half of the trip. The train ride would take three or four days, and he didn't want Peaches to be crammed up in an empty car for that long. The message seemed urgent, but Geronimo Park wasn't the kind of place he felt rushed to visit. He decided to ride with Peaches to the Government depot just north of the Apache border, then pick up a train the rest of the way down.

It had been four days since his departure from Little Raven when the Government depot crept into sight on the horizon. While the tracks were still technically run by the Government, only about one in four depots were staffed with Government clerks. The Natives operated the remaining depots at their own discretion. Wyatt preferred to stick to the Government depots most of the time. The Government clerks relayed messages to the marshals, updating them on tribal affairs or outlaw activity. The native clerks, however, couldn't read or write, let alone translate Morse, so no messages were ever transferred.

When Wyatt finally reached the depot, he tied Peaches to a large post near a row of benches, then headed over to the small depot building. All the depots looked identical, small metal cubes with dark tinted windows that masked whoever was inside. From what Wyatt could tell, all the clerks looked as identical as their depots. It made him wonder if they were all the same person. The black glass masked any details of their faces; for all he knew they could be faceless men, or maybe machines. He didn't know where they came from, but he was sure they didn't originate in the Western Heart. If that were the case they wouldn't be able to read or write or translate Morse. Only Government workers, like marshals and clerks, were taught how to read and write. Wyatt learned from the marshal before him, Bill Fuller. Bill told him that the Government's headquarters was somewhere far east, on the New Coast, that the clerks were sent from there. It must be a terrible way to live, Wyatt thought, trapped in a metal box waiting for a message to pass off to some stranger.

He walked up to the middle window. The glass opened, and a ghostly white hand crept out with a piece of paper. A faint voice murmured, "Message for you, Marshal." He laid down the piece of paper then shut the window. Wyatt gave the note a quick glance then folded it back up. He fiddled with the piece of paper as he walked back to Peaches. He was about to open it up to give it another read, but stopped when the train whistle rang out in the distance. Untying Peaches and stroking her smooth pale skin, he watched the train approach. He walked the mare alongside the behemoth machine as it slowly glided past. Glancing into each of the cars, he searched for one suitable for Peaches. There was usually an empty car, with pails of water and stacks of hay, reserved for horses. They could hold five or six horses at a time, but Wyatt couldn't remember the last time he opened one that wasn't vacant. He found the car and slid open the large steel door, then pulled a ramp out from the floor. A normal horse would have to be led up the ramp into the pitch-black room, but because Peaches was blind it didn't make a difference to her. She walked right up the ramp and lay down in the darkness. He blew her a soft kiss then slid the door shut.

Once Wyatt boarded the train he saw a Native boy standing inside the car, as if he had been waiting for the marshal to enter. He was thin and his body was trembling. Wyatt pulled a lever and closed the door behind him.

"Everything alright, boy?" Wyatt asked.

"There is a man on the back of the train... he's got a gun," the boy said.

The train began to shake then started forward down the tracks. Wyatt looked down the hall, over the boy's shoulder. "Has he threatened anyone, hurt anybody?" Wyatt asked.

"No sir," said the boy, "He's just playing with his gun and talking to himself. My grandma is worried, and no one even saw him board the train. He's a pale-face like you."

Wyatt tugged on his belt and pulled up his slacks, "I'll have a word with him. Why don't you take your Grandma and go find another place to sit."

"Thank you, Marshal."

He walked through the cars down to the far end of the train where the boy directed him. Other than a few elderly Natives and the boy, the train was practically empty. He passed car after car without noticing anything unusual, until he arrived at the final car door. He peered through the window and saw a man sitting at one of the booths all alone. A pistol lay in front of him on the table. He stuck his finger in the trigger loop then spun the gun around it and watched it whirl. He had a white cloth wrapped around his head. It looped under his jaw and was tied into a neat knot at the top of his skull. It was tied so tightly that it pinned his mouth shut, making him resemble a bulldog with his bottom lip pushed up just beneath his nose. He was mumbling to himself just as the boy described. Wyatt couldn't hear him from the other side of the door, and he couldn't read his lips either, not with only his bottom lip squirming around like a worm on a hook.

Wyatt entered the empty car and walked over to the booth. Standing by the table, towering over the bizarre stranger, he pushed his poncho aside and exposed the silver star pinned to his pocket. "This seat is taken, friend?" Wyatt asked.

"Kept it open just for you," the man murmured almost inaudibly.

The man reached for his gun, but as Wyatt slid into the booth he grabbed his hand and stopped him from holstering it. "Let's keep that right where it is," Wyatt said. He slipped the gun out from under the man's hand and slid it to the far end of the table. Wyatt took a good few moments to examine the stranger. He looked fragile, with bony hands and sunken cheeks. His hair was greasy and unkempt, and his porous skin was clogged with dirt. Wyatt pointed at the bow tied to the top of his head. "What happened there?" he asked. "You take a tumble?"

The man giggled and slapped his hands against the table. "It was quite the tumble, Marshal! Let me tell ya'!" Reaching into his vest pocket, he pulled out a deck of cards and tossed them on the table. "Do ya' fancy yourself a gambling man?"

"Can't say I do. Card games have never really been a strength of mine," Wyatt said.

"Oh c'mon, Marshal, no self-respecting man should ever turn down a game of cards. I know every game, name any of your liking and that's what we can play." He pulled the cards out of their pack and shuffled them on the table.

"Well, I don't play games with strangers," Wyatt said.

A wicked smile slithered across the man's face. He bridged the cards and they fell into a neat stack that he pushed in front of Wyatt. "Well, how about this," he started, "you pull the top card from that deck and if I guess it right then I'll tell ya' my name. That way we won't be strangers. Then we can play a game or two... deal?"

The stranger's presence would certainly be disturbing to most, but to Wyatt it was almost amusing. He pulled the top card off the deck and before he could flip it over the man shouted, "Queen of Hearts!"

Wyatt flipped the card over in his fingers, he smiled and let out a laugh. "How'd you know that? Are you just lucky or something?"

The man leaned forward and winked. "Sometimes you gotta make your own luck... I slipped the card on top right after I shuffled them." He leaned back and giggled once again. His hands slapped the table, and his feet kicked against the floorboards. "Now, I owe you my name," he stuck his hand out, "Chance Havoc! Pleased to meet ya', Marshal!"

Wyatt grabbed his hand and gave it a firm shake, "Wyatt Cole," he said. "It seems like I owe you a game of cards then."

"What's your game of choice, Marshal?"

Wyatt pondered for a moment. He hadn't played a game of cards in ages. "I used to play gin with my old man, guess that will do."

"And what are we gambling for?" Chance asked.

"These days words are a scarce currency. Loser has to answer whatever the winner asks."

Chance took the deck and shuffled it once again, "I like the way you think, Marshal. Ya' got yourself a deal."

Wyatt snatched the cards out of Chance's hands and

shuffled them himself. He didn't plan on getting tricked again. He dealt ten cards to each of them, then flipped the top card of the deck over and placed it to the side. "You can start," Wyatt said.

"Let's see what we can do," Chance chuckled. He took the face up card and replaced it with one in his hand. "Gin!" he exclaimed, then laid down his hand for Wyatt to see.

Wyatt stared at the man's cards in disbelief. There's no way he could have won on the first turn, he thought to himself. But sure enough, he saw two three of a kind and a run of four. "No shit," he said.

"What made you become a marshal?" Chance asked. His once cheery tone had now slowed and gained a sense of seriousness.

Wyatt handed Chance the deck to shuffle. "When I was just a boy, a marshal saved my life, and he taught me a thing or two about the world as well. He felt that even though our world was gilded in dirt and grime, there was still a beauty at the center of it." Chance dealt out the cards, and the two of them began discarding from their hands into the middle pile, and drawing from the deck. "He showed me what that beauty looked like and the more time I spent with him the easier it was for me to see. The only way to let that beauty flourish is through order... That's what Bill believed and that's what I believe. That's why I became a marshal." Wyatt drew another card then threw one out of his hand. "Gin," he said, and laid down the cards in front of him.

"Well now," Chance said, "it looks like I'm not the only one with luck on his side."

Wyatt neatly piled together his cards and handed them to Chance. "What do you have that cloth tied around your head for? I'm guessing it isn't meant to be a fashion statement."

"No, it certainly ain't meant to be fashionable,"

Chance said as he shuffled. He bridged and cut the deck several times before he dealt. "This cloth is here for one simple reason, Marshal... Love."

"You're in love with a dirty old handkerchief?"

"You don't expect me to believe you're that empty inside, do ya' Marshal? Say it ain't so."

Wyatt chuckled, "It ain't."

"No, I am not in love with the cloth, but I've got to wear it *because* of love."

Wyatt didn't care for riddles. He preferred straightforward conversation, and what little fondness he had for Chance was quickly fading with every word he muttered. It was hard enough to make out the actual words he was saying, let alone try to put any meaning to them.

"Pardon me, Chance. But I have never been the smartest man in the room. You're going to have to elaborate for me."

"If you insist," Chance said as he began dealing out the next hands. "I've had a rather interesting life, ya' see. Luck has always been the one thing I've had on my side, but each coin has two sides. And the opposite side of that coin for me, is love. I ain't never felt the love of another, Marshal, not even from my own mama. She even tried to rake me out of the womb with an old stick before I could take my first breath. If I were to guess, I'd say the only thing that ever did love me was the ol' Grim Reaper himself. But my luck is the Reaper's oldest foe---he's tried to embrace me twice now and I've managed to slip through his cold grasp... virtually unscathed." Chance lifted his chin and adjusted the cloth. He exchanged a couple cards and switched them around in his hands. "Gin," he said. "Do you still see that 'beauty' in this world, Marshal?"

Wyatt drew a card, it was the Queen of Hearts, he

stuck it in between the Jack and King of Hearts he already held, then threw out the excess cards. "I still see it," he said while looking into the painted eyes of the queen of hearts, "even if it's hardly there, I can see it. As far as I'm concerned, the only way to keep it visible is to deal with the folks in this world that refuse to see it."

"Ain't nothing beautiful about this world, Marshal. This world that chews on your insides, and lets you rot in the heat rather than just getting it over with. It's a place where you can be hanged by the neck just for not loving the right person or even just for being the wrong kind of person. Do you know what it feels like to be hanged by the neck, Marshal?" Chance had stopped playing his hand. His cards were face down on the table in front of him and his once jolly nature had fully disappeared.

Wyatt drew once more, then slapped down his cards, "Gin," he said. Reaching into his pocket he pulled out the message he got from the depot. He opened it up and started scanning through it.

"Whatcha' got there, Marshal?" Chance growled.

Wyatt continued to read. When finished, he placed the piece of paper down on top of his cards. "Did you ever learn to read, Chance?"

"Course not. Only government types able to figure that stuff out."

"Well how would you like me to give you a reading lesson? I have here a message that came from the Sioux Nation, that's northeast of here," Wyatt said. "Now I'm not supposed to talk about Government messages, but I don't think anyone would care about one little time." His tone was sharpening. Just as Chance's persona had morphed, so too did Wyatt's.

"What do I care about what some featherhead has to

say?"

"Oh, come on now! I think you'll like this," Wyatt insisted.

"I don-"

"It says,

'Marshal, a violent killer has escaped out of Sioux land and was last seen heading west. He is responsible for the death of two Sioux girls. He was sentenced by Chief Nakota to be hanged by the neck until dead. When hanged the noose snapped and he managed to flee. Description: pale-face with broken jaw.'

...now isn't that quite the story?"

Wyatt stared at Chance with empty eyes. Chance, on the other hand, started to laugh uncontrollably. "Oh, Marshal, you ain't as dumb as you let on to be, are ya'?" He reached up to the bow on top of his head and tugged on one of the loops. As the cloth fell onto the table, his bottom lip dropped as his jaw gaped open lifelessly. He tried to laugh but all that came out was a low gurgle as his tongue flailed around his open mouth. Then he reached for his pistol at the edge table. He managed to grab it but before he could pull the trigger, Wyatt threw a heavy punch smashing into Chance's lower jaw. Chance fell out of the booth and rolled across the floor.

Wyatt exited the booth with a calculated tranquility. He swatted his poncho out of the way, and it floated by his side like a hawk gliding through the desert sky. Then drawing his pistol with deadly grace, he marched behind Chance, who was crawling toward the back of the train like a scared varmint.

Chance pushed open the exit door and braced himself against the back railing. Then he turned and fired a wayward shot that narrowly missed the Marshal. Wyatt pointed his pistol at Chance's chest and pulled back on the trigger, but before the hammer struck the bullet, the train took a sharp turn and threw Wyatt off balance. The bang from the gunshot echoed through the train, and the bullet whizzed past Chance's head. Between the shot and the sharp turn, Chance too lost his balance, and fell over the railing off the back of the train. Wyatt watched Chance's body disappear into the distance as the train sped on down the tracks.

"Damn it," he said. He holstered his gun and retreated inside the train.

The lofty gates of Geronimo Park were made of thick sturdy birch. Behind them was the largest bustling casino in the Southwest. It was home to the Apache but welcomed all the degenerate souls who roamed across the deserts. As Peaches trotted toward the gates with Wyatt on her back, they approached two guards veiled in the shadow of the young morning sun. Wyatt pulled back on Peaches' reins and hopped off the horse. His boots dug into the red dirt below, lifting a cloud of dust into the air around them. The two guards stood silently with their arms crossed, a stern look of discontent painted across their faces. Wyatt looked back and forth at the pair, wondering why the gates had not yet been opened for him. He pulled his poncho to the side and revealed the silver star clipped to his pant pocket. The guards took a step back; one turned around and waved his hand while the other ran up and grabbed Peaches' reins.

"Marshal!" the guard exclaimed, "Apologies for not recognizing you!"

"I thought Peaches here was enough of a giveaway,"

Wyatt said as he patted the horse's pale rear. The guard walked Peaches over to the stables and Wyatt headed toward the casino's front doors.

Chief Lipan's office was at the far end of the main floor. Although the casinos were not the Marshal's taste for entertainment, he couldn't help but to be quite impressed by the number of lights inside. The only places that had electricity were the trains and, somehow, the casinos. Loud noises reverberated from every inch of the room as he made his way to the Chief's office; bells jingled, alarms dinged, and people hooted and hollered. Mainly Natives roamed the casino floors, but occasionally one could find a Mexican or a pale-face playing a game of cards. If they weren't Native there was a good chance they were an outlaw, but the Apache could take care of their casino just fine on their own, so Wyatt didn't have to be on guard.

As Wyatt strutted across the gambling floor, a light yelp broke through the dinging and jingling. He looked over at the set of stairs, where he heard the sound originate. An old Apache man was walking up the stairs with two young women accompanying him. They were very young women---girls would be more accurate a term, no more than a third of the man's age. One of Geronimo's main selling points were its girls; a commodity attracting degenerates, loners, ne'er-do-wells, and romantics alike from all around the Western Heart. Wyatt didn't care to partake in any part of the casino life, gambling was never his strong suit, and delving into the abyss of the Geronimo's sex life made him uneasy, so he chose to avoid it. But he couldn't take his eyes off the one girl on the old man's arm, she looked so young and so pure even through her smeared make-up and dried tears. She reminded him of someone he knew, someone he hadn't seen in quite a long time.

A man at one of the poker tables scooped up his chips and jumped out of his chair just in front of Wyatt. The Marshal's eyes were focused anywhere but in front of him though, and right as the man turned around to take off, he bumped into Wyatt's chest and fell to the floor. His chips spilled across the green carpet, scattering far and wide. Barely affected by the collision, Wyatt looked around confused, not sure what had stopped him. Then he saw the man at his feet scraping to pick up every last chip. He looked up and stared angrily into Wyatt's eyes.

"Sorry friend," Wyatt said, "didn't see you there."

"Don't you damn pale-faces ever look where you're going?" the man snapped.

From across the room, the door to Lipan's office swung open, and a large Apache man walked out. "Marshal!" he shouted, "The chief is waiting for you."

Wyatt looked down at the man by his feet and tipped his hat, "Sorry again," he said. Then he stepped over him and made his way to the office. The man gathered his chips and fearfully watched as the Marshal, whom he had just insulted, entered the office of the great Chief Lipan.

Wyatt entered the room and the guard closed the door behind him. He scanned the room and saw a congregation far more important than he had expected. To his left, the man who had opened the door was Lipan's third son, Kuruk. Nitis, Lipan's second son, sat in the far corner just to Wyatt's right. Wyatt nodded to them both, then took the one empty chair in the middle of the room. In front of him sat Chief Lipan of the Apache, and to the Chief's right was his eldest son, Diablo. All the sons looked similar, the only way Wyatt could tell them apart was by how violently they looked at him. Kuruk looked at Wyatt with a subtle disdain, no different to the way any other Apache looked at him. Nitis' eyes were kind, Wyatt was no closer to him than any other member of the family, but he considered Nitis friendly at the very least. But Diablo's eyes were different. They burned with a scorching rage fueled by his hatred for anyone and anything unlike his own kind.

They sat in silence for a few moments as Wyatt surveyed the room. He quickly noticed there was a member missing from the family gathering. He rested his hat on the arm of the chair, then leaned forward to take a good look at Lipan. Lipan was an ancient man; Wyatt liked to count the number of wrinkles and rolls on his forehead, using them to guess how many decades he'd been alive. He counted 8, or perhaps 9, the old man's overgrown eyelids blended with the wrinkles on his forehead so it was hard to be precise.

"So," Wyatt started, "did you miss me, Goyathlay?" It was a name Lipan was given many years ago which meant, *One Who Yawns.* It was a fitting name since his eyes seemed to hardly ever open.

"You were expected here three days ago, Cole," Diablo said. "Did your train get derailed?"

Wyatt leaned back in his chair and threw his hands behind his head nonchalantly. "Peaches was getting a little cramped in the transport car, so I decided to ride with her after the first day."

"Your job is to patrol the trains for the tribe's safety, how are you supposed to do that if you don't ride on the train?" Diablo snapped back.

"Actually, my job is to patrol the *tracks*, so I rode to the side of them to watch out for any bandits. I'm sure you'll be happy to know that your tracks are clear," Wyatt said.

Then, slowly and shakily, Lipan pushed himself out of his chair---his old joints creaking louder than the rusted hinges of the heavy train doors. When he spoke, his toothless mouth flapped up and down slower than ever imaginable. "Not all the tracks are clear, Marshal," he said. "Not the tracks outside of the Navajo land." He shuffled over to Wyatt and placed his leathery hand on his shoulder. His umber hand blended so perfectly with Wyatt's brown poncho it nearly disappeared into the stitching. "If those tracks were clear," Lipan continued, "then my boy, Cochise, would still be alive."

Wyatt looked into Lipan's half-shut eyes, shocked and nearly lost for words. "Cochise is dead?" He asked.

"A few days ago, my youngest boy was shot, thrown off the back of a train, and left to rot right on the tracks. They say it was a Coyote who did it, a Mexican who resides in the pueblos outside of the Navajo camp," Lipan explained.

"Some poor scavenger stealing scraps from the back of a freighter?" Wyatt pondered how this could have happened, only members of big gangs were typically able to get their hands on firearms. "Do you know his name?"

"Two of our scouts went searching soon after finding Cochise's body. They intended on questioning the locals but all they found was an old man who had been shot to death." Lipan leaned in closer to Wyatt, then the faintest slits in his eyes began to open. Wyatt felt the man's piercing pupils bore into his own. "This Coyote killed my boy. He killed the old man as well and more are probably dying as we speak... I want him dead, Marshal. And I want the body brought back to me."

"I'm not a bounty hunter, Chief." Wyatt started.

"No, Marshal, you're not. But like it or not you share the same blood as my people. Yes, it has been tainted with the blood of that pale-face grandfather of yours, who stole away one of our women so many years ago. But have I not been merciful to your family? Did I not allow the old man to live peacefully on our lands? Your family owes a great debt to me."

Wyatt bolted from his chair and snatched his hat off the arm. "There you go about that damn debt again. I hardly knew the old man, I mean Bill practically raised me from the time I was just a boy. I never even saw my grandpa after I left the cabin. Now you're going to sit there and hold that grudge over my head with no intention of ever letting it go! Is that it?"

"Marshal," Lipan said. "you do this, and you can consider your debt paid and your family's transgressions forgiven."

Wyatt stood in silence, he nearly dropped his hat but managed to place it back on top of his dirty blonde head. He didn't know what to look at. He even thought he had gone blind for a few seconds. "The debt," he said, "paid?"

"In full," Diablo said.

Wyatt turned around and pushed open the office door. "Your scouts found him just outside the Navajo camp? Is that right?"

"That's right," Diablo said firmly. "I'll have the scouts show you which depot is nearest."

"No need... I know the area well."

Wyatt glanced over to Nitis, who hadn't spoken a word the entire time. They exchanged a friendly nod, then Wyatt left the meeting. As the door closed, Nitis got out of his seat and walked toward Diablo and Lipan. "Do you think he is that dull of a man, Father? We both know the scouts killed that old man, it is only a matter of time before he figures it out."

"He is dull enough to believe that any of us cared at all for Cochise, the fool." Diablo answered. "It was just a matter of time before he got himself killed." Nitis waited for his father to respond but Lipan's shriveled lips didn't move. "We have big plans, Nitis, and the last thing we need is a marshal interfering with them."

Lipan always sat with his head hung, if his eyes were

open, they would be looking just beyond his feet. Nitis sat down on the ground in front of him with his legs crossed. He stretched his neck so that his face was in clear view of the two small slits on his father's face where his eyes would be. "Look at me, Father," Nitis pleaded.

Lipan's old wrinkled eyelids began to lift open. "Your brother's words are my own…" he said. He reached out his hand and gripped Nitis by the base of his neck. "Our people are warriors; we take what we desire. The Arapaho, to the North, are led by a weak woman. Every tribe in the union knows the land is ripe for the taking. We do not need anyone interfering with our plan. Best we keep him occupied, then by the time he returns our advance will have already begun."

Chapter 3

THE COYOTE AND THE OWL

On the outskirts of the Navajo camp, a day and a half ride away from Juan's pueblo town, lived a woman named Kai. But Juan had no horse, so it would take him three days to reach the camp. A Navajo medicine woman and friends with Juan's father, Kai had treated Juan and Felina in the past when they were sick. He was not sure what good would come of seeing Kai, but as he trudged through the scorching hot sands of the red desert, he could think of no other options.

At the end of the second day, Juan set up camp near a large rock formation. The land around him was barren. There were no towns nor trains, so he wasn't worried about being caught by any Apache scouts. What did worry him was that he was nearing three days without food, and only a tiny amount of water. His stomach rumbled as he lay on the crimson clay ground. He reached into his bag and pulled out a hunting knife his father gave him. He rolled out of the dirt then went to find some supper.

After a couple of hours Juan returned to the rock formation with a bundle of dead twigs and a large jackrabbit. He piled up the twigs and pulled a pack of matches out of his bag. He found many useful little items over his years of scavenging through the Apache trains; matches were a rarity but always worth picking up. He pulled one out of the pack, quickly swiped it across the bottom of his boot and watched the tip flare up. He held the match upside down letting the flame grow, then he tossed it into the twigs. The embers leapt between the twigs until the whole stack was ablaze. The flames seemed to be alive, and within them he saw the cloud of dust that swallowed his sister, as well as his father's face as he died in his arms. Within the sounds of the twigs popping and crackling he heard Felina's screams and Roberto's fading breath. He backed away from the fire so his tears would not extinguish it.

His stomach growled again and he decided he should skin the rabbit. He stared into the flames as he reached down to grab the rabbit. He felt its long velvety ears as he wrapped his fingers around them, but when he tried to pull it off the ground, it didn't seem to want to move. Juan tugged and tugged, but for some reason he couldn't pick the carcass off the ground. He thought that perhaps it had come back to life and was trying to escape from his grasp, the same way his sister tried to escape from the grasp of the Apache scouts. He tugged once more but this time, not only did it not move, it pulled back. At last, Juan looked away from the fire and turned his attention to the rabbit. It was still dead, not reanimated out of the sheer will to live, but he realized he was not alone in the barren desert. A small tan snout and little white teeth gripped onto one of the hind legs of the carcass. A coyote pup was having a tug of war with Juan over who would be enjoying the rabbit for supper.

Juan pulled hard on the ears and the pup let out a weak snarl, then planted its feet firmly into the red dirt. Juan's stomach growled right back at the scavenger dog. He kept a firm grip on the ears, but just as he turned to face the pup head on, it let go of its bite on the rabbit's leg. The pup was shaking, and Juan could see its rows of ribs protruding from its sides. It must have been even hungrier than him---perhaps it had been starving even longer than he'd been. Juan ripped one of the hind legs off the carcass. The coyote cowered back again, this time at the sound of the tearing tendons and breaking bones. Juan solemnly glanced at the rest of the rabbit, then reluctantly tossed it to the pup.

He let the blade of his knife glide through the fur of the rabbit leg until it was bare. Then he stuck the tip of the knife into the meat and held it over the flames. He watched the meat blister and cook over the fire. He heard a wet smacking sound and looked over at the pup who had already begun to devour its supper. It was the first time Juan had smiled in nearly three days, and it felt like the first good thing he had done since getting on that train. He waited for the leg to turn golden brown then he pulled it out of the fire. He ate every last scrap of meat on the fragile little bone until it was completely clean, not knowing how long he would need it to hold him over. Juan fashioned his backpack as a pillow then turned over on his side and watched the little coyote finish the meal he so generously gifted to him, bones and all.

The next day Juan followed the rising sun in the East to make haste for Kai's hut. His canteen had run dry by noon and his lips began to chap and crack soon after. By sundown he stumbled at the entrance to Kai's hut and fell unconscious. He was unsure how long he'd been asleep, but when he finally awoke, he found himself inside the hut, stripped naked with a cloth on his forehead and a strange gel on his lips. The room was filled with thick smoke that carried a strong musty aroma. Juan pushed himself up and the cloth fell off his forehead. He looked around the smoky room and rubbed his eyes, trying to get his vision back to normal. Kai sat across from him on the other end of the hut. She held a long pipe festooned with feathers and packed the end with a brown substance.

The smoke rising from the fire in the middle of the hut

escaped through the hole in the top of the structure. As his vision recovered, Juan saw a bowl beside him filled with water, so he picked it up and took a sip. He could tell by the way the liquid burned his tongue that it wasn't just water, but before he could spit it out he heard Kai say, "Drink it all, it will give you strength for what is to come." He tilted his head back and let the liquid rush down his throat, he felt it burn all the way down until it hit his stomach. He coughed and gagged but could already feel his energy coming back to him. "You're in trouble, aren't you, boy?"

"Kai," Juan started, "I don't know what you have heard but-"

"Apache scouts came by yesterday. They said that a Mexican killed Cochise, the youngest son of Lipan," Kai said as she continued to pack the brown substance into the feathered pipe. "And here in front of me sits a young Mexican. Coyote is what they are calling you."

Juan recalled the instant he pulled the trigger of the newly found pistol; the explosion of the bullet exiting the barrel and plunging into Cochise's stomach. He saw the train spinning and tumbling as they fell off the back of it, and he heard the cracking of Cochise's ribs and spine as they landed on the tracks. He felt a fierce sense of guilt rush through his body, yet he couldn't find the words to express his shame. "Forgive me, Kai... I didn't know where else to go."

Kai stuck the end of the pipe into the flames until the brown substance started to spark. She wrapped her thin wrinkled lips around the tip of the pipe and gently inhaled its fumes. She let the smoke fill her lungs then slowly released it, it spilled out of her nose and mouth like a milky waterfall. The grey tint of her hair matched that of the smoke, such that the rising fumes resembled strands of her hair trying to escape off her head. She reached over the fire and handed the pipe to

Juan. He grabbed it and took a moment to admire its craftsmanship. Within the wood were the carvings of a raven, an owl, a dog, and a snake all wrapped around the shaft of the pipe.

"I have been watching you and your family, Juan. I have seen everything and know your truth. Partake in the peace pipe with me and together we will reveal the course to retrieving your sister."

Juan stared at the pipe and turned it around in his hands. He looked up to Kai and asked, "How do you know?"

She chuckled and motioned for Juan to inhale on the pipe. "The Owl can see all that is around her."

Juan stuck the tip of the pipe between his lips and inhaled deeply. He felt the smoke rush though his lungs and burn even more than the liquid he had just drunk. He felt the smoke coursing throughout every speck of his body until it traveled straight to his head where it began to form and solidify. After exhaling, he slowly opened his eyes. The inside of the hut had changed, he no longer saw the old wrinkled woman in front of him, but rather a shell of the woman, covered in feathers but still wrapped in her blue and white cowl. She had a small beak and two large round eyes on the front of her flat face. "The owl can see all that is around her," he repeated softly as he stared at her in awe. Her head began to spin around her neck---at one point her eyes faced directly away from him, then it rotated to stare at him once more.

"They said that Cochise was killed by a Coyote. It seems that those dull Apache were right for once," the Owl chirped. She didn't use words to speak, but Juan could understand the way she hooted. He looked down at his hands and realized that they were now paws; his once tan skin was now covered in a thick beige fur. He looked into the mirror at the far end of the hut and saw two yellow eyes staring back at him. He had a long snout poking out where his nose and mouth should have been, and his ears, now pointed, had moved to the top of his head.

"The flames, Coyote, look into the flames and they will light your path," she hooted. She pinched the brown substance between her feathered fingers and ground it together, then she sprinkled it over the open flames, and a thick smoke filled the room. "First, you will go east and find a One-Eyed Elk. He grazes on the dead plains with his herd of calves." The antlered head of a great elk emerged out of the flames, it marched through a barren wasteland surrounded by its tiny calves drinking from a boiling river and grazing on empty soil. The left eye of the elk was closed up by a large scar in the shape of a cross.

The owl continued, "Through the dead lands you will travel with the Elk in search of a Raven. The Raven's tears will heal any wound, and his gifts you will need." A mountain ascended out of the smoke with a giant black raven perched at its peak. A tear formed in its eye, and as it fell storm clouds swelled up around the mountain. The raven soared away from its perch just an instant before a bolt of lightning crashed into the peak.

"Beware threats both large and small. The Wolf hunts for the pack and will run its prey down for miles. But do not underestimate the destruction that can be caused by the diseased bite of a single rat." A ravenous wolf pounced out of the heat of the flames, while within the smoke a pack of rats scurried throughout the hut, trying to avoid the jaws of the wolf.

"The path you must travel down, beyond the Rotten Plains, is a dangerous one. There you will experience wonders like you have never imagined. Be diligent and remember the words I have spoken to you. Find your sister, Coyote, and guide her back to salvation." Juan watched as all the animals that the Owl spoke of swarmed around him, and in the middle of the fire was a black cat, glaring at him with two flaming yellow eyes. He did not need the Owl to tell him who the cat was, he had seen those eyes glare at him his entire life, and he recognized the pitch-black hair that covered the cat's body. He was determined to find Felina and bring her back home safely.

He inhaled the smoke and watched the hazy animals dance around the hut. The smell was nauseating. The more he breathed in the fumes from the brown substance the more he coughed and gagged. He watched the feathers fall off the Owl, and when he looked at his paws, he saw the fur peeling off his skin. His fingers grew back to a familiar length, then his ears crept back down to the sides of his head and recovered their normal roundness. The noxious congestion of the room became too much for Juan. He fell on his hands and vomit spilled from his mouth. He quickly lost consciousness and fell asleep.

The sun rose early the following morning. Its light snuck through the crevices in the walls of the hut, and its warmth gently woke Juan. His clothes laid next to him, neatly folded and freshly washed. It was the cleanest he had seen the old rags in months. In fact, he had forgotten that his shirt had once been white; it had been so infested with red dirt and dust that he started to think it had always been tan. Resting on top of his fresh clothes, was a new accessory, a black leather hat with a large round brim. He looked around and saw no sign of Kai, so he took the opportunity to get dressed---he wished not to expose himself to the old lady any further.

He crawled out of the tent and walked over to the well

at the far end of the camp, where he saw Kai tending to it and filling a pail full of water. He tossed his folded shawl over his shoulder and neatly placed his new hat on his head, angling it so it tiled to the side ever so slightly.

Kai smiled as she saw him approaching. "Seems like you're a real outlaw now," she teased, "a true outlaw always has a signature hat."

"Whose was this?" he asked, pulling the hat off his head and inspecting it closer.

"I made that for a man who once told me he would come run away with me and take me to paradise. He died before he could ever steal me away, but he was a good man."

Juan placed the hat back on his head and knelt to fill his canteen. He could see a slight reflection as he stared into the pale of water. The black leather matched the tint of his hair and eyes almost perfectly. He could also see Kai's reflection as she stood above him, watching. He glanced up at her and saw a look of sorrow fill her gaze. She reached out her hands and held his face.

"Don't let your sister learn how it feels to not be saved. It would kill me if she found out that pain."

Juan tightened the cap on his canteen and strapped it around his shoulder. He stood up and wrapped his hands around Kai's. "Thank you for showing me where to go," he said, "I refuse to die until she is safe."

"You have been here too long, Coyote," she said as she lowered another empty pail into the well. "There is a horse tied to a post just past the hut. Take her and head east toward the Comanche, once you cross into their lands you best hug the border and head north. That is the safest way into the Rotten Plains where you will find the One-Eyed Elk."

"Gracias," said Juan. "I don't know how I could ever repay you."

"You can repay me by leaving here before the Apache find me aiding you. Now go!"

Chapter 4

THE MEXICAN MAIDEN

As a train hurried for the western edge of the Apache Nation, Felina and three others were crammed together in a dark car. While Felina thought of herself as a woman---a young woman at that, she found herself feeling much older due to her surrounding company. The other girls were much younger and some looked quite exotic. To her left was a girl whose hair was much the same noir tint as Felina's, but her skin was much lighter in tone, her eyes were thinner and her nose much smaller. To her right, a girl with skin even lighter than the first, it was so fair that it almost seemed to glow in the darkness of the cold shaking train car. The second girl's hair was almost the same color as her skin. Felina's father once told her that he met a man who came from the North. He said his hair was the color of the sun, but she had always thought that was just a story.

The third girl sat directly in front of Felina. Although she was not unique looking in any way, her presence in the car was the most disturbing. The girl was clearly a native---from what tribe unclear. Felina could not understand why she was there. She was the youngest looking of the bunch; she could not have been older than 12. She looked at the swarm of goosebumps that crept up the skin of the native girl's arms. Her face was drenched from the tears falling down her cheeks. Felina tore off some of the fabric from the bottom of her dress and leaned forward. She pressed it to the girl's cheeks to absorb the falling tears.

The gesture only seemed to make the girl cry more, but the tone of the tears had changed, there was less of sadness now and more of appreciation. Felina looked at the blanket the girl had wrapped around her; the pattern woven into it resembled the blankets that her father would bring home from Lady Kai's.

"You're Navajo, aren't you?" Felina asked.

The girl didn't speak but nodded. She grabbed the piece of cloth from Felina and blew her nose into it. When Felina asked what her name was she told her, "Doli."

She asked why the Apache would take a Navajo girl like her. Doli explained that she was to be offered to Chief Lipan as one of his son's potential wives. That the tribe would send the prettiest girl in the camp to try to impress the chief, and that it was better to be chosen as a wife than to be rejected and have to work in the Casino.

"But you are so young," Felina objected.

"It doesn't matter," Doli replied, "once you become a woman then you can be chosen to be sent." Doli pinched her knees together and curled her body up so that she was almost in a ball.

Felina pulled her in and embraced her. The other two girls tightened their legs together and curled up as well.

Juan had made his way into the Comanche Nation after riding for two days. When he crossed over into the new territory he was surprised to find small towns along his northbound route. Typically, they were only a single dirt road with some wooden buildings on each side. In one of the towns, he stopped into a saloon to see if he could fill his canteen. Inside the establishment was only a single other person, and it happened to be the man behind the bar.

"Haven't seen you 'round here, where'd you come from?" the bartender asked.

"I am... from the Apache nation. I'm looking for someone. Also, I am out of water and hoped you had a well that I could fill up at."

The bartender motioned his hand for Juan to come forward. "That accent you got there, I've heard it before... you're Mexican, aren't you?"

"Oh, si," Juan said as he handed the man his empty canteen.

"You said you're looking for someone?" the bartender asked, putting the canteen's mouth under a faucet, then pulling a lever to let out some water.

Juan watched in awe, he had never seen such a tool before, and he found it quite impressive. The bartender handed him the canteen and asked him who he was looking for.

"I don't know his name," Juan remembered the image of the elk that appeared in the flames of Kai's hut and the scar it had over its eye. He took his finger and ran it down his eye in the cross shape he had seen on the elk. "But he has one eye, and a scar that looks like this."

The man laughed, then he bent over the bar and whispered, "You gonna kill him?" Juan saw the man's eyes shift toward his right leg. He remembered he had the pistol hanging from his hip. "After all, you ain't no stranger to killing anyway."

Juan heard a click from behind the bar. It reminded him of the click his pistol made when he pulled the hammer back. Juan slowly stepped away from the bar.

"You think just because you crossed into Comanche

land that you ain't being looked for no more?" said the bartender as he lifted a rifle out from behind the bar. "Them natives don't take kindly to an outsider killing one of their own, especially when it's a Chief's son. Word travels fast around these parts, word that a Mexican with no name might be traveling east toward the Comanche."

Juan's hand hovered over the ivory grip of his pistol as he stared down the barrel of the man's rifle.

"Got anything to say for yourself, boy?"

"I'm sorry," Juan said.

"Sorry...huh?"

"Si, if the Mexican you are looking for is one with no name, then I am sorry to disappoint you. My name is Juan Coyote, so I'm afraid you have the wrong man. But I too have heard of this nameless Mexican you speak of. They say he can draw his gun and shoot in the blink of an eye." Juan's fingers rubbed together as he prepared to pull his pistol at the first sight of motion.

The two stood in dead silence. The sun that shone through the window highlighted the dust and dirt that filled the room. The bartender's eyes followed the dust as it fell to the ground, and he began to shake as Juan's hand appeared to creep toward his pistol. He lifted the barrel of his gun in the air. Juan's hand grabbed the ivory grip, but he didn't pull the gun out of its holster. Not when he saw that the bartender lowering the rifle back behind the bar.

"They didn't say nothin' about a boy named Juan," the bartender said.

Juan lifted his hand off the grip of his pistol. He took a few cautious steps back toward the bar. The bartender pulled out a glass bottle and twisted off the cap. "Deacon..." the bartender said.

"Hmm?"

"The man you're looking for, with the scar on his eye, his name is Deacon."

"You know him?" Juan exclaimed.

"He spent a few years roaming around these parts, preaching some nonsense about a fire talking to him, the man is insane," the bartender explained.

"Do you know where to find him?" asked Juan.

The bartender filled a glass with the clear liquor inside the bottle. As the drink poured out the fumes made their way into Juan's nostrils, and the familiar scent of tequila filled his head. His father used to make his own tequila. He used to let Juan have a bit on special occasions. It always left his insides very warm and his head feeling light. The bartender pushed the glass toward Juan, and the boy immediately took the glass and pressed it to his lips, slowly letting the spicy fluid fill his mouth.

"I just told you, kid, the man's head ain't right. Why could you possibly want to go looking for him?"

Juan swished the tequila around until it lined his entire mouth and burned his tongue. He placed the glass back on the table and let out a satisfying "Ahh." Leaning against the bar, he curled his finger to motion for the bartender to move closer. The bartender moved his ear closer to Juan. Juan whispered, "He is going to lead me through the Rotten Plains so I can make my way to Geronimo Park and kill Chief Lipan for taking my sister."

The words coming out of Juan's mouth resembled the snarl of a wild animal. The bartender began to tremble with fear. His lips and throat were dry from too much tequila that day, so he struggled to form any words in response to Juan's declaration. His hand was under the table and moving toward the rifle. But his hand was shaking, and he was not as stealthy as he thought.

With his left hand, Juan grabbed the bartender by his collar, while his right hand pulled out his pistol pointed it into his chest. "I already killed one of Lipan's sons, and I will kill 100 more if it means I get my sister back. They want to know where I am? You tell them to travel north to the Rotten Plains and come find me. Now you have five seconds to tell me where I can find Deacon before I pull this trigger and let you bleed out the same way that Apache did."

The bartender continued to shake. He tried to reach for the rifle, but Juan had pulled him over the bar just far enough that the gun was out of reach. Juan pulled back the hammer on his revolver, making the bartender flinch at the sound.

"3 seconds…" Juan growled.

The bartender writhed and stretched his fingers as long as he could---just enough to brush the warm wooden stock on the rifle, but not long enough to grasp it. Juan moved the revolver up to the man's neck and pushed the barrel into his skin.

"10 miles!" he shouted. Juan pulled the gun away from his neck but kept a firm grip around the man's collar.

"Which way?" he asked.

"Go north! You'll see the edge of the Rotten Plains once you reach a creek with dead trees on the far side of it. Follow the creek east and you'll find where he and those little beasts he hangs around live."

"Little beasts?"

"Little deformed bastards. Ugliest things you'll ever see. They worship him like some king, the lunatic."

Juan finally let go of the bartender's collar. But the bartender was not ready, so he fell and slammed his head against the bar on the way down. Juan grabbed the bottle of tequila off the bar, turned around and started for the exit.

The four girls huddled together within the dark train car. An Apache guard had brought them all a small plate of food, little more than slop that was fed to pigs out of a trough. To Felina, the slop looked like the frijoles that her father would make for her and Juan, but the smell was awful. She offered her plate to Doli and the others, but they didn't even care to eat their own.

During the ride the girls spoke to each other and began to learn more and more about where they came from. The girl with the thin eyes and black hair was named Misa, when she talked about home it was clear that it wasn't the Western Heart. She was from somewhere east of the Heart, an area that neither Felina nor the others had never heard of or seen. She said that where she came from had many people that looked just like her.

The girl with pale skin and blonde hair, Dakota, had been given the ancient name of the land she grew up in. It was part of the Sioux territory, very far north. She lived in a small village with just a few different families. One day a group of bandits raided their homes and kidnapped her. They ended up trading her to the Sioux tribe who traded her to the Apache. There weren't many people with hair the color of hers so the rarity made her quite valuable.

The girls asked Felina, "How did you end up here?"

"It was my birthday," she started, "I was dancing with my father just outside our home. We were waiting for my brother, Juan, to return. He had gone off to find a gift to give me. Before he returned, two men---Apache men like the ones who brought us that slop---rode in and shot my father then they grabbed me and brought me here."

"They did that to you on your birthday?" Dakota asked.

"How old are you now?" Misa inquired.

Then Doli chimed in, "What do you think your brother was going to bring you back?"

Felina ran her hand through Doli's hair and pulled her in to embrace her. "I don't know what he would have brought me back. What I do know is that he still hasn't delivered me a gift, and I know in my heart that the gift he now plans on bringing me will not be a necklace or a charm. The gift he will bring me will be far more valuable than any of those types of things. I know he will not stop until he brings me freedom. And Juan is not alone, I know that *He* will find out what has happened and once he does, he will come after me as well."

"Who is '*He*'?" Misa asked.

"Your brother sounds amazing," Dakota added.

"Juan is fantastic. He is smart and cunning and most of all he is protective of me. We agreed a long time ago that we would never let anything bad happen to the other. The other man though, he is a man who made a promise to me a long time ago. He promised he would one day take me to Paradise. A place that would have no one but the two of us and we would not have to worry about tribes or bandits or noisy trains. I have waited for four years for him to return to me, and I know that somehow he will keep his promise."

"Wow, he sounds amazing," Dakota repeated.

Felina couldn't help but smile at the girl's reactions. As dire as their current situation was, still she found a way to smile, but she knew they had a long road ahead of them, and there was no guarantee that Juan or the other man she spoke of would ever find them.

"Doli, Misa, Dakota," Felina said sternly, "I don't know if any of you know where we are being taken, but I assume that Doli and I both have the best idea."

"Geronimo Park," Doli answered.

"Yes, I don't know if we will be able to stay close while we are there, or what exactly they will have us doing… But I want to assure you that I will do whatever it takes to keep the three of you safe. I believe that my brother and the man I told you about will come to save me, and when they do I know they will save you as well, but what I don't know is how long that might take. We have to be sure that we don't do anything that will get us into trouble while we are at Geronimo Park. The Apache are ruthless, they killed my father in cold blood, and I have no doubt that they will do the same to us if we get out of line. I am just asking that we all do our best to endure whatever comes our way and have faith that we will be saved. Can you do that for me?" Felina pleaded.

In unison, Doli, Misa, and Dakota all confirmed that they could. Then after, Doli looked up at Felina and asked, "This man who said he would take you to Paradise, what is his name? And why do you have such belief that he will come find you?"

Felina thought back to four years ago, in her mind was the image of the man in her bed, sickly and worn down. She remembered holding a small silver star that he had attached to his pants and remembering how it was the shiniest thing she had ever held.

"His name… is…" she choked as tears began to build up in her dark black eyes, "His name is Marshal Wyatt Cole! And I believe in him because he is the man that I love!"

Four Years Earlier

Juan and Felina sat on the porch of their little pueblo house. It was winter, and the desert was cold, even during the day. Juan was tossing a ball in the air as he lay flat along the single step of the porch. Felina was sitting in her father's rocking chair as she finished knitting a new shawl for her brother. She didn't want to make him a poncho like she had made for their father, because Juan was growing fast and he would only fit in it for a year or so. The shawl on the other hand was more of a wearable blanket, one he would be able to utilize for a much longer time. She promised him that once he stopped growing she would make him a poncho, one with nice patterns and traditional colors.

It had been four days since they had last seen their father. He said he was going to see Lady Kai to stock up on medicinal herbs in case any of them got sick during the winter. Felina watched as thick haunting storm clouds began to creep over the horizon toward their home. She wondered if they would bring rain, or snow, or raging winds. The winters were unpredictable and uncertainty scared her. Juan, on the other hand, did not seem to care about the approaching storm--- uncertainty was the driving principle the boy lived by.

"We should go inside, Juanito. It is going to get cold soon." She instructed.

"Just a little longer... Just to see if Papa makes it home," Juan objected.

"He would not be traveling this late, especially not with a storm like that approaching."

"Just a bit longer," he said stubbornly.

"Hmph," she grunted, "fine, but once the winds pick up we are going in."

She continued to knit the shawl, and as she did the clouds moved closer and closer. As they filled more of the sky they also seemed to descend toward the ground, almost like a fog that swallowed the horizon. The scene made her nervous, even though the winds had not picked up---in fact it was even calmer out than a few hours before. Juan had moved off the step and was running around tossing the ball to himself, he threw it high into the air so it would disappear into the clouds, then he waited to see where it reappeared and ran to catch it. Felina finished knitting Juan's shawl. The winds had not yet picked up, but the air was beginning to chill.

"Juan!" Felina called from her chair, "I have finished!"

He waited for the ball to fall back down from the mist, and when he caught it he hopped and skipped back toward the porch. Felina walked down the couple of steps and held the shawl out to show to Juan. She spread the fabric out so that the pattern she had stitched could be seen in its full view. As she unfurled the shawl a great gust of wind blew past them; it grabbed onto the cloth and tore it from Felina's tired hands. She watched in utter shock as it was carried away by the cold winter breeze.

"I'll get it!" Juan cried out. He sprinted after the shawl and quickly disappeared into the fog.

"Juan! No!" Felina shouted. She ran a few feet from the porch, but already her view was blurred and she was afraid to move farther from the house. She strained her eyes as she tried to see where her brother went. She called out for him a number of times with no response.

Felina ran back to the house and grabbed a lamp off their dining table. She searched through boxes and drawers looking for a set of matches. It felt like an eternity before she finally laid her fingers on the small cardboard packet. She fumbled as she tried making her way back to the lamp, and most of the matchsticks fell, scattering across the floor. She picked one up, and with shaking hands, tried to swipe the match against the rough strip of material on the package to get it to spark. It took her several tries to finally light it. The winds outside started to howl like a pack of wolves, making her fingers tremble even more violently. Once the tip of the match finally sparked, she held it against the wick of the lamp and waited for it to catch. The flame lit the inside of the room and she headed back for the door.

She opened the heavy wooden door and lifted the lamp in front of her face. The light shone on a massive horse, its nostrils so close to her face that every time it breathed, she could see the clumps of mucus dripping out of them. The animal was terrifying, she had seen black horses, white horses, and spotted horses, but she had never seen a pink horse. It had no hair whatsoever, and its size was unmatched by any she'd ever seen. She stood paralyzed, flashing the bright flame into the face of the horse but it didn't seem to spook her. Felina felt a tug at her dress. Startled, she jumped away, but realized it was only Juan.

"Felina! This man! He is hurt, you have to help him!" Juan exclaimed.

"Man?" Felina mumbled. She tilted her head to look down the length of the horse and saw someone hanging over the side of the pale mare. Blood was running down his face and dripping off his fingers. "Juan, help me get him off, then go tie the horse to the post out front!"

They each grabbed an arm and tugged him off his mount. Once they managed to drag him off his legs flopped to the ground, like a lifeless doll. They wrapped the man's arms around their necks and pulled him inside to the bed in the main room. Juan ran outside and quickly led the horse to the post.

Trying to find where the man had been wounded, Felina began to undress him. She removed his hat and placed it on the ground beside the bed. Then she worked on pulling off the man's thick suede jacket, but it was so soaked in blood that it had begun to crust and harden in the cold weather. She had to brace her feet against the frame of the bed to pull the piece of clothing off him. As the jacket began to slip off his torso she could see his face wince in pain. That was the first sign of life she had seen out of him, and it filled her with the slightest glimmer of hope that she could help him. Once the jacket was removed she grabbed a knife out of the kitchen and cut through his shirt---she didn't want removing the shirt to be as difficult as the jacket, and she didn't want to put him through any more pain than he was already in.

She soaked a cloth in one of the jugs of water, then rubbed it gently along the man's bare chest to try and clean away some of the blood. As her hand moved over his muscular chest she felt the tips of her fingers slightly dip in a couple spots. There were two bullet holes, one through his right shoulder and the second just a bit lower in his chest. The bullet that hit his shoulder had gone straight through, but the shot in his chest still had the small metal projectile lodged in his muscle.

Juan came running back into the house and hollered over to Felina, "Is he gonna die?"

"No!" Felina responded, "but I need you to help me while I go grab some things to sew up these wounds."

She instructed Juan to take the cloth and press it firmly against both holes, then she went into another room to grab her sewing kit and her father's box of toiletries. She began to wind a piece of thread through the small hoop on the needle, but her shaking hands made it hard for her to slip the small string through the hole. Once she finally managed to do so she placed the needle on the bed and opened the other box. She pulled out a small pair of tweezers and asked Juan to go to the kitchen and grab a bottle of the tequila.

He came back with the bottle and watched as Felina soaked the tweezers in the spicy liquid. She removed the blood-soaked cloth from the man's chest, then used her fingers to try and spread open the hole. Carefully, she lowered the tip of the tweezers into the wound until she felt them tap against the bullet. She grasped the bullet in the tweezer tips and pulled on it until it popped out of his chest. Felina quickly poured some of the tequila onto the wound. The man's whole body appeared to tighten, and he moaned in agony.

"Is he okay?" Juan asked.

"Hand me a fresh rag," Felina instructed.

She wiped the blood and alcohol away from the wound then took the needle and began to sew up the hole. She then cleaned and closed up the hole in his shoulder, then tightly tied one of Juan's belts around it. She couldn't find anything large enough to wrap around his chest though, so she ended up covering the wound with a rag and using her hand to keep pressure on it.

Felina fell asleep, knelt beside the bed, keeping the rag pressed against the wound. Her head laid against the man's chest, his steady heartbeat acted as a natural lullaby. The way her head moved up and down as air filled his lungs then rapidly left them made her feel like she was being rocked to sleep. The pouring rain and howling wind blanketed the house in a soothing embrace. Juan, however, didn't sleep. He spent the night cleaning up the blood and the rest of the mess around the house.

When the sun arose the boy went outside to check on the horse. He had scraped some corn off the cob and into a bowl for the horse to eat. The animal was so large Juan could barely hold the bowl up high enough to reach its mouth, but once it smelled the sweet corn it lowered its head and began to lap it up greedily. He ran his hand over her snout, and was amazed at how much darker his skin was compared to the bald horse's. After it finished the corn he walked around the mare and noticed that its body was covered in goosebumps---he assumed it must be freezing since it didn't have any hair. So he ran inside and grabbed the blanket off his bed and threw it over the back of the horse.

"That should feel better," he assured it as he continued to stroke the underside of its neck.

Juan went back to the house, and inside he saw that Felina and the stranger were now both awake. He watched as Felina lifted the man's head and helped him drink from a bowl that she had filled with water. He could see that Felina was smiling. It wasn't often that she smiled, he wondered why now of all times she would be happy.

Over the next two days Felina stayed by the man's side; she nursed his wounds and helped him eat and drink until he was able to do it on his own. Juan for the most part stayed in his room or tended the man's horse, only occasionally checking in on his sister. Their father had taught them to be wary of strangers, but also to help those in need. Juan fought with the two sentiments, not knowing which one best fit their situation.

On the third morning Juan pulled Felina away from the man's side and took her outside to discuss his concerns in private.

"Should we be helping him?" he asked nervously.

"Of course we should be, he would have died if it wasn't for us."

"But what if he is a bad person? He was shot, Felina, aren't outlaws and bandits the ones who get shot?"

"He is not a bad man!" Felina argued. "Why don't you talk to him yourself and ask him?"

Juan pushed his sister to the side and stormed into the house. He dragged a chair from the kitchen across the room to the man's bedside. He hopped on the chair and stared down at the stranger.

The man's eyes fluttered open, as if he hadn't already been awoken by the ruckus the boy had just caused. "Well, hi there kid," he said softly, "you must be Juan."

"That's right," Juan snarled, "and I am sick of wondering just who the hell you are!"

The man pulled his arm out from under his blanket. Juan panicked and nearly fell out of his seat. The man stuck out his left hand in front of Juan and just kept it there. "I'm Wyatt," he said, "Wyatt Cole."

Juan fixed himself so he was sitting upright once more, and stared at the man's hand but did not shake it. "Why were you shot?"

Wyatt grinned and pointed his finger at the small table by the bed. Juan looked over and saw a small trinket laying there. He picked it up and inspected it, it was a small silver star with markings on it that Juan couldn't read.

"Know what that is, Juan?" Wyatt asked. Juan shook his head and continued to run his fingers over the shiny metal. "I'm a marshal, do you know what that is?"

"No."

"Well basically it means that I roam around and protect the trains from robbers and bandits and-"

"And outlaws?" Juan butted in.

"That's right."

"So, why were you shot then?" he asked, no longer in a threatening tone.

"Well, I was patrolling a train that was making a shipment west, and on the same train was a gang of about six men who had snuck on at the depot and were planning on hijacking it. They wanted to steal all the goods on that train, and they were willing to kill anyone who got in their way." Juan listened in awe and fantasized about the event as Wyatt continued his story. "They were ready to kill me, had their hands on their guns and all, ready to draw."

"What happened?" Juan begged to know.

Wyatt leaned in closer, and his motion pulled Juan's ear in closer as well. "I was quicker," he whispered. "But… six to one is quite the advantage they had on me. I was able to take them all out but not before a couple of them got a shot off."

Juan looked at Wyatt's chest, at the belt wrapped around his shoulder and the cloth that Felina had been pressing against his other wound. Wyatt was still holding out his hand for Juan to shake. The boy looked at his hand and grabbed it firmly. "Okay," he said, "you can stay until you are healed or until my father gets back."

Wyatt chuckled and shook Juan's hand back. "I will be out of your hair in no time."

Two more days passed and Felina continued to nurse Wyatt's wounds. Finally, he was able to get out of bed and move around. He would spend most of the day outside with his horse, Peaches, feeding and bathing her. Felina followed him wherever he went. She said it was to make sure his wounds didn't open up, but that wasn't an actual concern of hers. She asked him one day why his horse looked the way it did, bald like nothing she had never seen.

"I found her in a place called the Rotten Plains," he explained, "the whole area is diseased and most of the animals that reside there only slightly resemble their cousins you would see in the natural world. She was just a colt, but she was already the size of a full-grown mare."

"What were you doing there?" she asked.

"I was chasing a bandit group. They often think that since the natives don't control the area they'll be safe, but it's a horrible place, and they rarely know how to navigate it properly. My old teacher, he used to take me there for months at a time so I would know where to go and where not to go.

There are a lot of abandoned Government outposts there as well. I liked going there because they had a lot of books they had confiscated and there was so much to learn."

"Books?" Felina inquired, visibly confused.

"When you work for the Government, you're taught how to read and write. Books were collections of written words that told about things that had happened, things that might happen, and things that could never happen, but were interesting to think about."

The next day Wyatt and Felina woke up early and were sitting on the porch watching the sun rise. The colors in the sky were the same tint of pink as Peaches' skin, and the red dirt blended with the orange glow of the sun.

"What were some of the things you read about in those books?"

Wyatt mulled over his answer for a few moments; he had read many of the confiscated books. "Well, they were about a lot of things. The ones that I enjoyed the most though were about how this world was in the past. It is hard to imagine it but so many things were different... Felina?"

"Yes?" she replied.

"Have you ever heard of a sea?" She shook her head, never having heard the term. "A sea is a great body of water, one so massive that you couldn't possibly see where it ended. Well, there are many kinds of seas, but there is one that I read about that was located right in the middle of a desert. Most seas are abundant with life, they have fish in them, just like you would find in a river or a creek, but this sea was different."

Felina imagined what the horizon would look like if the red sand was to be replaced with deep blue water, how the sun would not blend in with the horizon but reflect off it. "What made it so different?" she asked as she stared blankly into the distance.

"This sea couldn't breed any life…" he said. Felina turned away from the distance and saw the sun reflecting its light off the tears that were building up in Wyatt's eyes. "The water was poison… fish couldn't live in it, birds couldn't swim in it, and people couldn't drink from it."

"Why was that your favorite? That sounds horrible."

"It was horrible. But that was hundreds of years ago. Hundreds of years ago there were also beautiful places, with farms and millions of people who wanted to live there, but now those places are gone, and they can't harbor life any more than that poisoned sea could." The tears that were filling Wyatt's eyes finally began to roll down his cheek, trickling into the corners of his mouth. "Things change in this world, Felina, but what I have learned is that change isn't good and it's not bad. It is just neutral. But if there were beautiful places that are now desolate and unlivable… well then maybe the places that were once desolate and unlivable are now beautiful. Maybe the absolute worst places of the past are the most perfect places now. Did you know that there is a word for a perfect place?"

"What is it?" Felina asked as she too felt a few tears welling up.

"Paradise… My dream is to find Paradise. I can't explain it, but I know that that sea is where I will find it."

Felina looked back out toward the horizon and imagined what a perfect place would look like. She pictured warm weather and trees that would provide enough shade and fruit that you would always be comfortable. She imagined that the sea would be filled with cold water that you could drink and immediately feel cooling your insides as it reached your stomach. She imagined watching the sun set into the sea with Wyatt beside her as they ate the fruit that fell from the trees that shaded them. She moved her hand toward Wyatt's until her thin fingers ever so slightly brushed against his. Neither of them reacted to the sudden touch, it felt too natural to have any reaction.

"Will you take me there someday?"

"Sure… but first I have to pay someone's debt. After I do that we can go."

That afternoon Roberto returned home. He apologized to Juan and Felina for his trip taking longer than expected. The harsh weather had kept him stuck at Kai's for a few days. Like they agreed, Wyatt prepared to leave just as Roberto arrived. Juan had warmed up to Wyatt and told him that he did not have to go so soon, but Wyatt insisted that he could not intrude any further.

That evening he filled up his canteens, and in Peaches' saddlebags packed some food that Felina had made for him. As he was untying her reins from the post outside the house, Felina came running toward him. She was carrying something in her arms. She stopped in front of Wyatt and extended it to him.

"Your coat was ruined. It is going to be too cold out to just wear a shirt, so I made this for you," she said. Wyatt took the gift and spread it open. "It is a poncho, it won't be as warm as your coat, but it-"

Before she could finish Wyatt grabbed her and embraced her. He held her tightly with her face pressed against his chest. She wrapped her arms around his waist and wished that the embrace would not end.

"Thank you, Felina," Wyatt said, his voice breaking slightly as his body flooded with emotions.

He stepped back and threw the poncho over his shoulders; the brown cloth draped perfectly over his torso, falling just past the silver star that was clipped to the pocket of his slacks. Wyatt kicked his leg over Peaches' saddle and mounted her. He tipped his hat at Felina, then slowly rode away.

"Wyatt!" Felina called out. He did not turn around, but Peaches stopped walking. "Promise you will come back! Promise that one day you will take me to Paradise with you!"

The massive horse reared her head around until Wyatt's gaze met Felina's. "I promise... I promise I will return to this spot as soon as I am free to do so."

He whipped the reins and kicked his feet against the horse's sides. They took off into the horizon, and as Felina watched, she imagined them riding across a massive sea, galloping on top of the cold water. The mist that splashed off Peaches' hooves washed over Felina's face, it ran down from her eyes and dripped off her chin, but left her face feeling refreshed.

Chapter 5

OUT OF THE DESERT AND INTO THE PLAINS

Wyatt sat on a rotted log and listened to the crackling sound of the burning campfire. Across from him was the beautiful Arapaho chief, Cheyanne. "*My people have enemies all around us, and those enemies see our land as ripe for the taking,*" she said repeatedly. They were the words she had said to him before he left Little Raven en route to Geronimo Park. Every time she repeated that sentence another face appeared in his mind. At first he saw Chief Lipan, then Diablo, then Kuruk. It was obvious to him that the Apache were planning on moving north in an attempt to take over the Arapaho lands.

Wyatt looked to his left where he saw his old teacher Bill, rolling a cigarette and whistling an old tune he had heard too many times. "*There's a lot of beauty in this world, Wyatt. Keeping order is the only way we can protect that beauty,*" Bill said as he stuck his fresh cigarette into the fire and took a long draw.

Wyatt slipped down the log so that his head rested against it and stared up at the starry sky. "*Promise you will take me with you to Paradise one day,*" said another familiar voice. He looked to his left and lying beside him was an older version of the girl who had once asked him to keep that promise. Her hair was still as black as the night sky that surrounded the bright stars, as were her eyes.

"*My people have enemies all around us, and those enemies see our land as ripe for the taking,*" he continued to hear in the background, mixed in with the crackling of the fire.

"*Order, Wyatt. It's the only thing that can protect that beauty,*" Bill repeated.

"*Promise you will take me to Paradise with you one day,*" Felina said again.

"*You know what it feels like to be hanged by the neck, Marshal?*"

Wyatt's attention shot toward Cheyanne, where he heard the last voice come from. It continued, "*I'm sorry Marshal, ain't nothing beautiful about this world. This is a world that will chew on your insides, and let you rot in the heat rather than just getting it over with.*" From out of the shadows, behind Cheyanne, emerged the slender man with the cloth wrapped around his head. He had a revolver in his hand and was spinning it around his middle finger.

"*My people have enemies all around us,*" Cheyanne repeated as Chance stopped spinning the pistol and placed the barrel against her temple. "*And those enemies see our land as ripe for the taking.*" Wyatt watched in despair as Chance's finger slowly tightened around the trigger, seemingly taking an eternity to fire it. The hammer pulled back into position then sped back to ignite the gunpowder.

BANG!

The room car shook and Wyatt sprung awake to the loud rumble. He almost forgot he was riding on a train. He looked out the window and all he saw was red dirt and large rock formations. He remembered those same rocks and dirt from four years ago. The train came to a halt. Wyatt made his way off, and walked toward the back car to grab Peaches. He hopped on the giant horse and headed for an old adobe house he had waited a long time to return to.

The temperature had dropped rapidly in the handful of miles Juan had just ridden. He wrapped his shawl a bit tighter, and adjusted it higher to cover the lower half of his face. He had heard stories of the Rotten Plains; how its weather patterns were even harder to predict than the rest of the Heart's. The days were still long so Juan expected hot weather. He was surprised when he saw his breath evaporating in the frigid temperatures. It was the coldest weather he had ever experienced. He assumed he must be close to Deacon's camp from what the bartender told him, though the area did not look right---he thought the Rotten Plains would be flat and open. What he saw in front of him was a dense forest, with trees colored red and orange as though it was autumn.

He could feel the temperature drop another degree with every stride forward his horse took. He wished he had a pair of gloves. He looked at his fingers and had never seen such pale skin. He wrapped the leather reins around both his hands to keep them warm, but his skin was raw and the stiff leather began to peel the flesh off the top of his hands and his palms. He watched as steam began to rise off the drops of blood that leaked out of the leather. Between his legs, he could even feel his horse's abdomen shivering.

It was so cold that he even thought he heard the trees beginning to shiver. He gazed all around at the wooden pillars that encompassed him. He had never seen so many trees before. Their crimson hue matched the tint of the desert sands, and it comforted him. While he observed the oddly colored leaves something else grabbed his attention. The trees continued to shiver, and he noticed a figure moving from trunk to trunk. He pulled on the horse's reins, then hopped off his saddle. He pondered what it may have been---perhaps just an animal. He hadn't eaten since leaving Kai's, and a fresh piece of meat would be more satisfying than a stale piece of bread.

He kept one hand on his horse's mane, partly to keep it warm, but also to feel if she made any sudden moves. The horse could hear and smell better than Juan, and she would be able to sense their visitor quicker. He listened closely, but kept his eyes fixed forward. He could see steam rising from the ground in the distance; the same way it did from the drops of his blood. Would the creek's water be red like the trees? He thought to himself. As he made his way toward the steam he heard no further rustling from within the trees, but he assumed whatever was following them was still close. Stopping to fill his canteen would be the perfect way to lure out their visitor.

There was a small creek where the steam was coming from. He imagined the water having a scarlet tint that matched the leaves and his blood. He pulled the canteen off his horse's saddle and knelt by the water. The creek was unlike how he imagined. It bubbled and sloshed downstream carrying a sickly green tint. As he stuck the canteen into the creek he could tell the water itself was clear, but the dirt below was what gave it its leaden sheen.

Through the ambient noise of the flowing creek he heard his horse beginning to pace up and down. Spraying dirt and crunching twigs with every stomp of its hooves. Its breathing became loud and uneven, and it started to make a low murmuring noise from deep in its belly. Juan's hand stayed still on his hip, just above his holstered pistol. He moved the opening of the canteen toward his lips and prepared to take a drink.

"WAIT!" a mysterious voice called out from behind one of the trees.

Juan quickly drew his pistol and fired a shot. The bullet tunneled into the tree nearest the mysterious voice's origin. The boom echoed through the forest and caused a blanket of leaves to fall from the treetops, descending to the ground like bright red snowflakes and piling up on the dirt.

"I know you are still there, show yourself! But slowly," Juan directed.

From behind the tree, only a couple of feet from its base, a small hand reached around and grabbed onto the rotten bark. A small bald head peeked out from behind the tree; its scalp wrinkly and blistered. It moved slowly as Juan had instructed until its entire face emerged from behind the trunk.

It is ugly, Juan thought to himself. He had never seen such a deformed face before. Its right eyelid was so swollen that it couldn't even open, while the left bulged so far out of its face that it looked like it might pop out.

"Why were you following me?" Juan asked.

"You are not from these parts. We do not get many straight-backs roaming through these woods."

"Straight-backs?"

"That canteen of yours, you best not drink from it. In fact, just toss it into the creek before it melts," the small man advised.

Juan began to smell a dank musk, he glanced at the canteen and saw a puff of smoke rising from the bottom of the leather. The water inside started to drip out and puddle into the dirt. Juan lowered his pistol and tossed the canteen into the creek.

"I apologize for following you, I don't mean to cause you any trouble," said the hidden man.

Juan fell back onto his rear and sat with his legs crossed. He squinted his eyes and studied what he could see of the small person. "Why don't you come all the way out from there," said Juan, but the man timidly stayed put. "Look, I apologize for shooting at you. I see that you were just trying to help me. I would like to talk to you, come out from there and get off your knees while you're at it."

The stranger crept out from behind the tree so that his full face was in view. He had large lips and a crooked nose shaped like a pig's snout. He removed his hand from the trunk of the tree and pushed his fist into the dirt. He hopped away from the tree in the oddest manner Juan had ever seen, and he quickly realized that the stranger was not on his knees at all. He was only about three feet tall. His legs were little more than stumps, proportionally small even for his tiny body. His arms were much longer in comparison though, so long that he used them as sort of a crutch to move on, occasionally not even using his stumpy legs. The last anatomical mystery that muddled Juan was the stranger's posture. He was so hunched forward, with a massive lump on his back, that he imagined the stranger could be a good two feet taller if only he could straighten his spine.

"What… are you?" Juan asked in utter bewilderment.

The stranger hobbled quickly through the dirt toward Juan and stopped just in front of him. He stood perfectly eye level with the seated Juan. The hunchback had mucus dripping from his pig-like nostrils, which he would frequently sniffle and suck up back into his skull.

"I am a man just like you… well perhaps only half a man if we are only speaking in terms of stature! Haha!" the stranger exclaimed as he erupted into laughter. "Your dialect is quite unusual, where is it that you are from?"

Juan found himself lost for words, staring dumbfoundedly at the *man*.

The little hunchback lifted his hand from the dirt and ran his stubby fingers down the soft shawl wrapped around

Juan's torso. "Mmmm, now that is NICE!" he said, as a massive smile crept over his face, revealing his mouthful of only a few teeth and even more spaces.

"Who are you?" Juan finally managed to ask.

The tiny man jumped back and glared at Juan, then leaned back in, his smile growing even wider than before. "The name is Hans!" He lifted his right hand and gave Juan a wave. Juan watched his hand and noticed that he had a sixth finger just outside of his pinky.

"I'm Juan, pleased to meet you, Hans." The Mexican couldn't help but get a chuckle out of the little man.

"Please Juan, you must tell me where you got that wonderful blanket you wear. You see, clothes don't quite fit my kind very well, but that seems like an excellent garment to help keep warm!"

"Felina made it. She's my sister," Juan said, feeling the fabric between his fingers.

"Take me to her! I want her to make me one!" Hans cheered as he hopped up and down in excitement.

Juan pushed himself off the ground and walked over to his horse. He dug through his saddlebag until he found a small red and green colored cloth. He sat back down beside Hans and handed it to him.

"She made this for me when I was just a niño. I outgrew it years ago but it should fit you fine."

Hans gazed at the garment, enchanted. "Why would you…"

"It is the least I can do to make up for trying to shoot you. Plus, if it was not for you my insides would be looking like that old canteen by now."

Juan let the shawl unfurl, then he draped it over Hans' shoulders and wrapped it around the hunchback's oddly shaped body.

"Haha!" Juan laughed, "you look more like a Mexican than I do!"

"Hmm… Mexican huh? Is that why you say *chu* instead of *you*?" Hans inquired.

"Must be," Juan said as he patted Hans on the shoulder.

Juan walked back to his horse and hopped on his saddle. He tipped his hat toward Hans and kicked his horse to start moving.

"Wait! Where are you going?" Hans called out.

"I don't know exactly. I am searching for someone and can't waste any time."

"Who could you possibly be looking for out here? There are more beasts than there are men in these woods."

He was right, and Juan knew it. He had no idea where to find the One-Eyed Elk, and the forest was frightening enough in the daylight. He couldn't imagine what he would find at night. Juan hopped off the horse and knelt beside Hans. He ran his finger down his left eye and then across it.

"I am looking for a man with one eye, and a scar in this shape," Juan explained.

Hans' eyes followed the motion of Juan's finger as he drew the shape of the scar. His eyes lit up, and his patented smile appeared back on his face. "Deacon! You are looking for Deacon!" he yelled. Hans hopped up and down and jumped onto Juan, embracing him. "I can take you to him! Your steed is strong enough to carry both of us. Let's go, and I will take you to him!"

"You know Deacon?" Juan asked.

"Everyone knows Deacon, you fool!" Hans exclaimed.

Wyatt found an old shovel in the shed behind the pueblo. He used it to pierce the firm red dirt outside the house. It was cloudy and not exceptionally hot out, for that he was grateful, but he was saddened to see that Roberto had died without having a proper burial. From the necrotic look of the man's skin he assumed it had been a bit over a week since he passed. There was no sign of Felina. Dry blood was splattered along all the floorboards. All he hoped for was that she was nowhere near when her father was killed.

It took an hour for Wyatt to dig a sufficiently deep hole to bury Roberto. He piled the dirt back over the body and went inside to search the cabinets for some homemade tequila. There was one bottle left, and he was pleased to see that it was nearly full. He found a cup then took a seat in Roberto's old rocking chair and poured himself a drink. There was a cool breeze and a bright purple sky as the sun began to set. He drank glass after glass; the tequila warming him even better than his poncho. The winds chilled the tears that ran down his cheeks, paving icy trails down to his chin.

"Where are you?" he asked.

Wyatt drank until the sun finally set behind the dirt plateaus and passed out drunk moments after. He woke up with the sunrise the next morning---feeling only slightly dehydrated but overall well for polishing off an entire bottle of the spicy alcohol in one evening. He filled up his canteen at the well behind the house, then hopped on Peaches. He started north toward the Navajo camp, the nearest native settlement. Whoever killed Cochise would have headed there. It's the middle of nowhere, he would need to take shelter somewhere, the marshal thought to himself.

As he headed north, the image of Roberto's dead body lingered in his mind. He began mulling over what had happened to him, and to Felina, and to her brother. Roberto had a gunshot wound to his chest, he thought, and their pueblo was only a few miles from where Cochise was shot. Felina and Juan were nowhere to be found though. If the man who killed Cochise also killed Roberto, then why would he not kill Juan as well? It has been a long time since I saw them, Juan would be a man by now, no one would think twice about shooting him to get something they needed. It would make sense if he kidnapped Felina, but why only kill Roberto? Unless for some reason Juan wasn't around. He could have passed away in the four years since I'd been there...

The endless questions about the pair's whereabouts plagued Wyatt's mind, but it was clear to him that whoever shot Cochise was most likely responsible for Roberto's death as well. Hopefully wherever he was, Felina would be as well. He was headed back toward the depot to catch a train to the Navajo camp. It was the only large settlement close by and even if the killer didn't stop there, he knew he would hear rumors at that camp.

He neared the depot after a short time of riding. He hopped off Peaches and walked alongside her up to the steel box. It looked identical to all the others. The more he inspected the structures the more curious he found them. They didn't even appear to have doors. He imagined the clerks crawling through the small windows when they needed to get in and out.

"Marshal Cole..." the voice from behind the tinted window projected.

"Any messages for me?"

The clerk didn't slip any paper through the opening nor did he respond immediately. He paused for several moments then said, "No."

Wyatt slapped the cold steel wall and started to turn

around to head for a bench, but he was stopped by an unexpected response from the clerk.

"But… I would like to run something by you…" said the ominous figure behind the tinted glass.

Wyatt chuckled and moved his face so close to the opaque window that not even a speck of dust could slip through the gap. He tried to make out any definition in the man's face, but it was no use. "I didn't know you people were allowed to say more than two words at a time."

"Well, that is typically the case."

"But this case isn't typical?" Wyatt questioned.

"The depot just north of the Apache border, in the Arapaho Nation, you were there not long ago, is that correct?"

"That's right. I was headed down from Little Raven to stop by Geronimo Park."

"Did you happen to open the entrance to the depot? Interact with the clerk in any way?" asked the hidden man.

"Didn't know there was even a way to open one of these boxes."

"There isn't… for the most part. Only marshals possess the key to unlock the depots, but you don't seem to be privy to that information."

"I guess it was something Bill thought I best not know about. Now if you don't mind my asking, what exactly happened?" Wyatt adjusted his hat and impatiently tapped his boot up and down in the dirt. Having such a long conversation with a faceless man was unsettling.

"There seem to be a few discrepancies that may have taken place from what I have seen, and not seen over the last week or so. First, the aforementioned depot was breached just around the time you arrived there. There has been no activity through that depot since. Second, our Marshal in the Eastern Territories has not been heard from in the past two weeks.

Third…" The clerk paused.

"Third?" Wyatt insisted on knowing.

"There has been activity on the decommissioned tracks within the Quarantine Zone."

"Someone's been running a train through the Rotten Plains?" Old tracks had been laid throughout the plains, but were deemed unusable for centuries after the incident with the nuclear waste contaminating the region.

"From what the logs show, yes. That seems to be the case," the clerk confirmed.

Wyatt reached into his back pocket and pulled out a small, folded piece of paper. It was the note that the clerk had given him, notifying him about Chance just before they encountered each other. He took a minute to read over the message, then he handed it to the clerk.

"These depots share all of the same logs, correct?" Wyatt asked.

"That is right. I can look up any message that has been sent within the system."

"This is the message the clerk at that depot gave me that day. I want you to look it up," the marshal instructed.

Wyatt heard a cacophony of clicks coming from within the box. Only a few places had the type of machines that the clerks used. He remembered reading that they used to be common centuries ago. After a few moments the clicking stopped.

"No message was ever sent from the Sioux Nation… but this script is certainly an official clerk's handwriting," the clerk explained nervously.

Chance, Wyatt thought to himself. He reached in through the gap in the window and grabbed the note. "If we assume the Eastern Marshal is dead, that means we have no one commissioned in that region, correct?"

"That is correct."

"I don't know if your big fancy Government has any reserves they can send out, but if they do now is the time to do it. Which is the nearest decommissioned depot in the Rotten Plains?" Wyatt asked as he grabbed Peaches' reins and hopped onto her saddle.

"Lima depot, just north of the Navajo complex."

"Then I guess I'm better off leaving now on horseback than waiting all night for the next train." He whipped the reins and Peaches took off directly north for Lima, the first depot within the Rotten Plains.

Juan sat on his saddle with Hans in front of him. They rode carefully through the cold woods while the little hunchback directed where to go. The little man had not stopped talking since they left the creek---yammering on about things Juan had never heard before. He spoke of strange stories about people with odd names and said that he had read them. Juan could not read and found it hard to believe a creature such as Hans would be able to.

"Are we close?" Juan asked, simply to try and get a word in.

"Oh yes, oh yes, just up this path and we will get to Deacon's camp!" exclaimed Hans.

As they made their way up the narrow curving path Juan could hear the same rustling in the trees that he heard by the creek. He examined his surroundings. He could see small figures peeking out from behind the trees, and could hear whispers bouncing back and forth from trunk to trunk.

"Do not fret, Juan. If you are with me then they have no reason to fear you. Just don't be shooting at any of them like you did me, and they will like you!" Hans teased.

"I didn't know people even lived in these parts," said Juan, in a tender tone of sorrow.

"My people were all but forgotten," Hans sighed, "but that changed when Deacon found us. Now we will at least be remembered by one."

Juan's horse suddenly halted. She began shaking her head and puffing harsh breaths, just as she had done by the creek. He felt her belly pulsing and shivering between his legs. He watched as Hans leaned over her neck and began stroking her with his blistered, six-fingered hands.

"We have arrived," said the hunchback.

Hans hopped off the horse and instructed Juan to do the same. Right when Juan's boots hit the ground Hans grabbed his hand and pulled him forward as he bounced around in excitement. Juan was surprised at how fast he could move considering his most curious anatomy; he was fast enough for Juan to have to proceed with a light jog. They ran up the path a few meters until they reached the gate to the camp. It was a small wooden fence running all the way around the complex. There were houses inside, built like the saloon he had stopped by. These were constructed out of wood, unlike his home that was made of adobe, or Kai's hut made from buffalo hide. He had never seen a village that looked so beautiful.

"Hans... how did you... find this place?" asked Juan, admiring the fascinating town.

"Find it?" he asked, "we did not find this place, we built it! Of course we could not have done it without the help of Deacon."

"Hmm... Deacon, huh?" Juan turned his attention away from the buildings and over to Hans. "When can I meet him?"

"Right now sounds good," boomed a voice from within the gates. His voice was deep and powerful, but his words were a bit muddled and slurred.

He walked down the main road of the town and pushed open the gate, then stood in front of it, blocking the path. His name was Richard Deacon; a name that had made its way through many towns around the Western Heart. He towered over Juan, staring down at him with only his right eye, his left concealed by a leather patch. He had a burly grey beard and wore a large coat that was made from an assortment of animal hides. His hat looked ancient, with a massive brim and a top that was tall and rounded.

"Hans," Deacon said calmly, "what kind of man have you brought to our gates? Do you dare let a snake into our garden?"

Hans unwrapped his new shawl off his torso and handed it to Deacon. "I said I liked the one that he wore, and he gave me this one. He said it would fit me better."

Deacon felt the fabric with his fingers and spread the shawl out to get a clear view of it in its entirety. He looked it over for at least a minute---his eye tracing over every stitch. Then he folded it and handed it back to Hans.

"Why did you give this to the boy?" he asked Juan.

Hans turned Juan with an apprehensive look in his bulging eyes. Juan could tell that the Hans wanted him to keep the attempted killing secret. He realized it was only the second time he had ever shot the pistol, and he hadn't even thought about pulling the trigger, there was no hesitation at all. He knew right where Hans was at the time he shot. If he wanted to, he could have hit him, yet he wasn't sure why he had missed.

"I gave it to him in hopes that he would forgive me for shooting at him," said Juan.

"I see," Richard said. He then turned around and walked away, back up the street he had come from, leaving the gate ajar behind him.

Juan and Hans glanced at each other; Juan looking bewildered and Hans smiling from cheek to cheek. "I think he likes you," said the little hunchback.

Juan chuckled then followed Richard and Hans up the road.

The sun fell behind the mountains that surrounded the woods soon after Juan arrived. The town had torches that lined all the roads, lighting the town even at night. The flames helped to warm the town, making it even more comfortable than during the day. His hands were still cold but not as much as earlier. All the light made Juan almost forget that it was nighttime.

Richard Deacon invited Juan to stay in his cabin for the night, saying that he wished to know more about why the young man had been searching for him. Juan sat at a circular wooden table in the middle of Richard's home. There was a large pot hanging inside the stone fireplace by the table. Richard offered Juan a bowl of stew, but filled a bowl for him before he could answer. Then he poured a bowl for himself and sat down in the chair across from Juan.

Richard removed his hat when he sat down and let his long grey locks fall past his ears, then he stared at Juan with his one good eye. Juan was about to take his first bite of the stew when he noticed his host's piercing gaze. Juan saw that Richard's eye was focused on his hat, which he was still wearing. He placed the spoon back in the bowl and removed his hat, placing it on the table just as Richard had. He looked back at Richard, and the old man was already digging into his bowl of stew.

"Eat up, son... stew is getting cold."

Juan chuckled and spooned a bite into his mouth, letting the savory broth coat his mouth and warm his insides. It had large chunks of meat that fell apart as soon as they touched his tongue. He had never tasted anything quite as good.

"Juan," Richard said as he continued to spoon bites of the stew into his mouth, "what stopped you from killing Hans earlier?"

Juan chewed on some meat while considering his response. He remembered the bark exploding off the trunk of the tree and Hans jumping out from behind it. He saw the smoke rising up from the leather canteen as the toxic water burned through it. He gulped down the chunk of meat and placed the spoon back in the bowl.

"He was only trying to help me. I only shot at him when I thought he was a threat, but if I had killed him then I would have drunk from that creek. I would have died as well… I guess it was just luck that I decided to hear him out," Juan explained.

"Luck huh? Is that all it was?"

"What else could it have been?"

"Was Hans just lucky that your initial shot did not hit him? Did you intend to kill him when you shot at him?"

"I… I know that I could have killed him, I don't know why I missed," Juan said. He started to nervously rub at the raw spots on his hands left by the reins.

Richard continued to eat, but Juan's appetite had begun to dwindle. After only a few large spoonfuls Richard cleaned his bowl out. He tossed the spoon into the empty bowl and finally turned his attention to Juan.

"You do not seem like a killer to me," Deacon said comfortingly.

"But I am. In fact I have the entire Apache tribe looking for me."

"How many men have you killed?"

"Just one… but it easily could have been three by now."

Richard stood up and walked to the kitchen. He grabbed a large jug and a couple of glasses. He poured a glass for himself and one for Juan, then he placed the jug on the table in between them. He gulped down the entire glass in one swig then poured another.

"If you were a killer then you would have killed three by now. I have killed many things but only one man. The way I see it though, I am even worse than a killer, because for a long time I sat by and let men get killed. I could have stopped it, but I convinced myself that I couldn't." He downed the second drink and poured another.

Juan took a sip of the liquid. It tasted nothing like the tequila he was used to, but it burned even more. "But I killed the son of a chief."

"Why did you do it? Would you do it again if you could?"

Juan saw the face of the little red-haired girl in the train car. He wondered what happened to her if she was still alive or not.

"There was a girl in the train car I think they were taking her to the Apache casino to work. She was so young and so afraid. I thought the man was just a guard, he must have been as big as you, he was going to kill me… so I shot him… I don't know if the bullet killed him or the fall off the train did but either way I killed him."

"So would you do it again?" Richard insisted.

Juan took another sip of the liquid and swished it around in his mouth, ignoring the intense burning. "Suppose I would. It's not like he was a good person."

Richard dropped his glass and it crashed against the

table. It quickly rolled off and shattered on the ground. The sound nearly sent Juan falling out of his seat.

"What's wrong?" Juan asked.

"A good person? You said... you said he was not a good person," Richard said. His face void of all expression.

"I did."

"What is a good person?" asked Richard. He lunged across the table and grabbed onto Juan's shirt, knocking over Juan's glass and spilling the drink across the table. His eye had grown bloodshot and the liquor was dripping off his beard. Either sweat or tears were pouring down Richard's face, but Juan could not tell. "Are there any left in this world?" Richard howled.

Juan tried to pry Richard's hands off him, but the rawness on his palms made it hard to get a grip on Richard's dry calloused skin. "I... I don't know," was all that Juan was able to choke out.

"Tell me Juan, are you evil?" Richard demanded.

Juan clutched onto Richard's hands, ignoring the pain that shot through his palms, but the old man's grip was too strong for him to break free. "I don't know what that is!"

Richard violently shook Juan. Through the commotion Juan could tell that they were indeed tears pouring down Richard's face.

"WHY THEN!" Richard yelled, "Why do you speak of good without knowing of evil? Why have you forgotten the ways of God!"

"Deacon, please! I don't know what you are saying!" Juan cried.

"Why, God? Why have you shown yourself to me once and then never again? Why have you damned me with fruitless minds so ignorant to your calling?" Richard howled as he looked up to the ceiling. He let go of Juan, tossing him out of his seat, then Richard too fell to the ground and lay there with arms sprawled out.

Juan, still in shock from whatever had just occurred, was worried about Deacon. He rushed around the table and patted the old man on his cheek. His eye fluttered open, and Juan waved his hand over Richard's eye, trying to catch his attention. As his consciousness returned, Richard saw the blur of Juan's hand stroking back and forth in front of his face. He watched it rock to and fro like the pendulum of a grandfather clock, but instead of a golden ball moving from side to side, he saw a red bloody circle in the center of Juan's palm.

Juan could tell that Richard was coming to, so he started waving both hands, a bit quicker now. Richard's eye stopped fluttering, instead it was stayed fully open. He traced the path of Juan's hands as they swung in front of his face. Juan stood up and offered to help Richard back to his feet, extending his arm, waiting for him to grab a hold.

Richard grabbed on and Juan pulled him to his feet, but the one-eyed-man did not let go of Juan's hand. Instead he reached for his other hand and he stared at the wounds on Juan's palms. Two bloody spots directly in the center of the young man's palms. He turned them over and saw identical spots on the back of Juan's hands as well.

"Hmm…" Richard muttered, then turned his head up toward the ceiling, "What a fool I am for ever letting my faith in you falter."

"Deacon…"

"Forgive me boy. It is clear you are not evil, and that there are still good people in this world. I know it."

"Deacon," Juan started, "I still don't have any clue as to what you are saying."

"Don't worry… you will learn," Richard said as he slapped Juan on the shoulder.

The two woke up at dawn the next morning; Richard told the young man that there was something he wanted to show him. They gathered their things and headed off into the woods, west of the town. Juan was surprised how well Richard moved considering how old he was. His strength was also surprising, as he remembered Richard's iron grip around his collar the night before.

As they walked through the red trees Richard expanded on some of the concepts he had spouted earlier. "The world we live in used to look a whole lot different, and in the relative view of the world, it really was not that long ago. But many lifetimes have passed in between I suppose."

"How did it look different?" Juan inquired as he trudged through the cold mud.

"Well about 200 years ago these lands were well inhabited with large cities spread about," Richard explained.

"What is a city?"

"Well it is like the little complex I have established here with the outlings, but much larger in scale with thousands of people living in them."

"Outlings?" It was a term that Juan had never heard before.

"Hans' kind. Personally, I feel dirty calling them that. They used to be human just like you and me, but over centuries of living in these lands they have been turned into abominations. The little ones like Hans and the others in the complex are peaceful and actually quite intelligent. But generations of living in toxic lands and inbreeding have given them shortened lifespans and... unappealing features."

Juan was having a hard time taking in all of this new information. It seemed like in a matter of hours the world he knew had expanded tenfold. He felt sorry for Hans as he listened to Richard describe the hand that his kind had been dealt.

"Deacon, how do you know all of these things?"

"I read about them. I was blessed to be taught how to read when I was young. It's funny how little we know and how quickly that can change by only being able to understand some markings," Richard chuckled.

Juan noticed a familiar steam rising up from the ground off in the distance. It was the creek from earlier. He was surprised it ran this far through the woods. As they approached the creek Richard unstrapped the bag he was carrying around and placed it beside the edge of the creek. He knelt in the dirt and Juan knelt beside him. Juan watched Richard fold his hands together and start to mouth some inaudible words, then Richard cupped his hands together and lowered them into the steaming creek.

"Wait, what are you-"

Before Juan could finish Richard scooped out the toxic water and pressed it to his lips then proceeded to drink it. He made loud gulps as he drank the poison. In a terrified stupor Juan knelt in the dirt and watched as Richard seemingly try to kill himself. "Deacon," he murmured.

Richard drank the last drop then let his head fall back. "Ahhhh," Richard sighed. He looked over at Juan, who was close to tears after watching what he had just done. "It is fine, Juan. God has blessed these waters. If you have faith then you can't be hurt by the creek's venom."

"Who are you talking about?"

"If you are a man of faith then you will drink without having to know the answer to that question," Richard said, his voice quickly dropping to a more serious tone than Juan had heard before. "And if you do not drink then I cannot help you find your sister... I refuse to continue assisting those who lack faith."

"How did you know I was searching for Felina?" Juan asked. He dropped to his hands and stared at his reflection in the creek. The warm steam rose off the water and covered his face.

Richard stood up and began walking away. "Drink," he said, "let the waters answer your questions."

What is faith, Juan thought to himself, and how in the world will it help me fix the mess that I have caused? I saw the water from this creek burn right through my canteen, if I drink it then surely my insides will rot. Maybe that would be for the best. The Apache man, Father, Felina, how many more people need to be hurt because of me?

He cupped his hands together just as Richard did and he lowered them into the water. He could feel the poisonous fluid seeping into the wounds on his palms. It burned, but its heat almost felt healing. He scooped the water out and watched it oscillate in his hands.

Richard had stopped walking away. He turned around to watch what Juan would do, but the boy was just kneeling by the creek motionless, gazing at the water he was holding. Please God, let him be the one, Richard thought.

Juan's hands were shaking. The water started to splash and spill over the sides. Kai, Juan thought, why would she have me seek him out if he were to only try to kill me? She wouldn't… there must have been a reason she sent me here. Juan saw his jet-black eyes staring back at him from within the water in his hands. They looked like his sister's, and they begged him to be reunited. He pulled his hands apart. The water dropped back into the creek and Juan fell back on his hands.

Richard watched in disappointment. He thought that this time would be different, that he had finally found someone like himself, but he was afraid that it was not the case. He walked back toward the creek and called to Juan, "come on, we can head back-"

SPLASH!

Juan dunked his head into the steaming creek. He grabbed mouthful after mouthful of the water and gulped it down. He came up for air, only for a moment, then dunked his head right back under and continued to drink. Richard ran over and grabbed Juan by the collar of his shirt. He tugged hard trying to pull him away, but Juan's hands dug into the soft dirt on the creek bank. He resisted Richard, not letting himself be pulled away until his stomach was full of the creek's liquid.

"Damn it, son! You made your point!" Richard hollered. He planted his feet and pulled so hard on Juan's collar that they both went tumbling backwards. Juan took a deep breath and started coughing up some of what he had just drank. Richard slapped Juan's cheeks and asked, "Juan, are you alright?"

Juan eyes fluttered open, and he saw Richard's face only inches from his own. "Faith..." Juan said, then coughed up some more water, "did I do it right?"

Richard burst out in laughter, then pulled Juan to his feet and embraced him. "I couldn't have done it better myself," he said as he began to tear up and sniffle uncontrollably.

"Deacon?" Juan asked.

"What is it, kid?"

"Help me get Felina back... please."

Richard picked up Juan and threw him over his shoulder then headed back toward the town. "Don't worry, son. We'll get her."

Chapter 6

SLACK JAW, SILVER STAR, BLACK CLAD

He pulled the trigger of his pistol, and the loud bang echoed through the train car. Chance heard the bullet speed past him then watched the clouds run across the sky as he fell off the back of the train. Ain't my time yet, he thought to himself as he laid on the tracks coughing up specks of blood. He heard the thumping of hooves digging into the dirt around him. Two men rode up beside him. One of them had his face covered with a bandana and wore a short brimmed black hat, dark round glasses, and a black coat. The other had a brown leather jacket lined with wool and a silver star clipped on the right breast pocket.

The man in black hopped off his horse. He picked Chance off the ground and flung him on top of his horse. "You get him?" he asked.

Chance continued to cough, staining the horses rear with splotches of his blood. "I will," he said.

The man with the silver star let out a chuckle, "I guess you really are marshal-proof, we just can't kill you."

"That is enough, Falkner," said the man in black, "he is hurt. We need to get him back to the depot and treat him."

"C'mon, we both know there ain't no killing him," Falkner called out as he kicked the sides of his horse and sped off in the direction they came from.

The man in black hopped back on his horse and

followed closely behind Falkner, keeping a firm grip on Chance to making sure he didn't fall. Chance continued to wheeze; he could feel the muscles contracting around his broken ribs with each hack. He had not felt such intense pain since that day.

Chance stood atop the gallows, staring over the horizon and watching the sun creep over the distant mountains. The Eastern Marshal, Falkner, walked up the wooden steps of the gallows, readying the noose meant for Chance's neck. He climbed the short ladder up to the top beam where he tied the rope. He had hanged many from that beam, and Chance would soon be like all the others.

"So, is this how you planned it then?" Falkner asked, "Kill them two little Sioux girls, then what? Just wait around for my ass to show up and bring you over here to hang, huh? You must have been dropped on your head as a kid, is that it? Because you have got to be the stupidest killer I have come across, or maybe you just have a death wish."

Chance laughed; his slender frame quivered with excitement. "Oh Marshal, a death wish is the last thing I have. I have avoided death's cold clutches since the day I was born, and I'm starting to think the bastard just has it out for me."

Falkner finished tying the knot then dropped down the ladder and walked the noose over to Chance. He flung it around the man's skinny neck and tightened it.

"Also, I wasn't dropped on my head as a little one, but you could say that this ain't the first time I've been hanged," Chance chuckled.

"What do you mean by that?"

"Well, I suppose that I was just never wanted in the

world to begin with---nature tried everything it could, right from the start, to get rid of me. As a baby I came out ass first with the cord tied around my tiny neck, even tighter than you have this noose tied. I'm sure it did a bit of damage but not enough to finish the job."

Falkner tightened the noose once more, but Chance's neck was so slim that a small gap still lingered. The marshal grabbed Chance by the shoulders and peered into his hollow eyes. He said, "Don't worry, you ain't dodging ol' death's clutches today... I can assure you of that."

"Are you a gambling man, Marshal?" Chance asked, scratching at the coarse rope around his neck like a rodent combing through its diseased fur.

"I might be, but you have 30 seconds before I pull this lever and shut you up for good," Falkner growled.

"Well, I most certainly am a betting man, and why not go out with one more bet of a lifetime?" Chance started. "The both of us know this is a miserable world, and that it don't want either of us in it. You marshals are nothing but the dogs of the Natives. You bust your asses running errands for them knowing damn well they'd rather see ya' dead. Because to them all you represent is a shit stain in their history that they can't seem to wash out."

"15 seconds," Falkner announced, gripping the wooden lever.

Chance began laughing maniacally as he felt the cold hand of death reaching out to him once again. "You people sit back and accept the orders of a people who despise you and all that you represent, while you actively rid the world of the very people you share the most commonality with. People like me!"

"5 seconds... still ain't heard a bet."

"You pull that lever, Marshal, and if it goes as planned you keep living your pathetic life! But let's say, by some slim chance, I don't die right here and now. Let's say I live. Then why not ride with me into a world that we deserve!"

Falkner pulled back on the lever. Chance felt the floor fall from beneath him. In the blink of an eye he dropped through the hole, and the marshal heard a loud crack as the rope lost its slack.

"Ain't escaping a broken neck," he mumbled to himself. He turned to walk away but stopped when he heard another crack---a long-drawn-out creaking that sounded nothing like the one before it. He looked up at the top beam, where he had tied the rope, and saw the wood beginning to splinter. In an instant, the entire structure collapsed and fell through the hole in the floorboards.

Falkner hurried down the steps and into the small opening in the base of the structure. Chance's body lay on the ground, covered in the broken wood that he had been hanging from. As he tossed aside the broken boards, he noticed the noose was no longer wrapped around Chance's neck. He slapped Chance's face to wake him up. His eyes shot open and he began to cough and wail in agony. Falkner saw Chance's mouth agape and realized that he'd slipped through the noose, breaking his jaw in the process.

Let's say I live. Then why not ride with me into a world that we deserve! Falkner heard Chance's words repeat in his head. He picked Chance up and carried him to the well behind the gallows. He sat him up against the stone cylinder and pulled a long white handkerchief out of his coat pocket. He tied it around Chance's head, keeping his jaw good and shut, then he filled a bucket of water and splashed it onto Chance's face.

Chance was laid out in a cot in the living quarters beneath the depot. His body was still in excruciating pain from his tumble off the back of the train, and he didn't even attempt to sit up straight. Turning his head, he saw the man in black sitting beside him and Falkner at the other end of the room, drinking out of a large jug.

"He's nothing like you, Falkner," Chance said, still coughing up bits of blood.

Falkner set down his jug and wiped his mouth on his sleeve. "He learned from the old marshal, Bill Fuller. Stubborn old bastard must have really got in the kid's head. Probably better off just killing him."

"Reports have been coming in," the man in black started, "saying one of Chief Lipan's sons has been murdered. It is likely that the marshal will have his hands full searching for the killer. Best that we continue with the plan as is."

Chance laughed, but it quickly turned into a cough then a painful moan. He managed to sit upright and adjusted the bow on his head, then a thin smile crept across his face from one cheek to the other. "See, Falkner, I told you our little John Doe here would be helpful. The poor bastard, hauled up in a shit shack like this with nowhere to go for who knows how long. Well, it's no wonder he's more than willing to help change things."

"Falkner," John said, "Chance needs to rest until he can move again properly. You should be able to deal with the Comanche on your own while we continue our business in the quarantine zone."

Falkner bolted to his feet, knocking over his chair. He marched over to John and grabbed him by the collar. "I've taken orders from freaks like you for long enough. I ain't going to tell you again. The only instructions I take now are from Chance." He pushed John back into his seat. John fell back and tumbled to the ground.

Falkner looked down at Chance, waiting for him to give him an order. "John is right," Chance started, "he'll send a message to the Comanche, and they'll let you walk right in. I don't care how you do it, as long as Chief Nokoni dies. That's all that matters, but the more the merrier."

"I'll head to Buffalo Hump as soon as John calls a train this way then. Where should we meet once it's finished?"

"Don't know yet. Just bust into whatever depot is closest to Buffalo Hump. If you can convince the clerk then bring him along, and give him a better name than John Doe so we don't get them mixed up. If not, then use him however you can and shoot him when you're done with him."

John pushed himself back to his feet and brushed the dirt off his black outfit. "Fort Young is where we will set up our camp in the quarantine zone. Meet there once you've finished it." Falkner nodded at John, then he left the quarters. The door shut, and John turned back to Chance. "How did you ever manage to convince that one to follow you?" he asked.

"He didn't have a choice," Chance chuckled. "He lost a bet."

"Well, looks like I lost our bet," Falkner said, handing Chance a flask full of liquor. "If I'm being honest, what you said up there kind of got me thinking."

Chance cupped his lip in a way that the booze could seep through his teeth without having to open his mouth. Falkner had tied his handkerchief quite tightly around Chance's face---hoping that he wouldn't talk so much. Chance let the liquor pour out of the flask, but most of it escaped his mouth and ran down his face, soaking his shirt and puddling up in his crotch.

"So what's your plan then, how do you plan on changing this world?" Falkner asked.

Chance giggled and winced in pain all at the same time. He slapped his knee then grabbed onto his face. Every action he took resulted in his face aching. "C'mon now Marshal! Plans and procedure is what got you into the position you're in today. I ain't got a plan, that is my plan."

"I would rather you don't call me Marshal. I gave that title up the moment I decided not to finish you off. My name is Falkner."

Chance presented his hand to Falkner, "Chance Havoc, pleased to meet ya!"

Falkner looked at Chance's bony hand for a few moments, then he gave it a lackluster shake. "So, what are we here for then? If you really want to change the way things are, then what does killing two little girls have to do with it?"

"That was just so I could get your attention," Chance answered, his tone much sharper than before. Falkner said nothing, but the look on his face illustrated his confusion and interest in Chance's answer. "Just because I ain't got no plan doesn't mean I don't know the steps we gotta take for things to change. You just happened to be the first step is all."

"Is that right?" Falkner said as he pulled out a pack of tobacco and started chewing on a plug.

"Now then, are you ready for the next step?" asked Chance.

The next day the two men arrived at the Crazy Horse Casino, the headquarters of the Sioux leadership. With Chance's hands tied behind his back, Falkner pushed him through the gates of the casino---nearly empty but for a few old Sioux men playing cards at one table. Falkner marched Chance through the halls then up the stairs to the office of

Chief Nakota. Falkner busted open the office doors and kicked Chance through. Chance rolled across the carpeted floor until he slammed against the Chief's desk.

Nakota stood out of his chair. He looked down at the pathetic man squirming around on the floor, then he plopped back into his seat. Falkner sat in a short leather chair in the back corner of the room.

"What is this all about?" Nakota asked. He was a young man, not as young as Chief Cheyanne of the Arapaho, but a lifetime younger than Lipan of the Apache. Falkner had never cared for Nakota, or his late father; there were plenty of things they had commissioned him to do that he wasn't fond of.

"He's the one that killed the two girls in the diner."

"So why is the pest still alive?" Nakota snarled.

"Tried hanging him, but your gallows were shit, the thing broke right when I opened the floorboards."

"Then why did you not shoot him? My father was right, you pale-faces really are half-brained!" Nakota snapped. He waited for Falkner to respond, but the marshal said nothing. "I want the rat out of my sight, Falkner!"

Falkner laughed, then he took off his hat and began fanning himself. He slapped his leg then wiped a few tears out of his eyes and said to Nakota, "You dumbass, he's *been* out of your sight!"

Nakota stood up to get another look at Chance, but he was no longer on the floor. He turned around and saw Chance standing behind him. Before he could react, Chance swung and struck him in the face with the butt of his pistol. Nakota fell over his desk and hit the ground where Chance had just been lying. Chance slid over the desk, and he landed right on top of Nakota, digging his boots into the man's stomach and groin. He bent over and struck Nakota across the other side of his face. He stuck his hand in the chief's mouth and grabbed onto his upper jaw. He dragged him out of the office and over to the balcony railing that overlooked the main floor.

"C'mon Falkner, give me a hand!" Chance called out.

Falkner got out of his chair and walked over to the railing. He picked Nakota up by his feet, then the two men hoisted him over the rails and watched him plunge down to the first floor. His body crashed onto the table where the old men were playing cards. The chips and cards went flying, and the two men fell back out of their seats.

The old Sioux men crawled over to the chief and felt around his neck and chest for a pulse. Then a loud bang echoed throughout the casino and a bullet rifled through the chief's chest, splashing blood on the old men's faces. They looked up to the second floor and saw a puff of smoke rising up from the barrel of Falkner's pistol. Chance aimed his pistol down at them, then he and Falkner proceeded to fire all their rounds down at the Chief.

The bullets rained down from above, plummeting into Nakota's body while all avoiding the two old men. Falkner and Chance walked down the stairs to the main floor, passing by the elders like they weren't even there. They headed for the bar on the far end of the room. Chance spun his pistol around his finger while he skipped through the casino like an excited child. Falkner followed closely behind, his hands in his jacket pockets as casual as ever.

Chance sat atop one of the barstools. The bartender backed up cautiously until he hit the wall of booze behind him, knocking over some bottles and sending them crashing to the floor.

"Hmm, what a waste," Chance growled. He raised his pistol and shot the bartender in his left shoulder. The bartender cried out in pain and fell to the ground, right on top of the broken liquor bottles. The shards of glass stuck into the man's rear, which only sent him into more of a fuss.

Falkner hopped over the bar, pulled a bottle off the shelf, and stuck it in his back pocket. Then he knocked over and threw more bottles around the floor of the casino. The wooden floors soaked up the liquor and began to exude a whiskey aroma. Chance and Falkner started for the exit, and Falkner opened the bottle in his pocket. As they walked, he let its contents spill out, leaving a trail in his wake. Chance pulled out a small pack of matches from his shirt pocket. He removed a single match and pressed the red tip to the rough strip on the box. He prepared to strike it.

"Hold on," Falkner stopped him, "almost forgot something." Then he ran back into the casino.

Chance stood impatient, dying to strike the match and set the whole building aflame. He saw Falkner walking back toward the exit, dragging the two old Sioux men behind him; they were bawling and covered in the chief's blood.

"Now what is the point of that?" Chance asked with a noticeable tone of annoyance in his voice.

"They can run along and tell the rest of the tribe what happened. Send the whole nation in a frenzy," Falkner explained.

Chance laughed, then he struck the match. He tossed it onto the alcohol-soaked wood and watched the flame travel across the ground to the bar. The bar ignited, engulfing the casino in a raging inferno. The bartender's screams echoed for miles as the flames consumed him. The Sioux leadership had been burned to ash.

Chance and Falkner sat atop their horses, looking over the

horizon of the Sioux Nation. They were on top of a hill and below them was a government depot---one Falkner had frequently used to board trains running up and down the eastern nations.

"Are you sure this is going to work?" Falkner asked as he flipped his silver star around in his fingers.

"That badge of yours is the only way for us to get into one of those depots. If we really want to change things then we need a way of moving around the Heart faster than on foot or horseback," Chance explained. "Those clerks are cooped up in those little shacks from the moment they get shipped out here. If anyone has the potential to hate this world, it's them. They just need a little talking to."

Falkner laughed and kicked his horse forward. "How are you going to convince him without a noose around your neck though?"

They rode down the hill toward the depot. No trains had passed through in quite some time; the East did not have as much traffic as the West. Chance rode to the front of the depot while Falkner rode to the backside.

Chance investigated the tinted windows, trying to make out any details of the clerk within. It was a cloud covered sky though, so all he could see was a general outline of the man's head. "Well howdy, Mister," Chance yelled as he manically knocked on the window.

"I am only permitted to converse with the Marshals, please leave," said the man from inside the metal box.

Chance smacked his hand down on the steel counter and pushed his face up against the window. "You conversed with me just now though. Already broke the rules, so what's it going to hurt if you exchange just a few more words with me?"

"Please move along," said the clerk. Then a steel sheet dropped down from behind the tinted glass, fully enclosing the metal box. Not even the outline of the man's face could be seen anymore.

"You're doing great. Keep it up," Falkner hollered from the back of the structure.

Chance marched around back and pushed Falkner aside, swiping the silver star out of his hand. There was a small slit in the back wall of the building---a couple of millimeters wide and a few centimeters tall. Chance knelt down and pushed the star badge into the slit. A series of clicks and rattles shook through the building, then the back wall popped open at the corner. Falkner helped Chance pull back the opening so it was wide enough for them to fit through.

The room was dark and filled with stale air; it carried a musty aroma that reeked of death. The clerk sat at his desk, not caring to turn around or acknowledge their entry. He wore a black suit and a short-brimmed hat. He appeared to be bald, as there was no hair sticking out of the bottom of his hat. The skin on the back of his head was so white it seemed translucent. Clearly, he had not been outside the confines of the metal box for a long time---perhaps he'd never even left the structure.

"Marshal Falkner, do you care to explain the meaning of this most unusual encounter?" the clerk asked.

"Not really," Falkner answered. "He does all the talking, I'll leave it to him."

"I am not permitted to converse with anyone outside of the Marshal Service."

Chance flipped the clerk's chair around so his pale face looked straight at him, but the clerk was wearing glasses with blacked out lenses so he couldn't look into the man's eyes. "Then don't speak, but listen," Chance started. "What you have been told to do or not to do means nothing. The men that shipped ya' off here and locked ya' inside this cage don't actually give a shit what you do. They only hoped you'd do as they say…but if ya' don't… nothing's gonna happen. They've already given up on this world."

"Chance, he ain't going for it, let's just have him call us a ride then kill the sorry bastard. I mean look at him, he doesn't even know what living is. It wouldn't make a difference," Falkner said as he removed his pistol from his holster and pulled back the hammer.

"I know you didn't choose to be here," Chance started. "Those Government pricks stuck ya' here against your will then tricked ya' into thinking it was all fine. Like I said, they already gave up on this land, why don't we help this land give up on them as well?" Chance took a step back from the clerk and reached out his hand, waiting for him to grab it.

The clerk gazed at the bony fingers in front of his face. He couldn't remember if he had ever seen another person's hand. "I do not know why I am here," the clerk started, "I don't even know who I am, or what I am. All I know are these tracks, and I know you, Marshal. In fact, until today I didn't even know that there was a way to open this box. This depot is all I have ever known."

Chance reached down and grabbed the clerk's arm. The clerk's attention shot to Chance's touch---he had forgotten what the touch of another person felt like, it was a most shocking sensation.

"Listen to me," Chance said, "your ignorance is the product of this world. This cage is the product of this world. Shed your ignorance… along with what you know this world to be. Authority is what has kept ya' in this box, it's what has forced Falkner to do things he hasn't wanted to do, and it's what's tried to expel me from this world since the day I was born."

The clerk looked over to Falkner. The rays of sunlight

ignited the marshal's silhouette, and they brushed upon the clerk's white cheeks. "What about you, Marshal? I assume you have broken protocol as I just have. Perhaps now there is no way to undo our actions?"

Falkner smirked, then turned around and started for the door. He opened it as wide as he could to let in as much light as possible. As the rays washed over the clerk's face, his skin began to sizzle and small puffs of smoke rose out of his pores.

"It is painful," the clerk said, but he did not scream or writhe in pain. A few tears rolled down his cheeks, that were blistering as the room grew warmer and warmer from the sunlight. "It feels much more pleasant than feeling nothing at all."

"Look, stranger," Falkner started, "do whatever you want. I ain't doing this because I did or didn't break protocol. I lost a bet is all, and to be honest I enjoy the change of pace." Then he walked out of the depot.

Chance strolled over and shut the door, but not fully, so that the sun would stop burning the man's skin. He reached into his pocket, pulled out a long black bandana, and handed it to the clerk. "If ya' want to come with us, ya' best cover your face. I don't know how long you'll last out in the sun. What are you called anyway?"

"Clerk..." he said.

"Hmm, in the old days they would call someone without a name John Doe. That will work for now. If you come up with something better just say it."

Chance rolled out of bed and let his feet touch the cold ground of the depot. John watched as the frail man tried to keep his balance.

"You have been in bed for five days, you don't have to rush yourself up," said John.

Chance's wore only his underwear, but his torso was tightly wrapped in medical cloth. The wrapping highlighted his skeletal figure, dipping between the crevasses of his ribs, which were clearly still broken.

"How is your jaw? Do you still need that ridiculous looking cloth?" John asked.

His mouth was still pinned shut by the long handkerchief. Chance inspected himself in the mirror hanging above the room's small sink, running his bony hand over the deep bumps and valleys of his thin face.

"I'm starting to like it actually… I think I'll keep it."

"We should start moving east if you feel up to it. I imagine Falkner will arrive at Buffalo Hump soon."

Chance nodded then looked around the room with great curiosity. "Umm… John?" he asked.

John got out of his chair and walked over to the nightstand beside the bed. He picked up a folded pile of clothes and handed them to Chance. "They were filthy. I tried getting all of the blood out of them that I could."

"Well, we should get moving then. We have work to do," Chance said as he slipped his head through the collar of his tattered but now clean white shirt.

Chapter 7

FRIENDS AND FIENDS

Lima was the first Government depot on the southern edge of the Rotten Plains. Wyatt paced around outside the depot and fiddled with his badge, flipping it in between his fingers as he inspected the structure. This one was larger than the other depots, nearly twice the size. It used to house Government officials---they preferred a workspace more luxurious than the typical compact cube the clerks were confined to. The clerk said that only a marshal could open the depots, he thought to himself, I wonder why Bill never told me about that---he taught me plenty of things that the Government wouldn't want anyone knowing about... maybe he didn't even know about it.

Wyatt ran his hand up and down the walls of the abandoned depot, trying to find any imperfection in its facade that could possibly be used to open it. But it was completely smooth and tightly sealed.

It sure is getting dark, he thought. Even though I'm on the edge of the Plains, those things could still be nearby. Hell... it isn't exactly uncommon for them to creep outside the Plains. He was beginning to get nervous. Peaches' breathing was getting heavier; she was tired and there was no telling what would come with the darkness. He knew that they needed to find shelter quickly. The depot was large enough to fit both him and Peaches, but it was no use if he couldn't find a way inside.

"Hmpf!" he could hear Peaches making a fuss. It didn't help calm his nerves by any means.

He stepped up his inspection of the depot's outer walls, running his hands up and down the steel, desperately hoping to find any bulge or dip in the flat metal surface. Peaches was growing more and more nervous; he could hear her huffing and puffing as the sun crept behind the tree covered horizon.

"Damn it all," Wyatt exclaimed as he pounded on the thick sheet of metal. He could hear the boom from his strike echoing off the walls inside.

The ground was covered in leaves from the dead trees that surrounded the building. He heard them crunching all around, a crackling from all different directions. Footsteps from the North, then from the South, then the East and the West. Peaches became frantic at the incoming symphony of steps, and in her panic she took a few quick steps then collided into the depot's wall. The horse let out a shrieking cry that startled Wyatt. He turned away from the wall and drew his pistol from its holster.

The sun had disappeared entirely. Only the dim light from the sliver of a moon lit the woods. Wyatt crept toward Peaches. She was still upright even after bumping into the steel wall. He placed his free hand on her head and caressed her pink skin. From within the woods, a great many pairs of yellow eyes appeared out of the darkness. He had encountered wolves before, but the creatures within the Rotten Plains were not built like those in the natural world.

The pack enveloped the entire depot, and by the way the leaves crunched beneath their paws it was clear that they were heftier than normal wolves. The moon continued to rise in the night sky. Its light cast a line between the open area where the depot rested and the dense woods that bordered it.

Wyatt could hear growls rumbling about the vicious horde that surrounded him. The pair of eyes directly in front of Wyatt floated a bit higher up than the rest, and its growl was far more vicious. Wyatt cocked his revolver and pointed the barrel at the angry eyes. He took a step forward and watched as the alpha beast mimicked his approach.

Its snout poked out of the darkness into the revealing moonlight. Its nose was crooked, and the skin on its snout pulled back, revealing its sharp fangs and foaming gums. As it took another step into the light, its paw pushed into the dirt exposing the pale grey skin that covered its body. His paw was the size of Wyatt's hand, and its claws the length of his fingers. It continued into the revealing lunar spotlight, not at all intimidated by the marshal or his gun. Its body was muscular and defined, just like Peaches', and the only patch of fur was a long strip, like a mohawk, from the top of his head to its rear. The wolf stood nearly eye level with Wyatt, its tongue hung out the side of its mouth while it salivated at the smell of fresh human meat.

Wyatt stared at the wolf, disgusted and saddened by its crude appearance. It was a cursed beast, as was Peaches. The pestilence of this land had changed them, distorted them into a twisted shell of their natural form. It was not nearly his first encounter with such things, but he could never seem to cast aside his pity for them. As he approached the wolf, Wyatt aimed his pistol away from the animal's head and pointed it into the moonlit sky. He pulled the trigger, and the shot boomed through the entire forest. Peaches screeched in terror, the gunshot too much for her sensitive ears, and the wolf frantically backed away, retreating into the darkness. Wyatt took a few steps closer and continued firing his pistol into the air, each shot echoing through the forest over and over. He could hear the wolves begin to whimper, then the yellow eyes began to disappear. He heard the footsteps of the pack running through the woods back whence they came.

He holstered his pistol and hurried back for Peaches. Her body trembled with lingering trepidation, but the marshal's touch soothed her. He stroked her neck and sides, and he could feel her shaking begin to subside. Much as he worried about his horse being startled, he knew that the pack could very well return at any moment. The clerk told him he could open the depot, and he knew he must find a way if he wanted to survive the night.

He ran around to every wall and continued to search for imperfections, but the sides were flawless. He hadn't a clue where the entrance was or how he was supposed to open it. He walked to the back of the building, took a step away and gazed hopelessly at the depot. He plopped on the ground and his ass landed hard into the dirt. It's useless, he thought, the damn thing is sealed shut, there's no way of getting in.

The wolves' howls in the distance began to fill the surrounding air. Wyatt looked around to see if any yellow eyes were watching him, but he could not see any. He flipped his badge back and forth between his fingers, and the howls grew louder in the background. "Come on," Wyatt said to himself, "one more look."

He got off the ground and returned to the front of the building. He thought he could shoot out the glass barrier, but he realized that a steel sheet had been placed behind the glass at this depot, sealing it from the inside. The whole process exhausted him. He put his hand against the border of the glass and rested his head on his arm. He closed his eyes for a minute, only opening them to the sound of yet another howl. When they opened, he found his face very close to the window, and next to the frame he saw the slightest gap, only a few millimeters wide and a few centimeters tall. He stepped back and pulled his badge out of his pocket. He turned it around in his fingers then pushed it up to the small slit. The edge of the star poked through the opening, and it was suddenly sucked into the wall. Noises rattled from inside the depot, then a loud click echoed from the back of the building and his badge popped back out.

Wyatt ran around the building and saw the back wall had opened at the corner. Wrapping his fingers around the edge of the wall, he pulled it back so that it opened wide enough for Peaches to fit. He walked the horse inside and closed the wall behind them.

It was the first time he had been inside a depot. Bill used to take Wyatt to the abandoned forts when they would travel through the Rotten Plains, but those were much larger and better equipped than this. It was nearly empty inside. The lights had turned on once he opened the wall, but the main computer remained off. The computers held the logs and controls for the trains. There was clearly a power source inside the depot; he hoped he could use it to get the computer up and running. Bill taught him much about the trains that ran through these parts; they'd spent years inside the Rotten Plains, reading through old instruction books that had been stored inside abandoned Government compounds. Wyatt knew how to decode the logs and even had a general knowledge of how to navigate the trains, but his knowledge would be no use if the control mechanism was dead.

In the far corner of the room was a small cot---he hadn't slept in a bed, with a pillow, in quite a long time. Peaches had already curled up on the ground and fallen asleep by the building's entrance. Her calm snoring nearly hypnotized Wyatt to sleep. He stared at the blank computer, recalling the clerk telling him about the train activity within the Rotten Plains. That would be impossible if the system was dead. He took a deep breath and accepted that he would not be enjoying a mattress and pillow tonight. Wyatt removed his hat and threw it on the cot, then pulled off his poncho and neatly folded it. He rolled up his sleeves and got to work on bringing the computer system back to life.

He spent the night rearranging wires, cutting some, and reconnecting others. It took him until sunrise, but he finally managed to get the computer booted up. He stared at the unending dots and dashes of Morse messages littering the screen. All the logs from the past century were being uploaded into the system in an instant. It was a lot to unpack, but he only cared about the messages that had come through in the past week. He saw the message Chief Cheyanne had sent him, summoning him to Little Raven, as well as Chief Lipan's request for him to come to Geronimo Park. That had been around a week-and-a-half ago---since then the comms had gone silent. He checked through pages and pages of logs, and there had been no messages out of the East in weeks. Wyatt was beginning to question whether or not the Eastern Marshal had been killed. If so, there should have been a message sent out by the Sioux or the Comanche. It was hard to believe that affairs in the eastern nations would be so calm; it was uncharacteristic to say the least.

On the right side of the computer screen was a map of the Western Heart. A dot was blinking at the bottom tip of the Rotten Plains, above the eastern half of the Apache Nation. That was Lima, where Wyatt currently was. He ran his finger over the screen, tracing the squiggly lines that signified the tracks until he reached the first dot within the Comanche territory; another Government depot called Tango.

Wyatt typed out a message in Morse and sent it to the Tango Depot, knowing it shouldn't take more than a few minutes to receive a response. That was, of course, if everything was as it should be. He spent the next couple of hours studying the map and looking through the logs, trying to find out where the activity in the Plains was taking place. He found that all the unauthorized activity kept leading back to one spot, Fort Young. It was an old fort on the western half of the Rotten Plains---that Wyatt remembered visiting with Bill when he was a boy. Pinched in between two mountain ranges, Fort Young was a junction for five different sets of tracks. It was not too far from Lima. If he were to call a train to Fort Young, then whoever was there would easily know he was coming---there would be no telling what would happen then. He would have to ride Peaches around the mountain and through the Rotten Plains if he was to make it to Fort Young undetected.

He checked the logs one last time. There was still no response---the irregularity of everything made him feel uneasy. He studied the map, planning a route that would best get him to Fort Young while avoiding as much trouble as possible. Riding north to Fort Thompson was his best bet---from there he could cut west, straight to Fort Young.

Juan walked through the woods with Hans beside him. Every few steps they would find a stick that was suitable for a fire and tossed it in the bag Juan carried on his back. It had been three days since Juan arrived in the town, and in those three days he had learned much about his hosts. Hans stayed up every night and told him stories of all the things Richard had done in his life and for the town. He had been living with the little hunchbacks for nearly 25 years, Hans told him.

"How long has it been since Deacon left the village?" Juan asked as Hans handed him a group of sticks.

Hans hobbled along and thought hard about the question. "Well, he has been there every day that I have been alive for. So I would say that it has been at least 15 years since he left."

15 years? Juan thought to himself. Hans looked like he was closer to 40, and he was far smarter than Juan. It surprised him to learn that the little man was younger than himself. "Richard said that he would accompany me to Geronimo Park. Do you think he will be alright traveling all that way at his age?"

"Deacon has been on many adventures, he is no stranger to a long pilgrimage. Plus, he has waited a very long time for you to come here. I realize that all the times he spoke of God sending him a sign, that it was you he had been waiting on," Hans explained.

"You all keep referring to that man…God. I don't know who he is, but he seems quite famous around here."

Hans burst out in laughter, he dropped to the ground, spilling all the sticks he had gathered. "You really aren't a smart man are you, Juan?"

Juan knelt down, gathered the spilled sticks and placed them in his backpack. "That seems to be quite obvious, doesn't it?" He reached out his hand and helped lift Hans off the ground, then brushed the dirt off the shawl he had given the little hunchback. "But I really don't understand," Juan continued, "who is he?"

"Do you remember the water in the creek where we first met?" Hans asked. Juan nodded his head in confirmation. "You saw the water from the creek burn right through the leather of your canteen, but for some reason when you went down to the same creek with Deacon, you still decided to drink the water, and in quite the dramatic fashion I am told. What compelled you to drink from something you knew would kill you?"

"I… I don't know," Juan answered honestly. He imagined the steam that arose from the flowing creek, and the smoke that puffed up from the leather of his canteen. "I just did it."

"And why didn't you shoot me when you had the chance to, back in the woods where we first met?" Hans asked. He moved his blistered boiled face closer, and his one bulging eye stared directly into Juan's.

"I…I-" Juan choked as he felt a wave of shame and guilt rush through his veins.

Then Hans grabbed Juan by the wrist and gripped it firmly with his six fingers. "I will tell you why! You didn't choose to dunk your head in that creek, and you didn't magically decide to spare my life. *He* commanded you to, *He* was the one who forced your head into that creek and *He* was the one who moved the barrel of your pistol away from my head. That is who *He* is, Juan. When you realize that, you will see that anything can be done if you act on his behalf. So do not doubt Deacon, and do not doubt yourself, just listen for when He calls to you, and do as He commands, and you will surely save your sister!"

Tears began to fall from Juan's eyes. He fell to his knees and embraced Hans. He squeezed the little man into his chest, and Hans returned the embrace. "Thank you, Hans. I promise I will try to understand. I won't doubt him."

"Come on now. If you stay bent over like that for long your back will start looking like mine!" Hans joked.

Juan stood up and saw Hans' giant smile gleaming at him, then the two burst out in laughter. "I think that is enough wood for tonight, let's head back to the town," said Juan.

Later that night the outling villagers made a giant bonfire in the center of the town, and a feast was prepared to send off Juan and Richard with good tidings. A mash-up of exotic meats cooked over the bonfire, filling the air with an ambiguous aroma. Juan wished to not know exactly what he was eating; the taste was not horrible, but with the strange forms that plants and animals took on in the area, he decided that ignorance was bliss for the night.

Hans hobbled over to Juan and sat beside him at the long picnic-style table. From where they were seated, they could see everyone in the village gathered around the fire. They all looked just like Hans, with only minor variations. None of the villagers wore shoes, and the men wore nothing but poorly fitted shorts or sometimes skirts. The women wore a long cloth that covered their whole body, or a skirt, like the men, and another cloth wrapped around their breasts---which were typically uneven, making them hard to cover properly. The men were bald, while the women had small clumps of hair budding from several random spots on their heads.

"You haven't hardly touched your food," Hans observed, pointing his fork at Juan's plate.

Juan gazed down at his plate. The meats had a purple tint to them and were cut in little chunks, making it was impossible to tell what animal they came from. And the pile of slop beside it looked like the mud he would scrape off his horse's hooves. "The meat... it isn't as good as the stew Richard makes."

Hans chuckled and stuck his fork in one of the chunks then popped it in his mouth. "Well, the other stuff is just beans, from a can. They are salty so I think you'll like them. We only have a meal like this maybe once a year. We have to scrape together easier-to-find meats to feed everyone so well for one night... I think you chose..." Hans took a good minute of chewing the tough meat to be sure he gave a proper answer, "mmm, giant squirrel."

Juan's ignorance had been destroyed, and his appetite along with it. "I have never heard of giant squirrel," he said.

"They grow much larger out here. Unfortunately you didn't get the tail, that is the best part."

Juan took a long drink from his glass, gulping it down into his empty belly. Hans swapped his plate with Juan's, "I managed to get the last bit of fowl, you will like it more."

"Thank you, Hans. I don't know what I would do without you."

"Well…" Hans sighed, "I suppose you better figure that out before the sun rises."

"What do you mean?" Juan asked.

"You and Richard are going to embark on an extremely dangerous trek tomorrow, and I will be stuck here in this village, waiting to find out if I ever see either of you again. I know it is wrong, but I envy you and Richard. With this body I will never be able to go on a great adventure like you could."

Juan was constantly amazed by the little hunchback, and he was having a hard time imagining how the next part of his journey would turn out without Hans by his side. "What is stopping you from being like Richard or myself?"

"Deacon would never allow it. He told us that we should not ever leave the village. The things that are in this land would kill me in an instant, I can't run like you can or shoot a gun."

Juan slammed his hands against the table and bolted out of his seat. He turned to Hans and stared down at the little man. "How pathetic…" Juan said. He grabbed the shawl he gave Hans and pulled it off him. "Just today you told me I wasn't a smart man, and you were right. But I would rather be stupid than a coward. Deacon is an old man, with who knows how much longer to live---do you think he could outrun anything better than you could? I have an entire tribe looking for my head, do you think I have enough bullets in my gun to shoot them all? And you say that Deacon wouldn't allow you to leave. Wasn't it you who just today told me that our actions are commanded by God? I didn't know that Deacon was your god."

"Juan…" Hans' voice crackled.

"Do you know what the real difference between the two of us is, Hans? The real difference is that I could never know all the things that you know. That mind of yours is something else." Juan stuck his arm out, dangling the shawl in front of Hans' face. "The only way I am giving this back to you is if you wear it all the way to Geronimo Park and tell my sister what a beautiful job she did making it!"

"What is all the fuss about?" Richard's voice boomed across the courtyard.

Juan and Hans hadn't noticed, but the entire village had gone silent and all eyes were fixed on their altercation.

"Deacon…" Hans mumbled, "Juan, he is… he wants me to come with-"

"You should know better Hans-" Richard started.

Before he could say anymore, Juan butted in, "Deacon! You can't keep Hans trapped here all of his life! All he wants is to see the world!"

"That is enough out of you, Juan… Hans is my family, and it is rude to get involved in another family's affairs," Richard declared. Juan did not argue, but he looked back at Hans and waited for his answer. "As I was saying," Richard continued, "you should know, Hans… that you should never be so careless as to reject a kind gift from your neighbor."

Hans struggled to contain his emotions; he could hardly get a full sentence to exit his mouth. "Does that mean… are you s-saying that-"

"I am saying that you can make your own decisions,

117

but it is rude to reject such a lovely gift. And it would be a shame if you didn't thank the person who made it for you."

Juan crouched down to get eye level with Hans, and he pushed the shawl in front of his face. Hans wrapped his fingers around the green and red fabric and pulled it close to his chest.

"Well..." Hans started, "I don't want you or your sister to think I am rude."

A moment of silence followed his answer, then Richard and Juan smiled and began laughing along with the rest of the outling villagers. Juan hugged Hans once again, then they sat back down and continued with their meals.

"Juan," Richard called out, "come to my cabin once you've finished, I would like a quick word before you go to sleep."

Juan took his time finishing his dinner. He chatted with Hans and the other outlings for an hour or two, then he made his way to Richard's cabin. "I hope I didn't keep you up too late," Juan said as he poked his head through the door.

"Are you ready for tomorrow?" Richard asked. "Once we leave there is no turning back."

Juan sat on the floor beside the fireplace, where Richard sat in his rocking chair, and stuck his hands by the fire to warm them. "I am," he said, "I only wish that we were closer to Geronimo Park. I can't stop thinking about what might be happening to Felina."

"Well, while I don't agree with the way those girls are used in the casinos, the natives don't just senselessly kill innocent women. She is alive and that is the only thing we need to know."

"Si," Juan said, rubbing his hands together beside the fire.

"Tell me about your family, Juan. It is my understanding that most of the Mexicans moved south toward their homeland over two centuries ago. I'm curious as to why your family didn't follow suit."

"When I was very young," Juan started, "Abuela, my father's mother, told Felina and me stories that had been passed down through our family for many generations. I don't remember them too clearly, I was so little back then, they did not make too much sense to me. But she would talk about the journey my ancestors made, going north from the homeland to where I was born in the Apache lands, although it was called a different name a long time ago. Apparently things were quite different hundreds of years ago, people seemed happier. She would tell us how there were all kinds of different people who lived in these lands. I always wished that I could go back in time and see what the world used to be like. As for why my ancestors did not move south, I think it was to honor the dead, the ones who had sacrificed so much to make it north---I don't think they wanted to give up on this land."

"That sounds like a story I have read about many times," Richard chuckled, "about a man who led his people to a promised land. Those people held that land very dear to them after that."

"I would like to hear that story someday."

Richard reached over to the small table beside his rocking chair. He pulled open a little drawer, and took out a book. It had a navy-blue leather cover, and gold writing so faded it was impossible to tell what it said. He handed it to Juan, who took it and inspected it with great curiosity.

"Everything I truly know, I learned from that book," Richard said, "I want you to have it, and to learn from it as I did. I hope that you can carry on what I have started here. That is all that I ask in return for helping you find your sister."

"Richard, I can't learn anything from this if I don't know how to read," Juan lamented.

"Hans will teach you, he is indeed a bright man. So all you have to do to fulfill your debt to me… is keep Hans alive."

"Si," Juan replied.

"I need you to swear it to me, Juan," Richard demanded, fixing his attention on the young man. His eye glowing with the same seriousness as the other night when he nearly pummeled the boy. "Place your hand on top of that book and swear you will do everything you can to keep Hans alive."

Juan held the book in his hands, riveting at the rough blue leather. He pressed his right palm against the cover; it was warmer than he expected it to feel. But then again, he thought, I am sitting very near to the fire. "I swear it, Deacon. As long as he is by my side, he will live."

Staring into the fire, Richard reached out and wrapped his fingers around Juan's arm. He kept a firm grip on him, firm yet gently, and loving. Juan rested his hand on top of Richard's and held it there. It reminded him of his father's touch.

"One last thing," Richard said.

"What is it?" Juan replied.

"I am assuming that someone instructed you to come find me. What did they say exactly?"

"It was Lady Kai, she is a Navajo medicine woman. She was friends with my father, and the only person I could think to go see when I was on the run. She showed me visions, the first one was of a one-eyed elk that I needed to find. That was you."

"An elk, you say?" Richard asked, looking quite astounded by what he had just heard.

"That's right."

"How interesting, what else did she tell you?"

"The next thing I saw was a raven, it was perched at the top of a mountain… it looked like it was crying, and there was a storm. Then she talked about a wolf, and a rat, that they would both be threats. I think she was saying that one of the threats would be obvious, but the other not so much."

"Sounds like quite the woman," Richard chuckled. "Well, if we head straight west we will reach Fort Thompson. It is an old, abandoned government outpost, adjacent to a large mountain. Perhaps there is where we will find your crying raven."

Juan pushed himself off the ground and turned to Richard. "I should probably try to get some sleep, I don't plan on resting until we reach Fort Thompson," he said.

"I sure hope you're ready, son," Richard said, closing his eyes and rocking himself to sleep.

Juan, Richard, and Hans left the next morning at sunrise. Hans weighed no more than 60 or 70 pounds, so he rode with Juan on his horse---they decided taking three horses would only slow them down. Richard led the way through the woods while Juan and Hans traveled closely behind. Richard explained that the trek to Thompson would take around three days. The first day would be the toughest, seeing that they had no tracks to follow. Instead they would ride through the woods until they made it out the other end of the forest, where they would find an abandoned Government depot.

Sitting behind Juan, Hans turned to face his town and watched it shrink away in the distance as they rode deeper and deeper into the woods. Juan turned his head around to check on Hans periodically. Part of him worried that Hans would fall off the back of the horse, the other part of him felt guilty for dragging him away from his home.

"Did you say goodbye to your family?" Juan asked

him.

Hans continued to gaze into the distance behind them, even though the town could no longer be seen. "I don't have any family, my kind does not live as long as straight-backs, like Richard and yourself. My mother and father lived to be about 20 years old, they died when I was five. Richard raised me for the most part, but really everyone in the village plays a role in each other's lives."

"Are you sure you won't miss it?" Juan asked.

"Quite the opposite," Hans chuckled, "I already miss it greatly... but it does not matter, because I know that this is the path I am supposed to travel. I cannot imagine what the two of you would do without me around!"

"Well then, you best turn around and grab ahold of me so you don't fall off, wouldn't want to be losing you on the first leg of the trip now, would we?" Juan said. Hans laughed and flipped around to grab onto Juan.

Besides the occasional quick conversation with Hans, the journey was quieter than Juan had imagined. There were birds that chirped and twigs that snapped beneath the horses' hooves, but the land did not seem as dangerous as he originally thought. The colors of the vegetation varied greatly, and each mile they traveled looked vastly different than the last. There were spots of thick, blood-red trees, like the ones where Juan first met Hans by the creek, and other areas where trees were short and sparse, with normal green and brown leaves and trunks. The one thing that did not change, however, was the same bleak air that filled the entire forest.

Juan's shawl didn't do much to keep him warm, but luckily he had Hans' embrace that was better than nothing. Hans seemed quite content wearing only the shawl Juan gave him; he felt the little man's hands wrapped around his waist and they didn't seem to shiver at all. Juan remembered how cold it was when he first met Hans. He had hardly even noticed that the hunchback was wearing nothing more than a loincloth that covered his privates, much like the other male outlings from the town. If he was fine in that cold with no clothes then he must be quite cozy now with my old shawl, Juan thought.

The hours passed as the group rode through the forest, and not once did Richard look back at the boys. Juan was mesmerized watching Richard ride so stoically on top of his horse. At times he wondered if they were even moving; if it wasn't for changing colors in the leaves, he could have believed that he was just looking at a still picture for the entire ride. Hans would periodically adjust himself, his sporadic movements would help shake Juan back into reality if he fell too deep into the melancholy that was the cold empty woods. He tried to look around more and note the details and nuances that surrounded them, hoping that would keep him livelier. It wasn't until later in the day that Juan noticed the long rifle hanging off the side of Richard's saddle. He knew what it felt like to shoot his pistol, but could only imagine the kind of power packed behind a gun as large as that one. A pistol is plenty enough to kill a man, Juan thought, a single shot from that would go right through a row of at least three men.

At one point Hans tapped Juan on the shoulder then tugged on the brim of his leather hat, pulling Juan's attention to an adjacent spot in the woods. Hans hopped up on his feet as they rode atop Juan's horse, whispering to Juan, "look over there," he said, pointing his finger toward the branches of the trees. "It is that tasty giant squirrel you enjoyed so much last night."

Juan observed every one of the towering trees, but he didn't see any squirrel, all he saw was dead bark. "I don't see anything," Juan replied.

The little man pointed his finger more excitedly at one of the trees and nearly shouted, "Right there! Right beneath the first row of branches!"

Juan looked harder, trying to line his eyesight up with where Hans' finger pointed, and then he saw it. He saw a large ring of fur wrapped around the trunk; the color of the hairs blended so perfectly with the bark it was hard to notice. What was easier to notice was the large pink head glaring at them from behind the trunk. Juan was under the impression that squirrels were merely rodents, but this creature was closer to the size of a dog.

"Do you see it?" Hans asked, "Only their tails have that fur. They wrap it around their bodies to try and stay hidden better. Their skin is quite easy to spot in the woods. Most animals in the Rotten Plains look that way, bald and larger than they normally should be."

Juan turned around and looked at the little hunchback. He asked Hans, "What about your kind, why did the people grow smaller but the animals grew larger?" Suddenly Juan's horse halted. Juan quickly turned his attention back in front of him when he saw Richard turned around, staring at him.

"Hans' kind are special," Richard explained, "Do not be mistaken, Juan. The sickness of this land did not pick winners or losers. Most of the humans did turn out like these creatures you see---large, aggressive, anything but human really. And many of the animals turned out like the outlings from the village. You won't see them in these parts because those small ones are all dead now. Hans' kind were the only ones who kept any semblance of their humanity, and that is the reason they survived… We need to keep up our pace, the depot is not far now and we best get there before sundown."

Richard turned back around and took off in the direction they'd been heading. Juan instructed Hans to sit back down and to hold tight, then kicked the sides of his horse and they sped off behind Richard. "He seems in a hurry all of a sudden," Juan called out to Hans.

"We need to set up a fire before nightfall," Hans started. "Like I said, most of the creatures here are easily spotted because of their bright pink skin. Because of that most of them have grown to be nocturnal. The only reason the ride has been so calm is because the life here does not usually roam around in the daylight."

The three men arrived at the edge of the forest as the sun lowered to the tops of the distant trees. In front of them were miles of open lands, quite a different scene from what they were used to, but to Juan it seemed familiar---only there being more grass than sand. Richard explained that the depot was a few miles farther out, that they should have no trouble getting there by sundown. Off in the horizon, the silhouette of many buildings started to appear as they moved forward. Juan thought the depots were singular buildings constructed next to the tracks, but of course, things were quite different in the Rotten Plains.

They arrived just as the sun began to set. The depot was set in the middle of an old ghost town. The tracks ran through the center and buildings were placed on both sides of the tracks, about ten buildings deep on each side. Richard led the others to one of the buildings beside the depot. Once there, he hopped off his horse and walked up to the entrance of the building. Juan and Hans followed suit and ran up behind him.

"What is this place?" Juan asked, "I thought depots were just singular buildings."

The windows on the front of the building were still intact; most of the others had their windows shattered. Richard walked over and peeked through the crud covered windowpane. "This used to be a busy stop for government shipments. They would restock their food supplies, and it was a spot for the workers and passengers to rest. But that was a long time ago, before any of us were even born."

"So are we going in?" Hans inquired.

Richard walked back to his horse and pulled his rifle off the saddle. While standing by the door, Juan heard a rustling coming from within the building. He pressed his hand against the heavy wooden door and moved his ear closer, hoping to get a better listen. He heard a strange mixture of sounds, like snoring and wet lips smacking together. The nasal slurping was unlike anything he had heard before.

Richard walked back up to the door, taking loud heavy steps that shook the wooden foundation, then he checked the rifle to make sure a bullet was loaded. "Step back you two," he instructed, "Juan, have your pistol ready."

Juan gripped the ivory handle of his pistol, wondering what horrors they would see on the other side of the door. Perhaps it was a bear? One that looked like the giant squirrel with little hair and long claws, or maybe it was a mountain lion, with a long pink tail that would look like a massive worm growing out of its rear. Hans hobbled up to the door and gently gripped the knob. He turned it so slowly that it didn't even make the slightest click. Richard pressed the barrel of his rifle against the door and pushed it open. Standing to the side, Juan waited to draw his pistol.

The door swung open, revealing the mysterious creature behind the indiscernible sound. Richard pointed his rifle at the center of the room, but no shot was fired. Instead, the barrel of the rifle dropped, and he gazed at the sight in curiosity and horror, as did Juan and Hans. The smell reeking out of the room overpowered the sloppy sounds. The nausea forced Juan to his knees, while he used his shawl to cover his nose.

Juan peered into the room while holding back the strong impulse to vomit, and from the room a set of eyes stared back at him. They were either the eyes of a man or the eyes of a bird, like Kai's when she took on the form of an owl. He wore a cowl, with a mask shaped in the form of a long black beak---dark feathers woven through the fabric on his head and down his back and shoulders. His chest was scarred and bare, the pinkish tint of the scrapes and cuts popped out against the reddish tan hue of his skin. The nails on his fingers were long, dirt black, and pointed, they more closely resembled sharp talons than anything human. The two slits cut out of the mask shadowed his eyes, but Juan could see the two crimson irises gleaming from within. He was squatting over the body of what appeared to be an outling, but not one like Hans and the townspeople. This one was like the ones that Richard warned about. To think that it was once human was hard for Juan to imagine. The outling creature was massive, close to eight feet long, and was sprawled out on the ground with its arms and legs fully extended to its sides. Its features closely resembled those of the outlings Juan had seen, but its expression was far more nefarious and animalistic. Lacking any humanity that could be found in the faces of Hans or the others, it was more beast than man. The man in the bird-like cowl had a knife plunged deep in the creature's belly, and four similar knives had been driven through its hands and feet---immobilizing the creature as it was nailed to the floor.

Juan got back up on his feet, he still pressed his shawl against his mouth, but he moved past Richard into the room and walked closer to the nauseating scene. Even as he moved closer, the birdman did not seem to care, he continued to poke his knife inside the belly of the captured outling. Once Juan got close enough he could see the skin had been peeled away from the torso of the outling, exposing its perverse muscular tissue and organs. A large raven stood next to the birdman, it pecked at the removed skin, tearing it into small pieces and swallowing it. Every time it ripped a piece off, the lip-smacking sound rang out, followed by a gruesome snort as it threw its head back and forced it down into its belly.

"What the hell is that?" Hans yelled from back in the doorway.

His question was shortly followed by the screeching "KAW!" of the raven. Swiftly, it spread its wings and flew past Juan, knocking him to the ground. It sped out the door past Richard and Hans, who both turned and watched as the raven flew away, following the tracks out of the town. Juan grabbed onto his pistol and turned over to where the birdman was, but when he pointed his gun, the man in the black feathered cowl was gone.

Hans helped Juan to his feet, while Richard walked over to the carcass of the giant outling. The knives had been removed from its hands and feet, but a giant slash ran across the width of its neck. Blood leaked from all the cuts on the creature's body, and the stench within the room grew only stronger.

Richard squatted next to the body and stuck his fingers into the pool of blood. He pulled out a long black feather and held it upside down, letting the blood drip off the end. He turned to Juan and said, "I think we've found your raven."

Chapter 8

THE MAIDEN'S DANCE

"Diablo!" the Apache guard hollered from outside the large doors of the chief's office. "We have a new batch for you." The guard waved his hand over his head and motioned for the girls to follow in behind him, while another guard pushed open the office doors. Felina entered first, followed closely behind by Doli, then Misa, and lastly Dakota. They lined up in front of Diablo's desk, all of them holding hands, the same way they had on the entire journey to Geronimo Park. Diablo sat in a large chair with his legs crossed and propped up on the polished wooden desktop. The back of the room, where he sat, was elevated by two small steps, so that even while he sat carefree, he could look down upon the specimens being brought before him. His eyes ran up and down each of the girls, inspecting them from the comfort of his sturdy perch.

He started at the end of the line with Dakota, who seemed to pique his interest, so much so that he even got out of his chair and walked down the steps to get a closer look at her. He held his hand next to her face, squinting as he compared the stark contrast in their skin tones. It looked like a clump of clay had been dropped into a pile of freshly fallen snow as his reddish tan thumb caressed her cheek. He pinched a strand of her hair and ran it through his fingers. It was such a light shade of blonde that it almost blended in with her skin.

"You're an exotic one," Diablo chuckled, then he

motioned to the guard and said, "brothel."

Felina and the others watched as Dakota was dragged out of the room. Tears began to drip down Doli's face and her body began to tremble. Felina's grip tightened around Doli's hand to try to comfort her, but the gesture was of no avail.

Diablo moved on to Misa, squatting down so that he was eye to eye with the girl. He peered into her dark pupils, then he compared their skins just as he had with Dakota, but he quickly shoved her away. The guard walked back into the office, and he was met with Diablo's wicked stare.

"Where did you find something so ugly?" Diablo asked.

"Our friends from the East Coast sent her. I guess she didn't have much appeal for them either," said the guard.

Diablo pushed Misa to the ground. "She can serve drinks," he said, "if one of the degenerates with bad taste wants to take her upstairs then that's their choice." The guard nodded, grabbing Misa by the hair, and dragging her out of the office.

The few tears that fell down Doli's face had quickly become a monsoon of bawling, as she choked down each breath in an ugly fearful sob. Felina shook Doli's arm and whispered to her, urging her to stop her crying. Diablo skipped past Doli, paying no attention to the fit she was throwing, and moved right along to Felina.

"Let go of the girl's hand," he commanded.

Felina stared at him with her empty black eyes, and she calmly said, "No."

Diablo pulled his hand back and struck Felina across the face, with a loud clap that knocked Felina to the floor. She wound up pulling Doli to the ground too, as she'd refused to let go of the girl's hand. The guard walked back into the room and saw the two girls on the ground.

"Is there a problem?" asked the guard.

"The old one... where did you get her?"

"From outside the Navajo camp," he started, "there are not many of her kind left in the Heart. She's a Mexican, almost all of them live far south of our lands."

Diablo marched across the room, stepping right over the two girls. He grabbed the guard and shoved him up against the wall. The room shook furiously, nearly knocking over the mounted bison head. "I don't give a shit what she is! She is far too old, you fool!"

The guard coughed and tried to catch his breath, but Diablo's knuckles were digging into his throat. "The... the scouts that caught her said they saw her dancing---perhaps she could be good entertainment... besides, some of the men have a taste for more mature girls."

Diablo dropped the guard then stomped back to Felina and lifted her off the floor. "A dancer... hmm? Well then, perhaps we can find a use for you." He brushed his hand through her jet-black hair and began to admire her features. Although older, Felina's beauty was undeniable.

He tilted his head over her shoulder and looked back at the guard he had just assaulted. "You said you found her near the Navajo camp? Wasn't that where my brother's body was found?"

"Not far from there."

"Is that right?" Diablo smirked, then he pushed Felina away. "Wherever you put her, keep it near enough so I can see her."

The guard scurried across the room and dragged Felina out. "Doli!" Felina shouted, "Don't worry, Doli!" she yelled as the doors shut on her.

Diablo stood over Doli, gazing down on her with an endearing stare. He knelt beside her and moved her hair out of her eyes so he could see her face. He lifted his hand next to her cheek---the shades were identical.

"You will stay with me," he said in an almost comforting tone, "I have waited a long time for such a beautiful girl who comes from the blood of our land. Perhaps when my father dies and I assume the rank of chief, you can become one of my wives."

Doli's eyes once again filled with tears---she desperately wished for Felina's hand to still be clutched to hers. But instead she found herself being embraced by the man who stole her and her friends away from their homes.

"Shh, my dear," Diablo said as he wiped the tears from her cheeks, "you are home now."

A week within the walls of Geronimo Park felt like a lifetime for Felina, and even in that short span, she was already having trouble keeping track of the days. They had given her a stage, with places for casino goers to sit even though they never did, and they had a younger girl with her who could play the guitar. They told her to be a dancer, yet she found herself most often sitting on the stage while her *partner* played the same chords for hours on end. Her stage was not far from the Chief's and his oldest son's offices. Diablo was serious when he said he wanted to keep an eye on her, but the part of the casino floor nearest the offices didn't get any traffic, so she felt more like a trinket in the tribe's menagerie of girls---a menagerie only looked at by two to three pairs of eyes.

Felina didn't know what the guitar playing girl's name was; it hadn't even crossed her mind to ask. Throughout the day she would try to spot where Misa was on the floor, typically handing out drinks to the gamblers, and very rarely being grabbed at. Doli had been given to Lipan as one of his personal servants. Felina would see the little Navajo girl walk into his office in the mornings, and they tried hard to smile at each other, but then she wouldn't be seen again until the next morning. She didn't see little Dakota though, not since she was dragged out of Diablo's office that day.

When Felina was walking through the sleeping chambers one night, which were separated for the girls who worked the floor and the ones who worked the *private floor*, she had passed the door into the private girl's chambers. The door wasn't all the way shut, and when she glanced in, she noticed that all of them looked just like little Dakota. All the girls were just as pale as her friend, with varying shades of flaxen hair---not all with the pure whitish tint of Dakota's. Back at her own bed moments later, she looked around at the girls she was staying with, and with minor differences, they all looked quite like Felina. They had dark hair and dark eyes, some of them with lighter skin like Misa had, others with skin a bit darker than Doli's, but all similar even so.

Since they both were *floor girls*, Felina and Misa shared a sleeping chamber and were able to talk at nights--- quietly of course---but they enjoyed being able to stay close. Misa once asked, "Have you seen Dakota at all? She was the only one of us who was sent *upstairs*. And I haven't seen Doli either, I wish they were able to sleep with us. I wish they weren't so hidden."

"I see Doli every morning," Felina assured her. "We haven't been able to speak, but every morning before she goes into the Chief's office she smiles at me and I always smile back."

"Well that is nice that she smiles, really nice."

"But… I haven't seen Dakota," Felina sighed, "I walked by her chambers the other night and was able to peek in though!"

"What! You did that?" Misa exclaimed. Then they heard one of the old Apache women shush them loudly from across the room.

"Shhh... yes," Felina whispered. "There were almost as many girls in there as in our chamber, but it's... funny. They all look just like Dakota."

"I have noticed that from the other private girls I have seen." Misa looked around to see if the old Apache witch was still watching them. Then she leaned forward and cupped her hands over her mouth. Felina leaned in and pushed her ear to the little girl's hands and Misa whispered, "One of the girls had bite marks on her... Do you think the ones that look like Dakota taste better and that's why they all look alike?"

Felina moved back and looked at Misa with sad but hopeful eyes, saddened by the truth of the matter, yet hopeful toward the girl's innocence. She pulled Misa's head against her chest and they fell onto the bed and tried to fall asleep.

"Felina..." Misa whispered.

"Yes?"

"Do you think they *ate* Dakota?"

"No, Chiquita... I don't think they ate Dakota."

"You're right," Misa sighed, "she is way too thin anyway, not worth eating unless she got nice and fat."

"SHUSH!" The old Apache matron practically shouted from across the room.

Then for the first time in weeks, the two girls managed to let out a laugh.

So there Felina sat, on her stage, legs crossed in her new dress---which was just long enough to cover what ought to be covered in her current position. She didn't know what they had done with her old dress, but she no longer wore a long white one with red accent. They had given her a much shorter, all black dress. She liked that it was black, but this one was cut much lower at the bust and revealed quite a lot more than her father would have ever wanted a dress to reveal. She was happy Roberto was not around to see her in it, although she did think it was a pretty dress---she wondered if Wyatt would like it on her more than her white one. While she sat thinking about who would and wouldn't like to see her wearing whatever, Felina failed to notice, that for the first time, a seat had been occupied in front of her stage.

If it weren't for him letting out a slight cough she reckoned that she would have never seen the man. He was one of the men who looked like the chief---not old like the chief but sharing familial features. The only one of the sons she knew was Diablo, and she would have rather not known him. She knew there were two more but didn't even know what their names were.

He asked, "Is this some sort of foreign dance that I am not aware of?"

"A dance?" She hadn't realized it, but the guitar girl had stopped playing. She didn't know if she stopped minutes ago, hours, days?

"I heard that your people had a rich culture of different dances and music. If this culture is confined to sitting on your ass with no tune playing, well, then I don't quite understand what all the talk is about."

"I'm not dancing…"

"Blind or stupid, which do you take me for?"

"I'm sorry, sir… I don't understand."

"You're a dancer, aren't you?"

"Yes sir, but-"

"Then dance damn it!" he shouted.

Felina sprang to her feet. She turned to look at the guitar girl, but for some reason she wasn't there. She turned back to the man, with tears building in her eyes. "But there is no music," she said.

"Fine then, if you cannot dance then there is no reason to waste a stage on you. Get down from there and follow me to my office. You're mine now."

"But sir! Diablo wanted me in-"

"My eyes are just as good as my brothers, now get down from there and follow me to my office immediately."

Felina hopped down from the stage, and ran to the man's side, following closely behind.

"Nitis," he said without turning his head, and walking at a brisk place.

"Excuse me?"

"My name is not Sir, that is a title that pale-faces use. My name is Nitis and that is what I shall be called. Be it by you or anyone else in this world."

"Yes... Nitis," Felina said.

They arrived at Nitis' office, which was on the other side of the first floor, far away from where the chief or Diablo could see. Nitis closed the door quietly and carefully, while Felina stood awkwardly in the middle of the room. It looked similar to Diablo's room, only there were fewer ornaments on the walls, no animal heads or bloodied old weaponry, there was only the typical large desk and a couple of other chairs. He walked past Felina and moved the chairs against the walls, leaving only a large open space across from his desk. There was a small wooden box on top of the desk, it had knobs and buttons on it, but Felina didn't know what it was.

"You need music to dance, is that right?" he asked.

"My father or bro...guitar is what I am used to listening to," she said quietly, "I don't know what many other instruments sound like."

Nitis touched one of the buttons on the wooden box,

then slowly turned one of the knobs until the sound of strange music grew louder and louder from its direction. He walked over to Felina and took her hand in his. His fingers were quite warm and felt softer than she imagined.

Nitis mumbled a few words---he may have even spoken at a normal volume but with how loud he had turned up the music, Felina couldn't hear what he said.

"What?" she asked, feeling like she had to shout to make herself heard.

He spoke just loud enough to be heard through the tune in the background. "Dance with me," he said, taking her by the waist and pulling her close to him, so close that his lips were brushing against the hair that fell past her ears. They started to move together, but not fluidly---it was hard for Felina to figure out the tempo to move her feet to such foreign music.

They danced for a song or two, then Nitis began to speak into her ear. "You can nod your head, but do not answer me with words, understand?"

Felina tripped over his foot and nearly stumbled to the ground, but the momentum of their twists were enough for Nitis to keep her upright. He balanced her and asked again, "Do you understand?"

She moved away ever so slightly, and stared at him. She looked nauseated but not from the dancing.

"You don't have to fear me," he assured her, "but I need to speak with you. Only nod, do not speak, okay?"

"Oh-" she stopped, and nodded her head instead.

Nitis pulled her in again so that his mouth was right by her ear. From that distance even his whispers were fully audible.

"You are from the Navajo land, correct? Not far from their camps?"

She nodded and they continued to move.

"Did you know my younger brother was killed not far from your home?"

She shook her head, but her trembling hands made it clear that she was lying.

"There is no need for you to lie to me. I told you that you have nothing to fear. But I know you are related to the man who killed him... I assume he is your brother."

She didn't mean to, but her head nodded on its own.

"My brother was a brute, and so is the rest of my family. No blood deserves to be shed over the death of any one of them. They didn't even bother to shed a single tear for Cochise. But as of right now, I have reason to believe your brother is alive."

Her body tensed up, and she nearly tripped again. She tried to turn her head to look at Nitis, but his hand gripped her head and kept it in position so her ear would not move far.

"It appears that he fled your home east into Comanche land. Our scouts were on his trail, but the man they questioned refused to give up where he was headed. I applaud him for that. It is not often these days that you find loyalty amongst strangers. It is a shame the scouts killed him though.

"From what he told the scouts while he was alive, it seems that your brother is willing to go to some extreme lengths to find you. He apparently threatened to kill quite a few members of my tribe if it meant retrieving you."

Nitis' shoulder had quickly become soaking wet, as a flood of tears poured out of Felina's eyes, dripping off her chin and onto his shirt.

"I promise I will give you to your brother if he ever makes it here. He took my brother, but we took your father--- as far as I am concerned the score is settled. And even if it weren't... Well, I don't know, I suppose I simply lack the killer instinct so present in the rest of my family."

"Gracias," Felina sobbed, knowing she should not have spoken.

"From now on you will be my personal servant. You will dance for me, and you will dance better than you did today. Your young friend Doli has kept her entire sleeping chamber awake this week with her constant crying. You will stay with her from now on and keep her from getting herself in trouble at night."

And Felina nodded once more.

Chapter 9

WYATT AND THE BANSHEE

Falkner sat alone on the empty train as it hurtled through the rolling hills of the Comanche Nation. His handkerchief, once a pure white, was now stained a deep red as he wiped it across the long satin barrel of his pistol. He hadn't noticed how much blood had splashed onto his gun until then. Even the grip of his pistol had been stained, and it passed on a pinkish tint to his palms. He dabbed the bloodstained cloth into his cup of whiskey then rubbed it against the wooden grip. The blood had solidified inside the tally marks he had carved into the burgundy handle. The tallies added up to 23, but once he scrubbed them clean, he pulled out a small knife and carved in two more notches---25.

"Comanche Chief Nokoni and Maxwell Depot Clerk," he mumbled to himself, then he blew the splinters out of the freshly carved tally marks, "Join the club." He ran his thumb over the two new marks, caressing them with a gentle admiration, the wood still warm and slightly sticky from the whiskey residue.

The train began to rumble and Falkner felt a force pushing him forward as the behemoth started to slow. He looked out the window to his left and saw the reflective sunlight beaming off the steel cube that was the Tango Depot. It was his last stop in the Comanche Nation to try and recruit more clerks to Chance's cause. So far his stops had resulted in no new members, only more notches in his pistol.

He stood out back of the depot and pushed his badge inside the keyhole. His encounter began the way all the others had. Falkner cocked back his pistol and pushed the barrel into the clerk's mouth. "Times are changing," he said, "you can either be a part of the change, or I can just kill you now. What's it going to be?"

The computer behind the clerk lit up, and a message appeared on the screen. Falkner turned his attention, watching the dots and dashes litter the computer screen. He pulled the barrel out of the clerk's mouth then spun his chair around, facing him toward the incoming message.

"Well?" Falkner asked, nudging the barrel of the gun into the clerk's back, "where's it coming from? All of the depots in the East other than this one are vacant."

"It isn't coming from the East," the clerk muttered, "it is coming from the Lima Depot, on the southern edge of the quarantine zone."

Falkner holstered his pistol back on his hip and leaned over the clerk. He squinted at the coded message in bewilderment. "That ain't where the rendezvous point is meant to be. We're supposed to meet at Fort Young. What on earth are those two up to?" Falkner pondered verbally. He looked back at the clerk and lightly slapped the man on the cheek, "What else does it say?"

"Th.. they are asking if the Eastern Marshal is still alive... and why there have not been any comms coming from the Sioux or Comanche." The clerk turned his head upward to look at the underside of Falkner's face. "I apologize Marshal, but I cannot tell who is sending the message, all of the depots within the quarantine zone were shut down over a century ago."

Falkner stared at the map on the computer screen,

specifically at the light flashing above the spot titled *Lima*. Pointing at the flashing dot, he said, "I need you to call me a train to that station."

The clerk glanced at the map screen. There was fear plastered upon his colorless face. He wondered how the Marshal could go from sticking a gun in his mouth one moment to asking a favor so casually.

"Marshal," he squeaked, "the trains can't be run inside the quarantine zone from an outer depot---they have to be manually run, or connected to a depot within the quarantine zone."

Falkner laughed and squeezed the clerk's shoulders. "Well then! I guess it's a good thing I didn't kill you a minute ago, because now you ain't got a choice, you're coming with me."

The clerk nervously gulped down a wad of spit and nodded his head. "Marshal?" he asked, "Do you want me to send a response to the message?"

Falkner mulled over his response in silence, running his fingers through his black scruffy beard. "No," he said, "just call for the train and we will go there in person." Falkner pushed away from the clerk and started back toward the exit.

"Yes, sir."

"Oh, and Clerk," Falkner stopped, "No funny business, ya' hear?"

The clerk nodded and rose from his chair, then followed behind Falkner out of the depot. It was a dark cloudy day but, to the clerk, it didn't seem much different from within the confines of the depot. As he scanned the horizon, he realized that he had never seen anything so vast and open. Up until then his vision had been narrowed to only what he could see out the small murky window he'd been trapped behind.

"Hurry up and get on!" Falkner called from the steps

of the train. He waved his arm frantically, motioning for the clerk to enter the train. "I have some clothes for you to throw on. If those clouds break at all, you're going to be in a world of pain!"

The clerk hurried onto the train and threw on a scarf and hat that Falkner handed him. The two walked up through the halls of the train until they reached the engine. When Falkner pushed the door open, he was surprised to see that it didn't look much different than the inside of the depots.

"Make yourself comfortable," he said with a smile, pushing the clerk into the engine room. "How long until we get to Lima?" he asked.

The clerk sat behind the main computer and started plotting out dots, then short lines flashed on the screen connecting them. "It shouldn't take more than a day," he answered.

Falkner grunted, then he walked out of the engine room. He found a spot to rest in the next car back, then kicked his feet up and let the constant calm vibration of the moving train rock him to sleep.

"Ma...Marshal?" The clerk mumbled. Gently pressing his fingers against Falkner's muscular shoulder as he tried to wake him. Falkner was fast asleep; his snoring was almost louder than the idling engine of the locomotive. The clerk reluctantly pushed Falkner, nearly knocking him off the bench he was lying on. Falkner shook his head and opened his eyes at last.

"The hell was that?" he growled.

"We have arrived at Lima Depot, Marshal."

Falkner tilted back his hat, rubbed his crusty eyes with his knuckles, and surveyed the car for a few moments. "It's about time," he said, pushing the clerk back as he swung himself to his feet. "Stay in the car, I'll be back in a minute."

Falkner left the train and paced around the large depot. He found hoof marks in the dirt that led to the tracks, then turned up north. He walked inside the cold metal cube, quite easily since the hidden door hadn't been fully sealed. Inside he noticed the cot had been slept in, the computers had been worked on, and that there was a pile of horse droppings in the corner of the room, filling the entire space with its stench.

He inspected the computers and saw the message the clerk had received at the last depot. He studied the route that had been highlighted on the screen, leading directly to Fort Thompson, northbound, the same direction the hoof marks were headed.

Falkner stomped back onto the train and made his way to the engine, where he found the clerk patiently waiting. "Find what you were looking for?" asked the Clerk.

"We just missed him," Falkner said, "the prints in the dirt are fairly fresh. He must have only left a few hours ago."

"Are you sure?"

Falkner didn't respond to the clerk's question, instead he gave him a grisly glare that had the clerk regretting he'd ever asked it.

"Plot a course to Fort Thompson. That's where the bastard is headed. We should be able to get there before him, that should give me enough time to prepare for a little discussion with him."

"Yes, sir. Fort Thompson it is then," the clerk confirmed.

Falkner watched the clerk plot in the course to Fort Thompson then walked back to his sleeping bench and began to rest up for the ride.

Large pine trees filled the mountain forest where the boy grew up. He rushed through the woods, chasing after his barnyard cat, Otis, who was also chasing something. A little cardinal was flying low through the trees; when he wouldn't clap his wings just right, Otis would pounce in the air and try to snag him.

The boy and his cat weren't in the woods running around for no reason. They had a task to carry out, a task that had nothing to do with hunting a cardinal. The boy was in a rush to make it home before his grandfather noticed he and Otis had left the ranch. His grandfather had told him many times, "Keep that gate shut, boy!" And the boy would shut the gate, but he always seemed to forget to lock it. With no lock, it was easy for the animals inside the pen to escape---especially this one curious little mallard, who always seemed to be the culprit getting the boy in trouble with his grandfather.

"C'mon Otis!" the boy yelled, "We ain't got time for this!"

But the cat didn't care what his master had to say, for the cat's only true master was death, and this was a fact that the boy knew well. Otis was a killer, through and through. Once the lean cat caught the scent of his next hunt, it didn't matter what came before it, that scent had to be found, and killed, before anything else could resume.

The boy didn't fully understand it, but it seemed to him that Otis had a certain taste for birds. He liked to think that the cat held a personal vendetta against them---perhaps out of jealousy, for Otis was quite the killer, but if he were able to fly like those birds, then even more of the killer he could be. That must have been his motivation, jealousy---if only he had wings then he alone would become the apex predator. But Otis couldn't grow wings, and while the cat probably knew it, he still tried his hardest to fly. When he pounced at the cardinal he would leap six feet into the air, just nearly missing the tiny red bird.

The boy knew yelling at the cat was pointless. Plus, they'd been out so long, Grandpa had probably noticed they were gone already. He might as well let the hunt come to some conclusion, whatever it may be, and he was rooting for Otis.

After a few hundred more yards, the cardinal appeared to tire itself out, because it flew up a tree and perched on a branch, nearly 20 feet high, far higher than Otis could leap. The little cardinal sat on its perch and sang a mocking tune at little Otis, gloating in its victory of finding refuge. The boy knelt down and stroked the orange fur on Otis's back.

"You'll get him next time," the boy assured. "C'mon now! We gotta hurry up so we can get home." He turned away and started back on his path, but after a quick few steps he noticed that Otis wasn't following him. The little orange cat was still staring down his prey, perched up on its branch, mocking him.

Then the boy witnessed the most amazing sight he had ever seen in his short existence---he saw Otis grow wings. He couldn't actually see the wings, but he figured that must have been what happened. The cat took a position like he was ready to pounce, never taking its little yellow eyes off the cardinal, then he leapt toward the trunk of the tree. He gripped the bark with his little claws and propelled himself 20 feet up the trunk in an instant! He pushed off the bark and swiped his paw at the cardinal, who hadn't even realized Otis was no longer 20 feet below him. The little cat came gliding to the ground and landed on his feet. All that remained of the cardinal was a single red feather that floated down behind Otis. The cat had swallowed the bird whole---at least that is what the boy assumed had happened. He couldn't imagine the cat having enough time to chew in the brief moments it took to hit the ground.

He was a killer, in its purest form, Otis was. This, the boy had always known, and now would never forget.

"You've had your fun, now we gotta go!" he shouted at the satisfied cat. Then little Otis followed closely behind his master, deeper into the woods.

There was a pond deep within the woods where the culprit would always waddle off to. It certainly was a nice day for a swim, the boy thought, he couldn't blame the mallard for trying to escape, but he knew he'd get chewed out if he came home late and duckless.

As they approached the pond, Otis started to hurry ahead of the boy. Oh no, the boy thought, not another setback. He watched as Otis sprinted through the woods and pounced through the air for another kill. But he was quite far ahead and the boy couldn't see what he had caught this time.

It was no cardinal, no bird at all in fact, but it looked enough like an animal. Once he was close enough, the boy realized it was a man, an older man, but not as old as Grandpa. He had a messy brown beard with sprinkles of grey throughout; he could even see twigs sticking out of it. He wore a dirty suede jacket with a matching hat; their dark brown color made him blend it perfectly with the trees and dirt. The boy noticed one more thing. Something that stuck out to him the most, and stayed burned in his mind for quite a long time---to this day even. He had a shining silver star clipped to the pocket of his slacks. It was the only clean part about him, and it was mighty clean, not a blemish on it.

The boy watched as the old man stroked Otis with one hand, while the cat chewed on his other. The man was laughing and having a good time, even though Otis was tearing apart his hand.

"Best be careful, mister," the boy suggested, "Otis ain't no play toy. He's a killer, a real killer."

The man laughed and held Otis up to his face. The little cat swiped his claws at his thick beard. "He's the damn scariest thing I've ever seen, son."

The boy couldn't stop staring at the silver star. He fancied it, thinking that one day he might have to get one for himself. "Hey, mister. What's that you have pinned to your pocket? Think I could get one someday?"

The man stood up and handed Otis back to the boy. He pulled the star off his pocket and fiddled with it in his fingers. "You know what this is, son?"

"Nope, but I sure would like to."

"The only people in the whole world who have these are a part of the Marshal Service, and I'm one of 'em," he stuck out his hand for the boy to shake. "My name is Marshal Bill Fuller."

The boy grabbed his hand and gave it a firm shake. He liked the old man already. His hand was rough and scratchy against the boy's when they shook, but he had soft eyes, the same color as his jacket and hat and the dirt and the bark.

"Now, son. Where are your manners? I gave you my name. It would be rude if you didn't tell me yours."

"I'm Wyatt. Wyatt Cole. I ain't no marshal, but I'm a pretty good shot. My Grandpa gave me a .22 caliber rifle for my tenth birthday and I can shoot the ears off a rabbit with that thing."

"Well, ain't that impressive," Bill said, patting young Wyatt's head.

"I've never met a marshal before. What is it that you do?"

Bill sat back down in the dirt, patting a spot right next to him, inviting Wyatt to join him. At this point Wyatt had all but forgotten that he should have been home by now, so he happily sat down beside the marshal.

"What is it that I do…" Bill pondered aloud, "Well, technically I work for the Government. My job is to protect the tracks that run all throughout these lands and keep them clear of bandits and such."

"My Grandpa says that the Government is rotten… but you don't seem rotten. In fact, I think Grandpa would like you," Wyatt explained.

"Grandpa ain't wrong," Bill agreed, "but the Government doesn't have any power these days, not other than the Marshals. The native tribes run things now, I pretty much work for them. The Apache tribe out here always seems to have something for me to do."

Wyatt gawked at every word that Bill spoke, utterly fascinated by the man. "Grandpa once told me that his wife, my grandma, was Apache. Said that is why the tribe leaves us alone and doesn't mess with us."

Bill chuckled, "The Apache are a dangerous group. You must have some dangerous blood running through those veins. I'm sure no one is going to want to mess with you when you get my size, especially if you're as good a shot as you say."

"Well, I wouldn't say I'm as dangerous as Otis, but I'd sure like to be one day," Wyatt exclaimed as he began to wrestle with his cat. "So, Bill… Why did you become a marshal?"

Bill turned his head and looked at young Wyatt through his soft eyes. "Why? Well because there is a lot of beauty in this world. There is a lot of ugly as well, but being a marshal means I can do everything in my power to protect that beauty."

"What do you mean by beauty, Bill?" Wyatt asked

intently.

Bill looked around for a few moments, searching for an adequate example, then he stuck his arm out and pointed at the pond. Wyatt looked where he was pointing, and saw his mallard that he'd been after, swimming in the pond alongside another duck. The other was a bit smaller and had brown feathers instead of the colorful ones that his culprit sported.

"Those two right there," Bill said, "they're in love. I'm sure that male duck would do anything he could to go find his partner if they were to be separated. That right there is the beauty I'm talking about."

Wyatt watched as the two ducks swam along and realized that Bill was right. When the little mallard had escaped from his pen, he was just trying to be with the other duck. He realized that he'd been the one who was keeping them apart all these times, that he'd been the one stopping the beauty Bill so intently wanted to protect. He didn't like that; the realization made his chest hurt, and he felt like he wanted to cry.

"Bill?" he choked out, "Do you think I could be a marshal one day? I think... well, I think I'd like to protect that beauty as well."

"I don't see any reason why not," Bill started, "in fact, it would seem my best years are behind me now---it's about time I found someone to take over for me one day. But you must promise me, Wyatt-"

"Whatever it is I promise!" he chirped.

"That beauty I told you about is the most precious thing to me. If I were to one day trust its care to you, you would have to promise that you would die happily protecting it."

Wyatt pushed himself to his feet and stared down at Bill. His small fists were clenched, and he was crying. "Now I already said I promise! I'll walk back home right now and take a beating from Grandpa, happily even!" He pointed at the two ducks swimming in the pond. "If I were to take that little mallard back home then I would be the exact person that you protect against! Oh, Bill, I don't want to be that person!"

Bill watched the ducks swimming along. He was slightly confused at what the boy had said. "The ducks?" he mumbled. But he could see how upset the boy was, and it warmed him inside to have heard his response.

WWWWAAARRRRRUUUUUUGGG!!

Out of nowhere a blood-curdling cry burst from out of the woods and echoed throughout the trees. It rumbled Wyatt's eardrums and he dropped to the ground, clutching at his ears. Bill merely squinted and looked around trying to pinpoint where it came from. Bill took to his feet and picked up the shotgun laying on the ground beside him. After a long few seconds, the screeching subsided.

"Best you run back home and take that beating from your grandfather now, Wyatt. It's not safe for you out here anymore. Go! I'll come find your cabin once I've taken care of things here!"

Wyatt looked over at the two ducks, then he motioned to Otis and they ran back home to Grandpa.

Wyatt slowly opened his eyes, rubbing them to get the gunk out. He found himself inside the Lima Depot. He wasn't sure how long he had been asleep, but it was light out. He wondered why, of all the memories to dream about, that his first meeting with Bill was the one he had been playing over in his head. It happened a long time ago,14 years ago, maybe 15? It was hard to keep track of time these days.

He still heard the faint howling of the wolves, echoing off in the distance. They were no longer dangerously close, but they reminded him of that screaming creature from his memories. The natives had called it Banshee, an evil spirit that haunted the forests, at least that is what his grandfather had told him. Wyatt assumed it was just some way of keeping him from running off into the woods---it clearly hadn't worked if that were the case.

He got up to check the computer, reviewing the course he had plotted for Fort Thompson, and checking again for any response to his outgoing message. There hadn't been any. He pulled up the map and checked his course, there was a set of tracks he could follow alongside, nearly the entire way to Thompson, only having to veer off it for a few miles, through some tame wooded hills.

Wasting no time, he packed up his things and left the depot. Since the morning was young he could ride freely for a while without having to worry about those pesky hairless monsters trying to slow him down. Especially riding near the tracks, where the trees had been chopped down on both sides, the sunlight was abundant. The nocturnal population preferred to keep to the trees if they were even awake during the day.

The blanket Wyatt kept draped over Peaches helped her keep warm, though its main purpose was to keep her from getting burnt. The horses within the Rotten Plains were typically found in open "grassy" fields, although the grass of the Plains looked like anything but grass---it wasn't green and it certainly didn't feel good if it brushed up against one's skin. Although her kind was more exposed to sunlight than other species within the Plains, Wyatt preferred to keep his steed as comfortable as possible. Peaches was the closest thing he had to family, and she deserved the best.

Hours passed as they rode alongside the tracks. The

sun began to fall out of the sky, but was not yet setting. They had made good distance, and Wyatt still felt well rested from his ambiguously long sleep. He told himself it was only the one night, but it very easily could have been a few days. He didn't know, but it didn't worry him---all he could think about was his dream of that day he met Bill. He hadn't thought about that day for a long time. As the memories replayed through his head while he drifted along the tracks mindlessly toward Fort Thompson, he realized that there were many firsts from that day.

Yes, it was his first-time meeting Bill, a day that changed his life. It was like meeting the father he had never known. Sure he loved Grandpa, but not the way he loved Bill. Looking back on it, he realized his grandfather taught him nothing compared to what Bill had, even with that first simple conversation. He also realized that later that day he learned the truth about the Banshee. That its wretched scream was not a war cry, and it was not a howling wolf trying to signal to the pack. It wasn't even a growling bear preparing to feast on its prey. No, the Banshee's call was that of a sobbing infant, crying out in pain, fear, and confusion.

Its cry was haunting---even now that sound ricocheted off the walls of Wyatt's skull, bouncing about and aching on his mind. It sent tremors running through his fingers, down his legs, and out his toes. He was shaking viciously, but it wasn't a shiver. It wasn't the cold that made him tremble. It was the sound of that shrieking he heard in his mind, but it wasn't in his mind---it was there. It was alive, and it was growing louder and louder, like sharp nails carving into a steel wall and peeling the carbon away from the iron. It was different from what he remembered of the Banshee's scream, but it was just as awful---no, it was far more horrendous. He shook, and so did Peaches, but she never shook and even if she did, she couldn't hear the sounds within Wyatt's memories. The ride did not seem so calm now, in fact he could feel a behemoth force pushing up from behind him. A force as real as anything he had felt. And the screech only grew louder, and it approached with enormous mass. He could feel it right behind him. Wyatt turned around and saw a giant locomotive tumbling toward him with no sense of care for his wellbeing, only momentum, and the impulse to keep moving.

He didn't have to command Peaches---she knew what to do, and she sprung away from the trackside just as the train flew past them, screeching the entire way. Smoke and sparks flew off the rusted steel rails of the tracks, carrying a smell as nauseating as the sound. Watching the locomotive hurl past and fade off into the distance, Wyatt pictured in his mind the flashing lines of the computer screen all leading to Fort Young.

Gently, at first, his legs began to kick into Peaches' sides, but soon his delicacy faded and he began kicking her ribs firmly and he yelled, "Hyaa!"

The pale beast reared up on her two hind legs then took off down the tracks in a thunderous gallop. The pounding of her hooves made the ground tremble beneath her even harder than the train had. Wyatt whipped the reins with his left hand and held his hat tight to his head with his right. The smoke from the screaming train painted a clear path, even though it was not needed. Wyatt knew where the train was headed, and he felt lucky it was where he was headed as well.

Riding swiftly through the night, he followed the howling echo that rang through the tracks. He pictured Roberto, the chill of the night was as cold as the old man's skin when he laid him to rest. All around him he could hear the whining of the wolves within the woods, and it reminded him of the yapping of coyotes in the deserts. He pondered the severity of his situation, and the way he saw it, there were three fronts to his war. One with a face, another without, and a third that was only a faint idea.

The first was Chance. Based on their encounter, Wyatt assumed he would be west, likely the one already at Fort Young. The second was the Coyote. He surmised that he could be in league with Chance, their antics didn't seem far off from one another, but it was clear they were not the same man, being that the Coyote was a Mexican and Chance was not. Then there was the third. Who he was, to Wyatt, was more of a mystery---all he knew was that he was recently in the eastern nations, and most likely causing an awful lot of trouble.

The way he saw things standing was as so; Chance was behind the mysterious movement of trains within the Rotten Plains and most likely at Fort Young already. The Coyote may or may not be in league with Chance, but either way he posed a threat and needed to be brought to justice. Lastly, the man in the East was likely in league with the other two, or just another wild card. The train he was chasing, however, had come from the East and that he was sure of. It was likely that a marshal's star was on that train.

"It takes some amount of grit to kill a marshal and take his star," Wyatt murmured to himself, "but whoever has it won't be holding onto it for long."

So, throughout the night Wyatt rode up the tracks following the echo of the screaming train. Then, just before sunrise, he veered off the tracks to take a shortcut through the woods. He knew that if he stayed on the route he had previously planned that he could beat the train to Fort Thompson---the tracks had to wind through rough terrain that a train couldn't speed through. But a single horse could cut right through the trees and make it to Thompson in nearly half the time. Luckily, Peaches was well rested. Wyatt always rode her easy when he could, knowing that when times like these came around… she would be ready.

Chapter 10

TEARS OF THE RAVEN

"Juan!" Richard shouted into the evening darkness, peering into the distance with his one good eye. Hans' hands were gripping tight around Richard's waist as their horse galloped swiftly alongside the tracks.

"I cannot see him," Hans said into Richard's ear, "He's gotten too far ahead, can you see him?"

"I can't, and his horse isn't going to hold up much longer if he plans to keep up this pace." Richard cupped his hand over his mouth and hollered again, "Juan!" but the only response was the sound of his voice echoing off into the distance.

"Juan…"

He could hear the echo of Richard's voice, but he wasn't bothered by it, he was too focused. It was getting dark, but the black feathers that floated down from high in the sky were darker. He could see the raven sprinting through the air, bouncing from tree to tree, and resting periodically for just a few moments. Every time he would leap back into the air, a clump of feathers would fall from its wings, which paved a path directly in its wake for Juan to follow.

Juan kicked his feet against his horse's sides, keeping it at a full gallop. He could see the spurts of air blowing out of the horse's nostrils as it panted heavily. "We can do it," Juan assured his steed, "just a bit more and we can catch him... Andale!"

They had been following the raven for two days as it flew west toward Fort Thompson. As Juan chased it, he could not get the image of the mysterious birdman out of his mind. He was just like Lady Kai when she morphed into an owl that night in the tent, only he was... real, not an illusion like Kai. Kai was never able to change into an owl and fly away. But the birdman; his black beak and feathered cowl that he wore truly became a part of him as he morphed into the raven and flew out of that saloon. And he was able to restrain that monster--- the creature that so closely resembled the outlings from Deacon's village, but at the same time was far more perverse.

The night after their encounter at the saloon, Juan asked Richard, "Have you ever seen one of those things restrained like that?"

"No," Richard answered bluntly. "You don't restrain those brutes... either you kill them, or they kill you."

"You can't reason with monsters," Hans chimed in.

His comment made Juan smile, despite how disturbed he was. Richard had never spoken so easily about taking a life. In fact, he was one of the few people who even recognized the outlings as actual persons. Juan realized that he had greatly underestimated the true differences the mutations of the Rotten Plains could make.

"But what was he doing with it pinned down like that?" Juan pondered aloud.

"I don't know... I guess we will just have to ask him," Richard said.

Juan could feel the raven nearly within his grasp now, and he wasn't going to let Richard's or Hans' call slow him down, not when he was so close. He gripped the reins tightly with his left hand and held his pistol in his right. He knew exactly which tree the raven was perched, and he'd figured out how close he could get before the raven heard his horse's stomping and departed. He didn't know why the birdman was running from him, but the birdman didn't know why he was being chased. This was the next person that Lady Kai had instructed Juan to find. He wouldn't have a chance of getting Felina back if he didn't at least speak to the raven.

A hundred yards, that was how close he could get before the raven would take off again, and with the speed his horse was galloping, he wasn't planning on giving the raven much time to rest. The tree was 200 yards out now, and the gap was closing fast. Juan's horse kept its pace, it was panting hard, but even so it didn't relent. 150... Juan raised his pistol and aimed it near the raven's tree. He tried his best to steady his hand, but the terrain was rough and the ride was bumpy. 125... he cocked back his pistol and closed his left eye to get a better aim.

He saw the leaves of the tree start to shake then out came the raven, just as he predicted. Juan pulled the trigger and a loud bang echoed through the forest. He saw the raven struggle to stay in the air, then it swooped down to the nearest tree and a loud thump followed as it hit the ground.

Juan kicked his horse even harder. He couldn't afford to slow down now---he was so close, and this could be his only chance to catch the birdman. The horse's panting grew louder, and its sides shivered violently as it continued toward the trees. Juan kicked again, but the horse's legs buckled. It went crashing to the ground, and Juan flew off the saddle. He tumbled 50 feet, rolling through the dirt right to the base of the tree the raven had fallen into.

A cloud of dust surrounded Juan. He coughed up some dirt and noticed his pistol was no longer in his hand, but he hadn't holstered it. He felt around the dirt, searching for the ivory grip of his pistol, but all he felt was the leather brim of his hat. He placed it on his head and pushed himself to his feet. The cloud of dust began to settle, and he saw the light from the starry sky glimmering off the satin barrel of his gun. He took a step toward it but stopped when a knife came hurling through the air, sticking into the ground just past his foot.

"Not another---*kaww!*--- step."

Juan looked to his side and saw him; the birdman, still wearing his long black beak and feathered cowl. Juan raised his hands in the air as he turned toward him. "I just want to talk."

"People who want to talk don't---*kaww!*" the birdman coughed, "---don't try to shoot someone out of the sky."

"We have been chasing you for nearly three days, how else was I supposed to stop you?"

"You---*kaww!*---could have just left me a---*kaww kaww!*---*" he tried responding before having a violent coughing fit. He hacked so hard that it brought the curious man to his knees. "---Ugh... you could have left me alone."

The birdman continued to cough. Running his hands through his feathers and pulling at his beak, he looked like he was trying to rip off his face. While he writhed around in a furious commotion, Juan heard the pounding steps of Richard's horse approaching.

"Juan!" Richard called out. He and Hans rode up beside Juan, and Hans hopped off the horse and hastily waddled over to grab Juan's pistol.

Richard stayed mounted and watched the scene that the birdman was making. He appeared to be in a great deal of pain. All the feathers were falling off his garb, and he screamed as he began tearing off his mask.

"What's wrong with him?" Richard asked.

"I don't know," Juan mumbled.

"*Kaww! Kaww! Kaww!*" he cried.

Hans brought back Juan's pistol; in his other hand he held the knife that the birdman had thrown. "It's the same one that he used to pin the outling," Hans muttered to himself. Slowly, he approached the birdman, holding out the knife and pointing it in the stranger's direction.

"Hans, don't go any closer!" Richard hollered.

Juan held up his hand to Richard. "Hold on," he said, cocking the hammer on his pistol and readying it by his hip.

Hans crept closer. As he moved, the garbs of the stranger began to fall apart and morph. His hood and cowl changed into a thick blanket---with an intricate diamond pattern woven into it, possessing various shades of blues and reds. The bird mask simply disappeared, vanishing with the rest of the dust that surrounded them, and what remained was a young man's face. He had umber skin and black makeup smeared across his cheeks and chin. His long black hair was woven into two long braids that covered his ears and hung down just past his bare chest. He had light amber eyes that illuminated in the darkness and peered fiercely at Hans as he approached.

With only a couple feet between them, Hans stopped. He held out the knife with a stiff arm and offered for him to take it. "We just want to speak… we didn't mean to trouble you."

The man stared at the knife then ran his eyes up Hans' arm, then over his entire body. He reached his hand out, past the knife, and he grabbed Hans by his small, blistered arm. He ran his fingers over Hans' skin then touched his head and let his thumbs slalom over the bumps that covered Hans' head.

Juan and Richard watched nervously. Richard stepped off his horse and the two men moved closer. The stranger eventually took the knife out of Hans' hand and stuck it in the ground beside him. He shifted his attention to the approaching duo and stared at them with unexpectedly soft eyes.

"This one can speak… how incredible."

Juan and Richard shared a glance. Hans appeared calm as the stranger continued to run his fingers over his nearly hairless scalp.

"I have been studying his kind for quite some time out here," the stranger continued, "but I have never come across one this small and docile."

"I happen to have a name, you know!" Hans blurted out, yanking his body away from the man. "And I hear just as well as I speak."

The stranger was taken back by Hans pulling away, though his face remained expressionless. He turned his attention back to Richard and Juan. "You have trained him well. I didn't know that they had such capabilities."

Hans fell on his rear and sat in shock. Juan noticed a crude look of embarrassment and rage overcoming the little hunchback's face. He had never seen Hans in such a state. It almost made him worry, but he couldn't help but find the stranger's naivete slightly humorous. Richard walked over to Hans and propped him back up on his feet. He rubbed the little man's shoulders and tried to comfort him.

"It would be wise of you not to insult my friend there," Juan said to the stranger. "He happens to be one of the smartest men I have ever met."

"Man? Is he not of the same mutations as the rest of those beasts?"

"He has more humanity than most normal men these days," Richard protested.

The stranger crawled over to Han, inspecting him closer, and looking firmly into the little hunchback's eyes. He had to squint to get a good look, Hans' brow was quite swollen, obscuring his eyelids slightly.

"Yes I see… He does not have the eyes of an animal," the stranger started. He rested his hands on Hans' shoulders and gently rubbed them. "Forgive me, little man."

The rage that had engulfed Hans' face disappeared, but a hint of the embarrassment could still be found, illustrated by a small, awkward grin.

"What is your name stranger?" Richard asked.

"I am called Ashkii. Who is asking?"

Juan stepped forward and squatted down to get on eye level with Ashkii, who was still on his knees and holding onto Hans. "I am Juan. Behind me is Richard Deacon, and this is Hans. We are searching for someone. Lady Kai of the Navajo sent me to find what she called a Crying Raven-"

"That name," Ashkii interrupted, "what was that name?"

"Crying Raven?" Juan repeated.

"Not that one! The one before, did you say Lady Kai?"

"Yes, she-"

"I am afraid you have the wrong man. Lady Kai would never send someone to find me."

"Why is that?" Hans asked.

Ashkii patted Hans on the shoulders then rose to his feet, wavering slightly on the way up, still trying to find his balance. "I too am of Navajo blood. I was a medicine man in training, learning under Lady Kai, but she sent me into exile here within the Rotten Plains. I do not know who she instructed you to find, but I am quite sure it is not me."

Hans stared at the ground, looking at one of the black feathers that had shed off Ashkii's body. He picked it up and stuck it out toward Juan. He took it and stared at it solemnly. The pure black hue of the feather reminded him of Felina's eyes. A cool breeze blew through where the men stood. It lifted the feather out of Juan's fingers, and he watched it float away, toward a mountain range off on the horizon. The same mountains he saw the raven perched on within the smoky vision at Kai's.

"You are wrong," Juan asserted. "I saw it in the smoke. Kai told me it was a Crying Raven, and it was perched atop those mountains right there. The same ones you were flying toward before we stopped you!"

"In the smoke?" Ashkii mumbled. "You didn't say that Lady Kai gave you a vision."

"Well of course! In her tent, she had me smoke that strange pipe around a fire! I saw it all!"

Ashkii turned toward the mountains in the distance and pondered the meaning of what was happening. Then Richard stepped forward. "The same vision led him to me as well. I don't know what the woman's reasons were for sending you away from your home, but perhaps this is your shot at getting back."

"What was her reason for sending you into these lands?" Ashkii asked. His stare stayed fixed on the mountains, watching as a set of dark clouds moved upon them. "Why would she send you to trust me? Someone she lost all faith in long ago."

"We need to make it to Geronimo Park. The Apache stole my sister from our home and murdered my father... but due to my actions, we cannot move through the native lands. Kai sent me to find Richard, he knows his way through the Plains. I don't know what your part in all of this is but there must be a reason I saw you in the smoke."

"The Apache you say?" Finally Ashkii's attention turned from the mountain range. He peered into Juan's eyes, as though all of his doubts had suddenly left his body. "The Apache have oppressed my tribe for centuries, only keeping us around for our knowledge of medicine and to use our women as their playthings. The Apache are the reason I was exiled from my home. Those there?" He pointed at the mountains. "You said they were where you saw me in your vision?"

Juan looked toward the mountains where Ashkii was pointing. "Yes, that's right."

"There is a fort near those mountains. I will travel with you there, then it will be known whether or not I am the Crying Raven you foresaw."

The group started a fire and set up camp once the sun went down. Richard threw a small pot on top of the fire and cracked open a few cans of beans to heat up. They hadn't managed to trap any smaller animals over the last few days, due to the fast-paced pursuit, so brown slop was all they had to eat. Juan, Richard, and Hans all sat near each other on one side of the fire while Ashkii sat alone across from them. His nose twitched as the aromatic scent arose from the pot. Leaning in closer, he looked curiously at the dinner.

"Is this food?" he asked.

"It's nothing special, but it will fill our stomachs and help get us to Thompson," Richard responded while slowly stirring the pot. He scooped a couple servings into some metal cups then passed them around the fire.

"Where did you manage to find all of these canned beans anyway?" Juan asked.

Richard took a big mouthful of beans and slurped them down. "Back in my younger days I knew all the best spots to find abandoned government stockpiles. They had plenty of food reserves and no one around to eat them. When we started building the village, I took some time to gather as much as I could find from the surrounding spots. You'd be surprised how long those special Government rations can last."

Juan swirled the beans around in his cup. He couldn't

help thinking how old they were, 100 years, 200 maybe? He thought it best to not think about it and just eat them. They tasted fine, although it made him miss his father's cooking--- they would eat beans often but these were much different.

"I won't end up looking like the little one if I eat these, will I?" Ashkii asked.

Richard and Juan both turned to Hans then looked into their cups. Hans stared into his beans as well, then he slowly looked across the fire at Ashkii. "All this time I'd been hoping they would start making me look like the rest of you."

Richard chuckled, spitting some beans into the fire, which in turn made Hans laugh, and in a matter of moments the four of them were all sharing in the cackle. Juan couldn't help but be slightly amazed to see Ashkii laughing, only a few hours prior he hadn't even been sure he was human.

The laughter settled, and Ashkii began digging into his dinner, even seeming to enjoy it. Juan scooped out another spoonful and plopped it into his cup. He swished them around then looked across the fire once again.

"I am curious, Ashkii," he said, "why did Kai send you here?"

"I broke her trust. She was right to have sent me into exile."

"And you think she has no intention of forgiving you?" Richard asked.

"My transgressions are unforgivable. There was but one rule I was to follow while under her mentorship, and I broke it."

"When I had my vision," Juan started, "I saw Kai… morph. She took on the form of an owl, at least that is how she appeared. When we saw you back in the town, you reminded me of her."

Ashkii's face was filled with shame; some of the black

paint that was spread across his eyes had begun to melt and run down his face, like black tears falling down his cheeks. "There is a great taboo within my tribe. The skills of the Navajo medicine men and women are great, and one of those skills is darker---it's nefarious. What you experienced with Lady Kai was only a vision, but within that state she can change her form. She probably changed yours as well. I, on the other hand, learned how to manifest those forms outside of mere visions."

He reached into a pocket that was woven into his blanket, and pulled out a small bird's skull. Extending his hand, he showed it to the others. "The skinwalker. The art of taking on the form of an animal sacrifice. Medicine men are meant to heal---my killing of this raven granted me this unnatural skill, but it also led to my exile for breaking my oath."

Juan stared at the small skull then watched the tears drip off Ashkii's chin. "Why did you do it? You must have had a reason."

"For a long time, the Apache have oppressed my people. They use our medicines but give nothing in return; they only *take*, they *take* our girls, *take* our knowledge. But I thought that if we had a way to fight back, perhaps things could change. Hundreds of years ago, the skinwalkers were the most feared creatures in these lands. It wasn't even known if they were truly men. But I was wrong---I couldn't protect a tribe that didn't wish to be protected."

"God gives us all a path to redemption," Richard said, "I don't know about you Juan, but to me this man's involvement in our journey seems quite clear."

"I agree."

"Seems as though we have two feared creatures now!" Hans exclaimed. He hopped on his feet, threw his hands above his head, and let out a not-so-frightening growl!

Ashkii chuckled and took another slurp of his beans. "It's clear the Apache have caused both of us similar pain. Invading their stronghold will be a tough endeavor---perhaps I could be of some help. And you, old man, perhaps you are right about someone giving me a path to redeem myself."

"Ashkii," said Juan, "there is one other thing I am curious about."

"Hmm?"

"What were you doing with that outling? The one you had restrained back in the town."

"Oh that? Research."

"Research?"

"That's right," Ashkii said, "I have been researching what, if any, medicines can be used on the creatures within the Rotten Plains, or made from them. That is why the little one had me so interested. I haven't seen anything like him since I have been here."

"Any luck with that research?" Hans asked.

Ashkii looked down at Hans and shook his head. "Unfortunately, no. This land's inhabitants are still a mystery to me. But I have managed to make some new medicines out of the plants in this region. Good for normal men, at least."

"Sounds useful," said Richard.

"Mmm, I decided that my time in exile should not go wasted. I have continued my practice as a medicine man. Of course there has been no one to help in these parts, but I have prepared for the day that my services will be required."

"If we are to make it to Geronimo Park, it should be assumed that they will be needed at some point," Richard declared. He threw back his head and chugged down the last bit of beans remaining in his cup.

The men then rested until sunrise. Fort Thompson sat

on the far side of the distant mountains, just at their base. "I have plotted the lands quite thoroughly in the year I have been here," Ashkii explained. "Follow behind me and I will lead us up the shortest route to the fort."

"You don't have a horse," Juan interjected, "do you plan on running ahead?"

Ashkii laughed and brushed the dirt off his pants and blanket. "Don't worry about me, Coyote... Just try to keep up."

Coyote? Juan thought to himself. "How did you-"

"I see the things that Kai sees... Like I said, try to keep up."

Richard finished packing up the supplies they used the night before and slung them over his horse's saddle. "Time is of the essence," he said, "if you are going to lead the way, Ashkii, you best get to it."

Ashkii sat down and crossed his legs together. He draped his blanket over his body then a cloud of feathers exploded from where he sat, and out of them a raven took off, soaring through the air. The three others watched in awe as he flapped his large black wings and began gliding toward the distant mountains.

Hans hopped onto the back of Juan's horse and slapped his hand against the saddle. "Well men, we don't want to go losing him right away!"

Juan and Richard exchanged a confident nod. Then both quickly mounted their horses and whipped the reins. "HYAW!" they both shouted---and off they went in the wake of the raven.

Chapter 11

FORT THOMPSON

The black feathers spiraling down from the sky charted a path to a bare tree at the peak of the small mountains. Ashkii perched himself on a thin branch and looked out at the large fort, positioned at the foot of their mountain. The sound of two galloping horses followed closely behind. Juan, Richard, and Hans pulled up to the tree and quickly halted when they saw that Ashkii was no longer flying.

The clouds were low, just barely above their heads, and they cast a dark shadow over the giant fort below. The setting sun shed just enough light for them to see their final path down to Thompson.

"That didn't take long," a surprised Juan said, glancing over to Richard.

"We can make it down the mountain by dark," Richard grunted, "I'm sure our feathered friend knows a way in."

"*Kaww! Kaww!*" Ashkii yelled.

Juan couldn't help but feel relieved. It had been hard to believe what Kai had shown him, but as he looked toward the horizon at the landmark fort, he felt confident that they were on the right path.

"This is it. Isn't it Deacon?" Juan muttered. Richard furled his brow at Juan, unsure of what he referred to. "This is faith."

The old man smiled and adjusted his hat back,

pointing the brim upward and letting out his grey locks. "We have a long way to go, son, but you're getting it."

"We will do it, Deacon," Juan swallowed hard, "I know we will get Felina back."

"Do you guys hear that?" Hans then asked..

Juan's ears perked up and all the men went silent; even Ashkii stopped his cawing. Juan didn't hear anything though. He tried closing his eyes to see if that would help, but still nothing.

"It's coming from over there!" Hans yelled and pointed toward the setting sun, beyond Fort Thompson.

Juan opened his eyes and scanned the horizon, but all he saw was the fort. "I don't see any- wait!" Leading into the fort were a set of tracks that ran all the way past the setting sun, and in the glaring beams of light he could see a bright reflection---a reflection that was moving toward the fort. "There!" Juan pointed.

Richard pulled his rifle out of its saddle holster and he looked down the scope where Juan was pointing. "It seems that we aren't the only ones stopping by the fort."

"What should we do?" Juan asked, no longer feeling a swelling confidence.

"We should hurry," said Hans. "The more time we have there, the better prepared we can be to greet them."

Richard turned to Juan, putting his rifle back in its holster, then fixing back his hair and hat. "He's right. Let's move."

"*Kawww!*" Ashkii screamed, then he jumped off his perch and went gliding down the mountain trail.

Juan tried to kick his horse, hoping it would move, but his legs stayed still. He was frozen, and the high altitude was making it hard to breath. Richard rode in front of him and stared him dead in his eyes. "Don't let go of that faith yet,

son… this is where you need it most. Now come on, your
sister is waiting!" He whipped his reins and took off behind
Ashkii.

Hans rested his hand on Juan's shoulder, "We must
go, Juan. We will all be fine. There is a reason for this, have
faith."

Grabbing his shoulder, Juan ran his thumb over Hans'
hand. He nodded his head then kicked hard against his horse's
sides, and they took off behind the others.

The engine-room doors slid open and Falkner walked up
behind the clerk, who was sitting behind the control panel.
Falkner looked out the engine's windows at the dark silhouette
of Fort Thompson.

"We're almost there, Marshal," said the clerk.

"I can see that, and you're sure we will have made it
there before that man on the horse we passed?"

"If he followed the tracks the whole way, then yes. But
again, we can't be sure this is even where he was headed."

Falkner slapped the clerk on his cheek. "Oh, it's where
he's headed alright," he stated with conviction.

The clerk pulled back on a lever, and Falkner felt a
slight push as the train began to slow. Falkner reached for a
shotgun that was resting against the other seat. The barrel was
rusted, but the walnut fore-end was polished and looking
pristine. The slick wood gleamed with the reflection of the
overhead lights. He flipped it over, checked to make sure it
was loaded, then slung the strap over his shoulder.

"Now you're going to stay right here and wait for me
to get back, you hear? If anyone but me comes up to this train
you don't let them in," Falkner hissed.

"Of course Marshal, I'll be waiting."

Falkner slapped the clerk on the cheek once again. "You're alright, Clerk."

The exit door slid open just as the train came to a stop. A low fog blocked out the minimal light cast by the setting sun, and the steam emitted by the train clouded the air even further. Falkner marched into the fog, not able to see what was in front of him but knowing that the entrance to the fort was only steps away. An orchestra of noises echoed off the train behind him; gears crackling and pistons slowing down, but it was only a faint whisper to his ears compared to the slow rhythmic thumping of his heart. His breathing was even, and his hands did not tremble. He unstrapped the shotgun from his shoulder and readied it at his hip. After only a few moments, his eyes adjusted to the fog, and in front of him he saw motion--not a great motion but only a slight disturbance within the still mist. The air in front of him was moving, but he did not feel a breeze. Everywhere else around him, the cold air lay still. He pumped back the fore-end of his shotgun and pointed the gun toward the moving air, taking a few more careful steps forward.

He could hear another's breathing. As he got closer the breathing quickly changed into a grunting sound. Then the unstill air materialized into a large pink mass. A hairless horse the size of a mountain stood before him. It was tied to a post just outside the entrance of the fort, and from the sound of its grunts he could tell it was hostile. Part of him felt like going back to the engine room and shooting the clerk where he sat for not getting them there fast enough. He decided to keep his distance from the large mare and proceeded to the entrance without a hitch.

Fort Thompson was much different than the depots that Falkner had been accustomed to. Most noticeably, the fort didn't have a hidden door requiring a key, just large doors that were unlocked and opened quite easily. The Government abandoned the forts within the Rotten Plains long ago, and they decommissioned them with little care, not even locking the doors on their way out. Other than the extreme buildup of toxic dust that littered the large halls, the fort was in nice condition---fully enclosed and unexposed to the outer elements. Each step that Falkner took echoed through the abandoned rooms. There was a sour smell in the air, carried upon each flake of dust floating through the deathly still space. Falkner pulled a handkerchief out of his coat pocket and tied it around his face. He wasn't concerned with anything he breathed in, but couldn't handle the nauseous miasma. He despised the Rotten Plains---he even tried to convince Chance to set up a rendezvous point elsewhere. It pained him to know that after leaving Thompson he would still have to remain in the toxic wasteland.

He passed room after room, peeking his head into each one to see if his host was there waiting. He passed ten rooms on each side of the hall, and each one was empty. After the tenth room, the hall opened into a great courtyard with hallways extending down the east and west wings of the room. On the north end of the room was a large set of stairs leading to the mess hall. There was a large stale pond in the middle of the enclosed courtyard. Its deep green water reeked worse than the dusty air. He held his hand over the pond and felt a heat radiating off it---even without his fingers having touched the water, it still stung his skin. He strolled around the courtyard's pond and glanced down the east and west wing hallways as he passed them. He tapped the barrel of his shotgun against his shoulder repeatedly as he mulled over his choice of path.

After lapping the pond a handful of times, he stopped in front of the east wing hallway then started down the dimly

174

lit passage. But after one step, a faint noise in the distance grabbed his attention, a noise not originating from the east wing. It was a faint high-pitched tapping that made a not-so-rhythmic, *ding ding ding*'ing. Falkner turned back to the courtyard and carefully followed the dinging. It brought him back toward the pond then had him turning right up the large set of stairs toward the mess hall. The thumping of his boots up the metal stairs began to drown out the dinging, but he could feel the vibrations pulling him toward their point of origin. At the top of the stairs were the doors to the mess hall, one of them was shut while the other hung ajar, inviting him in. His grip tightened around his shotgun, and he once again readied it at his hip.

The mess hall was dimly lit when Falkner strutted in, but unlike the hallways, the lights were not flickering. There was a reflection glaring off a metal plate atop one of the tables. Sitting at the table, scooping an ambiguous slop out of a plate, sat a man wearing a tattered wide-brimmed hat, a brown poncho, and a silver star pinned to his pant pocket.

"I was hoping I wouldn't have to eat alone," said Wyatt. "Now I have three ideas who you might be, and be patient with me if I don't get it on the first try, I've never been the most clever man." Falkner stepped toward Wyatt but quickly halted while he continued to speak. "The one they're calling 'The Coyote'," he guessed first. "No, that can't be it--- they say he's a Mexican, and it might be a little dark in here, but I know white when I see it. Well, I would guess that slack-jawed big-talker, Chance Havoc... but no. I've met him, and I don't think he would have grown so much taller in just a couple weeks."

Falkner took another step forward, just enough of a step for the light from the overhead lamp to reflect off the star he had pinned to his jacket. Wyatt pushed himself out of his chair, his pistol already drawn and pointed at Falkner's heart.

"Ahh," Wyatt sighed, staring through Falkner viciously, although his eyes were still shaded by the brim of his tattered hat. "You see, I couldn't quite make out what the third guess was. I reckoned that the Eastern Marshal was out of commission, but I assumed that would only happen if he was dead. So, why haven't you been killed... Falkner, is it?"

"If it isn't the Marshal in the West... Wyatt Cole. I don't know, the way I see it, the Marshal in the East *is* dead."

"Well, that's good then. Just means I won't feel bad when I put a bullet through you."

Falkner raised the shotgun from his hip and pointed it up to the ceiling. "Put the gun away, Cole... I just came here to talk."

Wyatt holstered his pistol, then sat back down and promptly grabbed a spoonful of slop. "Well, it's been a while since I had a chat with anyone other than poor Peaches out there." Falkner set his shotgun on the table beside him, pulled a chair out and sat down.

"I was wondering who the hell could have sent that message from Lima depot," Falkner started. "From what I hear you've got quite the mess to clean up in your own house. From what I've heard about you, I didn't think you'd go running away from your problems, and to this wretched spot, of all places."

"Mmm, that's where you're mistaken, partner. I'm running right toward my problems, and I think I just got to the finish line," Wyatt said with his mouth half full of whatever it was on his plate.

"I suppose it is the end of the line... one way or another." Falkner's gently ran his hand over his shotgun. The orange rust built up on his fingertips, then sprinkled onto the table as he rubbed them together. He was no longer looking at

Wyatt, he couldn't bear it---his mere presence disgusted him. "What's the point of it all, Cole?"

"The point of what?"

"The Marshal Service! Hell, that old bastard dragged me into it when I was just a kid. I know it was the same for you."

Wyatt dropped his spoon and pushed the bowl aside--- with more force than he intended and it fell off the far edge of the table. He lifted his head just enough for the light to finally reveal his eyes, his cold eyes, his angry eyes. The disgust between the duo was mutual. "We're here to keep order. We may be the only two men in the world that still know what that means… or maybe now I'm the only one."

"Order," Falkner chuckled, "Keep order by blindly following whatever those damn Natives say?"

"Order isn't about the Natives, but they're the people of this land and they're who we're meant to protect."

"I've given the whole speech before, but what the hell has any of it gotten us? Havoc was right. There ain't no freedom or justice in this world. Not the way it is now!"

"Havoc?" Wyatt mumbled. "So, you are with him."

"I'm supposed to convince you to come along with us," Falkner grunted. "He knows that you'll be an issue. But you sure are a stubborn bastard, and I don't think there's much chance of you changing your mind."

"You're observant…"

"So I guess there's only room for one marshal in our new age." Falkner grabbed his shotgun and sprung out of his chair.

Wyatt remained seated, but watched as Falkner pointed the sawed-off barrel at his chest. Wyatt stared at the silver star that was pinned to Falkner's jacket, and he ran his thumb over his own badge, feeling the cold embossed letters that were carved into it, *MARSHAL,* they spelled.

"You're right, Falkner. And I'm going to make sure I rip that fucking star off your cold dead body."

Wyatt kicked his feet up to the table and pushed it over toward Falkner, then he rolled out of his chair behind the table. Falkner fired a shot, and the pellets scattered into the steel tabletop. He pumped back on the shotgun to load another shell, but before he could pull the trigger, Wyatt jumped out from behind the cover of the table. He slapped his hand against the hammer of his pistol and fired four rapid shots deep into Falkner's belly. The shotgun hit the ground instantly. Falkner quickly followed, slamming to the cement floor in a pool of his own blood. Wyatt flipped out the cylinder of his revolver and loaded rounds from his belt into the empty chambers as he stood over Falkner. After pushing in four new rounds, he flicked the cylinder back and holstered the pistol.

Falkner began hacking violently, while blood spurted from his mouth with each cough. Grabbing his stomach, he observed his crimson-stained palms and began laughing in between the coughing and spitting. He looked up at Wyatt's cold sharp eyes that were already locked on him. "You're in over your head, kid," Falkner said. "Don't say I didn't try to warn you."

"What happened with the eastern tribes? Falkner, what did you do?"

"Hahaha!" he tried to laugh but nearly choked on the blood that continued to spill out of his throat. "You can't have a tribe without a chief! Ain't no eastern tribes anymore, Cole!"

Wyatt knelt beside Falkner and looked at the blood pooling up around him, but it didn't bother him---not as much as the sight of the man's face had moments before. He wrapped his hand around the silver badge on Falkner's jacket and ripped it off.

"Don't move!" a sudden voice called out from the far end of the mess hall.

"This place sure is empty," Hans said as he and his band walked through the lonely halls of Fort Thompson.

"I reckon it's not as empty as we would like it to be though," said Richard, keeping his eye peeled as they took slow cautious steps down the halls.

"*Kaww!*" Ashkii shouted. He was farther ahead, hopping into the rooms one by one. "*Kaw Kaw!*" he repeated.

"I guess he found what he's looking for," said Juan. Guessing was the best any of them could do, communicating with a bird was not an easy task. They had tried to convince him to change back, but he argued otherwise, at least they guessed that's what he'd done---either way he continued as a raven.

They entered a large gathering room, an open space with a great long wooden table at the center. Like the rest of the fort, it was covered in dust and reeked of stale nothingness. Ashkii was perched atop the table and motioned his beak toward the wall closest to the entrance. There was an old map pinned to the wall. Richard pulled it off and laid it out flat on the table. The material was faded and tattered, but it was still readable, only barely. "Here," Richard pointed, "it looks like we came in through the northeastern entrance. These here are the tracks---the southern entrance is most likely where whoever is on that train will enter."

"Do you think we got here first?" asked Juan.

"I don't know," Richard replied.

"What about this, Richard?" Hans started. "It seems as though our end is on a higher level than the South. That should give us an advantage being higher up, should it not?"

"Hmm, it looks like this courtyard separates the northern and southern sections of the fort. If we can just get to the-"

BANG! A booming shot ran through the halls. The men, and bird, looked at each other, now fully aware they had not been first to arrive.

"That came from the south," Juan whispered. "Richard, we should go---the last thing we want is to be pinned inside this little room."

BANG! BANG! BANG! BANG!

"Hans," Richard started. "You and Juan stay here. I'll go on ahead and find out where those shots came from."

"But Richard-" Juan started, only to be stopped by Richard.

"Ashkii, come with me. If anything goes wrong you can make it back here and find a safe way out, even if you have to go back and find a way around the fort."

"*Kaww!*"

"Richard, it's better that we stick together! There are four of us," pleaded Juan.

"And what if there are five of them?" Richard barked. "Then all of us die and Felina stays right where she is until her dying breath. This is *your* journey, son. If you die then it's over. Now wait here with Hans until the bird or I get back." Richard didn't wait for a response, pulling his rifle off his shoulder, he took off back into the hall.

The door slammed behind Richard, right in the face of Juan who had tried to lunge after him. He ran up to the door and pounded it with his fist. "Damn it!" he cried.

Hans waddled up to Juan and shook him until the young man stopped pounding against the door. "Please, Juan! It's best we don't make noise. Remember what Richard told you earlier, now is when we need faith the most. He has lived through times tougher than these. We must have faith that he knows what he is doing. You have to for your sister's sake."

Juan tossed his hat to the ground and his black hair fell forward into his eyes. He hadn't realized how long his hair had grown until just then. He brushed his locks behind his ears and saw Hans' calm face looking back at him intently. It was so different from the face he saw staring at him in the reflection of the creek that day. This was a face void of fear or doubt, it was a face he wished to have himself. Hans is right, he thought to himself, I must have faith in Richard.

***

"Don't move!"

Wyatt slowly turned his head toward the back of the mess hall. He saw the silhouette of a large man standing in the doorway, and a long rifle pointed his way. "Easy there, partner," Wyatt said firmly, raising his hands in the air. He rose to face the silhouette, but could not yet make out the details of the man's face. He could tell, however, he was a large burly man, quite similar looking to his mentor Bill, at least from the outline. "What seems to be the problem?"

"I reckon the fact that you just killed a marshal."

"You friends with this man?" Wyatt asked.

"He's no friend of mine."

"What's your name, old man?"

"Deacon. Who's asking?"

"Well Deacon, my name is Marshal Wyatt Cole. Now I'm sorry for the misunderstanding but that there on the ground is nothing more than a good-for-nothing outlaw. I was just getting back this misplaced star."

Richard lowered his rifle and took a step closer into

the light. Wyatt started to lower his hands but stayed put where he was. "So, you say you're a marshal… did you get lost? You're quite a ways away from any of the native lands."

"No, I am right where I want to be. There seems to be a man who has made quite a mess in the Apache territory--- he's killed a handful of people including the son of Chief Lipan, an old man, and possibly a young girl and even younger boy. I have a feeling he might be strolling through these parts sometime soon." Wyatt's voice began to sound like the growling wolves at Lima.

"Sounds like quite the bad apple," said Richard. His hands were beginning to tighten around his rifle, and he could feel his pulse pounding through his fingertips.

"Maybe you've heard of him?" Wyatt snapped. "He's a Mexican. A rare kind these days. So, if you ran into one there's a good chance it was him. They call him the Coyote, seems like no one even knows his name."

"I haven't. I wish you luck finding him though," Richard said as he began to turn around. Ashkii was just behind him down the hall; Richard nodded his head and the raven took off back the way they came. Then Richard heard a faint *swoosh* followed by a slightly louder *click click click*.

"Not so fast, Mr. Deacon," said Wyatt. His poncho was flipped over his shoulder exposing his right arm, that was holding the cocked revolver. "You seem a bit older, so I'll ask again in case you didn't quite hear me the first time. Have you heard of this Coyote?"

Richard turned back around. He had the rifle pressed up against his shoulder, and the barrel was pointing at Wyatt. "Heard of him? Hell, I'm with him! That boy's on a mission, and I'll be damned if you're the one who's going to get in his way."

"Is that right?" Wyatt snarled.

With a burst of flapping wings, Ashkii sped through the hall. The hall was so dark that the raven was perfectly camouflaged, only becoming visible when he passed under the random flickering lights. BANG! He heard a shot ring out behind him, but his concentration did not waver. His hearing was not as keen in this form, so he could not make out which gun the shot was fired from. BOOM! He heard a body hit the floor shortly after. Then he heard a voice shout out, "Come out, Coyote!" The voice frightened Ashkii, which was quite the accomplishment in and of itself, but what frightened him more were the following shots that echoed down the hall, and the bullets whizzing past his small, feathered body. It was enough for him to lose his concentration, and in turn lose his current form. He had not been struck by any of the bullets, but still he tumbled to the ground as he morphed into his crude hybrid form. As he rolled along the floor he became entangled in his feathered cloak. He struggled to his feet and hurled one of his knives blindly down the hall. The blade dinged against the concrete floor just as another flash of light sparked from out of the darkness, carrying a loud BANG with it. The bullet sped past Ashkii once again, then the voice followed once more, "C'mon, Coyote!"

The shots shook the walls of the gathering room. Juan rushed for the windows by the door and tried to see what the commotion was. The room was well lit, but he couldn't see anything down the hall. He could only hear the fusillade of shots reverberating through the building. "Why are we not helping!" Juan cried as he pounded his fist against the glass.

"We are supposed to wait for Richard or Ashkii to

come! We have to believe in Richard and believe in the plan---
he will not lead us astray," said Hans.

"The plan is already astray, Hans!" Juan yelled,
scowling at the hunchback.

"You do not know that!"

"We should have gone with them. If we were only
there to help... what if Richard is dead?"

"Juan, all of this is happening for a reason. You just
have to have faith in *His* plan!"

"Damn it!" Juan slammed his fist once more against
the glass.

Then the window cracked and shattered with a great
explosion of force, and Ashkii came lunging through,
plummeting into the room. He crashed on top of the large table
and slid off the edge, finally coming to a stop just in front of
Hans.

"Ashkii!" Hans shouted, "What happened?"

Juan rushed across the room and helped lift up
Ashkii's cowled head. "A Marshal. He is looking for you,
Juan. He killed a man and shot Richard as well. He is
coming!"

"Coyote!" Wyatt shouted from the hall.

Juan drew his pistol and moved to the door. His hand
had never shaken so much, not even when he first rode into the
chilling forest of the Rotten Plains. Through the shattered
window he saw a man in a tattered brown hat walk by. He
could hear Hans and Ashkii saying words behind him, but he
couldn't make them out. Their words were drowned out by the
resounding noise made by the man's boots. *Tap tap tap*, he
heard bouncing back and forth in his mind. Juan tried to pull
the hammer back on his pistol, but his thumb missed. His grip
slipped and the revolver fell to the floor. Just as it hit the
ground, the marshal's foot pounded against the door, and the

entrance swung wide open. There Juan stood, under the gun of the Marshal. A man he had met once before, but didn't remember, because all he saw was the black hole of the pistol being pointed at his heart. Before he knew it he was on his knees, staring at the silver pistol he had just dropped, but he didn't reach for it. Part of him still believed that Richard would walk up behind the Marshal and save them all.

"That's Felina's shawl..." the marshal whispered. Though quiet, the words were clear as day to Juan.

"Felina?" said Juan. He raised his head to the man that towered above him. His honey-brown eyes seemed familiar, but he didn't remember why. The dirty blonde scruff on his face was unique, but he knew he had seen it once before. His tattered brown hat with a wide flat brim was awfully familiar, but the carefully woven patterns of the man's burnt umber poncho could never be forgotten. They were the same patterns woven into his own shawl, and woven into all the clothes that Felina made. "...Wyatt?"

Wyatt's pistol fell to the floor. He stumbled toward Juan and pulled off the boy's black leather hat. He grabbed his face and stared intently into his two pitch-black eyes. He held on dearly to Juan's face. "Juan? Oh, Juan, what's happened?"

Hans and Ashkii silently watched the spectacle unfold. "What is the meaning of this?" Ashkii whispered.

"Do they know each other? Juan never mentioned a marshal before," Hans pondered.

Tears streamed down Juan's face, streaking through the dirt that had built up on his skin over the past week. "I... I didn't mean it," Juan mumbled through his sobbing.

"What, Juan? Talk to me!"

"I didn't mean to kill him, Wyatt! I only wanted to find a gift for Felina's birthday, but I went too far into the train. That girl was so scared and then he came after me, he was going to kill me. I... I didn't want to kill him but I was going to die! And then they took her, Wyatt, they took her and killed Papa and it's all because of me!"

Wyatt shook Juan, trying to calm him from his manic state, and trying desperately to take in all that the boy had just laid before him. "Who, Juan? Who took Felina and killed Roberto?"

Juan buried his head into Wyatt's poncho---the familiar feel of the fabric in his hands was a powerful reminder of his sister. Then he muttered something into Wyatt's chest.

"What did you say?"

Juan lifted his head and stared at Wyatt with ravaged eyes. "The Apache!" he declared. Wyatt was baffled at the answer, but Juan continued. "We are trying to make it to Geronimo Park. I need to rescue her! And all of them have agreed to help me, Ashkii and Hans and Richard... Richard! Where is Richard?"

"Richard?"

"Richard Deacon!" Hans hollered.

"Deacon... the old man? I... He..."

"Richard!" Juan cried. Pushing Wyatt aside, he sprinted out the room and down the hall. Hans and Ashkii followed closely behind him. Wyatt paused for an extra moment but reluctantly followed down the corridor as well.

Juan knelt over Richard's large body, sprawled out on the floor, with blood all around. He pressed down on the hole in the middle of Richard's chest, but that didn't stop the blood from leaking out the back.

"What do we do?" Hans asked frantically. "Ashkii--- you're a medicine man! Don't you have anything that can help him?"

Ashkii examined the body through the dark eyeholes of the skull mask he wore. "The bullet entered close to his heart, it may have caught a piece of it. There is no medicine that can heal that."

Juan turned around and grabbed Ashkii, shaking him with great force then speaking with a booming passion. "We need him! And you are the only one who can help him. I know that Kai sent us to you for a reason. Now there has to be something you can do!"

Ashkii reached over to Richard and pressed his taloned fingers against Richard's neck. "It is weak but he still has a pulse. We do not have much time, and I do not know if I will be successful, but there is a ritual that could save him. I have never performed it though."

"What do we have to do?" Hans inquired.

"Help me bring him outside. Then I will start making the preparations."

Wyatt stood down the hall as the others conversed. He stared at Richard's body as it lay motionless. He couldn't stop thinking about the fear in Juan's eyes and the sorrow in his tears when he spoke. *The Apache!* he heard repeating in his mind. Also resonating were the words of Cheyanne. Those *enemies see our land as ripe for the taking.* Juan was his friend, and so were Roberto and Felina. They had saved Wyatt's life, yet Wyatt was sent to end Juan's. Plus, the man he had shot was a friend of Juan's. Wyatt couldn't help but feel an agonizing remorse. Tethered to his remorse was an equally painful conflict as to where his loyalties lied. Did they lie with friendship or with order? With Lipan's so-called mercy, that merely bound him to a life of misery? Or with Juan and Felina's grace, that saved him from impending death? He wondered what Bill would do, but he struggled to recognize any beauty in the situation. He found himself toying with Falkner's star, flipping it through his fingers. He looked past Juan and the others at Falkner's corpse on the floor of the mess hall, accompanied by the silhouette of a strange feeble man.

"Hey," Wyatt called out. "Stay right there!"

But the man did not stay. He abruptly turned and bolted out of the mess hall, then down the stairs back toward the courtyard. Wyatt pushed past Juan and the others, lunging over Richard's body, and sprinting after the man. He gained on him quickly---the stranger not seeming to know how to properly run. Just outside the doors, Wyatt pounced on the man, tackling him and tumbling through the dirt.

Wyatt grabbed the stranger by his clean while collar and pinned him to the ground. "Who are you?" he snapped. "How do you know Falkner?"

The stranger struggled to catch his breath. Wyatt could feel the man's heart pounding beneath his knuckles, which were buried into the man's chest. "Please, Marshal---I heard gunshots and felt compelled to see what was happening. Marshal Falkner instructed me to stay in the train, but I was just so curious."

"You work for Falkner?"

"Marshal Cole, you should know that we clerks work exclusively for the Marshal Service," he explained.

Wyatt loosened his grip on the clerk's collar. Then he noticed the ghostly complexion of the man's skin, the same pallor of the hands that would hand him messages all these years at the depots. He looked up, toward the western horizon, and saw the same screaming locomotive that had passed him earlier, sitting idle on the tracks with the door to its engine room ajar. Wyatt pushed himself off the ground and stood up. Brushing the dirt off his slacks and poncho, he pulled the clerk up off the ground and brushed him off as well.

"Do you know all of what's been going on lately?" he asked the clerk.

"No sir, I do not know everything---only the little that

Marshal Falkner mumbled to himself about."

"Are you willing to tell us what you know?"

"If you order it, sir! My duty is to the Marshals."

"Well that's good," Wyatt chuckled.

"Wyatt!" Juan called from the doorway. Wyatt and the clerk turned around to face the voice. "Ashkii thinks he might be able to save Richard. He needs us to carry his body out here, but I can't lift him on my own and Hans isn't any help. Please, I need you... Richard can't die."

Wyatt slapped the clerk on the shoulder, "C'mon, make yourself useful." And all three ran back into the fort to retrieve Richard's body.

Ashkii was outside mixing strange odoriferous ingredients into a small pot. He motioned to the others to bring Richard's body to him. "Quick, undress him," Ashkii ordered. The others stripped off his coat, then his shirt, pants, boots, and socks. "We are ready to begin," Ashkii announced.

"How long will it take?" Juan asked.

"The ritual takes time. I must sing the Night Chant and dress his body in the healing oils. I do this each night for the next three nights. In that time, Deacon will relive the most trying times in his life. His survival is strictly dependent on his will to live."

"And you're sure you know what you are doing?" Wyatt asked sternly.

Ashkii gave the marshal a wicked glare. "I promise I will do all I can to save the life of the man you tried to kill. But if it does not work then his death is on your hands, not mine." He turned to Juan. "I should begin."

"We will come check on you soon. Wyatt and I have to have a word with our new acquaintance," said Juan.

"Right," Ashkii nodded his beaked head and continued mixing the strange concoction.

Wyatt marched off toward the idle train in the distance. The clerk was waiting in the doorway of the engine room. Juan and Hans followed closely in Wyatt's dusty wake. Entering the engine, they all gathered around the map displayed on the computer, much like the one Wyatt saw in the abandoned depot. The clerk's snowy white fingers tapped nervously against the desk as he awaited questioning from a noticeably edgy bunch.

"Well," the clerk's voice trembled, "what is it you would like to know, Marshal?"

"We need to get to Geronimo Park as quickly as possible. From what I understand the fastest way to get there from here is by stopping off at Fort Young first."

"That's right. Any other path would take twice the distance and time to travel."

Hans wrapped his long fingers around Juan's hand and tugged at it. Juan looked down and listened to Hans' comment, "Something about this clerk seems off to me. Do you feel it?"

"He seems fine to me," Juan whispered back to him.

"But his eyes, Juan," Hans pleaded, "they're so cold, almost lifeless."

Juan looked closer into the clerk's eyes, and soon understood the feeling that little Hans expressed. The clerk hardly blinked in the time that Juan stood there staring at him, and his skin was so pale it was like there was no blood moving through his veins at all. The longer he looked the more disturbing the man appeared---even the sight of Hans when they first met was not so unappealing. He looked back down to his little hunchback friend and could see tears forming in his swollen eyes. Juan thought it almost impossible that a being that looked like Hans could feel pity over the appearance of another man, but it was understandable why.

"Richard's plan was to go to Fort Young after leaving

Thompson," Juan began as he tried shaking himself from the trance the clerk had unknowingly put him under. "Why would we need to find another route? We have a train now---so won't we only make it to Geronimo Park even faster?"

Wyatt removed his hat and slicked back his long dirty blonde locks. He waved his hand and motioned for the others to come closer to the map. "It's only faster if we don't run into any speed bumps. And we already have a big one with the Navajo trying to save Deacon. We have a potentially bigger one waiting for us at Fort Young. I checked the activity in the Plains a while back and it was all concentrated in and out of Young."

"That is due to it being the hideout for the Chance Havoc Gang," the clerk butted in. "It was where I was meant to take Marshal Falkner once he finished up here."

"You mean after he killed all of us?" Juan sneered.

"He was only planning on killing Marshal Cole. There is a chance he would have tried to recruit you and your friends, but he *could* have also proceeded by killing you."

Hans tugged firmly on Juan's shawl and glared at him angrily. Juan nodded to him with full awareness of his reluctance to work with the clerk.

"So, what do we do then?" Juan asked.

Wyatt studied the map, taking inventory of all the flashing lights and dots on the screen. He glanced back at Juan and saw the same black eyes that he shared with Felina. "I'm worried what Chance's plans are moving forward, but our number one objective is making it to Geronimo Park as soon as possible to rescue Felina."

"That is my only objective, Wyatt," said Juan.

"I understand, but if we don't deal with Chance first then we may never get her back. This man is a wild card, and he's already got it out for me. If you want my help then he is

191

going to have it out for you as well."

"So, we confront him at Fort Young, then go south to Geronimo Park and rescue Felina," Juan declared.

Chapter 12

NIGHT CHANT

Rolling thunder and titanic lightning crashed about the horizon. Ashkii danced around Richard, spreading the mysterious potion on and around his body. He sang a haunting tune, unlike any the others had heard before. He tossed some of the potion into the bonfire and its flames expanded in a furious rage! And so began the Night Chant.

"Ma! Hey, Ma! I'm heading out to go find some supper now. Hopefully I won't be long," Richard called out, but there was no response from his mother. She had been ill for quite some time and didn't always have the strength to holler across the room. Richard grabbed his rifle and made his way out the door. It was nearing the end of autumn in the North, where he and his mother resided. The skies were grey and cloudy, but the ground was not yet white. Soon the snow would start to fall, and the cold season would be upon them. Hunting became far more difficult in those months. Big game was hard to find as is, let alone in the cold of winter---luckily his mother could hardly eat solid food, so one buck would last a long time. He would make his mother broth from the bones, and leave the meat for himself. He would dry some out to make jerky, for the months where blizzards rendered it nearly impossible to go outside.

Their cabin was tucked away in the woods. It made them harder to find; most of the bandits in the area didn't stray far from the tracks. Richard tried to contain his hunting to within the woods---the birds and rodents and occasional deer sufficed during the warm months. But with winter fast approaching, he knew he'd have to catch something big to last him through. An elk, moose, or bison would do the job. They had plenty of meat and bones, enough to last for weeks, but nothing that large could be found in the woods. For that he'd have to make his way to the open meadows. He didn't like open spaces, it was too easy to be seen.

The tracks ran right through the open plains below the forest, and bandits always roamed near the tracks. Gangs camped out mere miles from the tracks, plotting out ways to derail a train or just waiting to see if it would happen on its own. Sometimes a train would come rolling through while a herd of bison or elk grazed along the tracks. Most of the herd would run off when the tracks started to shake, but there was always at least one that didn't make it. A foot would get caught, and they'd be left waiting helplessly as the train plowed through. Sometimes the entire animal would get hit and paint the whole front of the engine. Other times only its hind would get torn off---tough to watch, but it made for an easy time carrying only half a buck back to the cabin.

Richard rode on muleback through the dense forest. Ned was good at letting Richard know when game was nearby; he got nervous around large animals, and would slow his trot if he heard something approaching. Today Ned moved swiftly through the woods---a bad sign. Richard feared they would make it to the forest's edge without a hitch then be forced to roam the open plains.

"Whoa, Ned!" he called out. The mule slowed his

stride as the two exited from the cover of the woods and into the open meadow. The tracks laid across the entire length of the horizon, from the rising sun in the East to its setting in the West. A massive herd of elk were grazing around the tracks, and as far as Richard could tell, no bandits were nearby. He pulled a pair of binoculars from his saddle bag and took a closer look at the herd. There was one huge buck standing right on the tracks---an easy target for Richard. It was difficult sneaking up on a herd in such an open area. If he was caught, and they decided to run, there was a good chance the large buck would get his foot snagged between the tracks.

They were about a mile off in the distance. If he rode near the edge of the woods he could circle around them and cut the distance in half. Ned trotted along the tree line, just far enough off that they wouldn't startle the herd. Once they were close enough, Richard hopped off his mule and grabbed his rifle and knife. To get any closer he'd have to go on foot.

He walked through the tall grass until he got the bare patch that ran parallel to the tracks. Though it made him more visible, walking along the bare path was far quieter than rustling through tall grass.

The herd had crept in his direction while he'd been riding, leaving him only a short walk until he was in range. He had a powerful rifle with him, and its large scope allowed him to shoot from a far distance. His father had given it to him. He found it in a derailed Government car that was carrying confiscated goods.

Richard continued his approach, making it a couple hundred yards from the herd without startling them. It would be a stretch to pull off a good shot from where he stood, but he didn't want to risk getting any closer. He got down on his knee and pulled the rifle from his shoulder. He pulled back the lever to make sure a round was loaded, and it was. Then he locked the lever back in place and pressed the stock against his shoulder. The elk magnified as he peered through the scope. Feeling the breeze blowing slightly from his left, he adjusted his aim. He wasn't nervous, but he could feel himself starting to shake. Not enough to throw off his shot, but enough for him to focus a bit harder than usual. He took a few deep breaths, and when he was ready, he pulled the trigger.

The loud bang immediately sent the herd stampeding away, but the large elk fell to the ground. Richard looked up and adjusted his hat. He had done it. He took the elk down on his first try. He wrapped the rifle's strap back around his shoulder and ran down the tracks to grab the animal. As he ran, he could feel the ground shaking beneath his feet, and it sent him tumbling over. He turned around, and in the distance he saw the light from a locomotive blitzing toward him.

"Shit!" he yelled. He sprung to his feet, threw his rifle to the side of the tracks, and sprinted toward the elk carcass. The shaking of the tracks intensified once he got to the elk. He looked back and saw the full figure of the train racing down the tracks. He grabbed the buck by its antlers and tugged as hard as he could, trying his best to drag it off the tracks. Richard was strong, but the buck was tremendously heavy. It started to budge, but it didn't move far; what Richard had once hoped now cursed him. The elk's hind foot was caught in the tracks.

The train was closing in, but Richard wasn't letting go of his catch---without it they had no chance of surviving the winter. Hopping back on the tracks, he pulled out his knife. He bent down and thrusted the blade into the elk's hind leg. Sawing the knife back and forth, he tried to sever the foot. The tracks tremored beneath his boots, and the train screeched like a rabid grizzly. He pulled the knife out, and he gave the leg a vicious chop. Swinging the knife with all his might, the blade cut clear through the bone, lopping off the hoof and relinquishing it from the track's clutches. He grabbed a hold of the antlers, and with all his strength, hauled the carcass off the tracks. As he pulled the last part of the elk off the tracks, the train came plowing through with no regard for him or his catch.

He watched in awe as the behemoth machine stormed past him. Its immense size and power were something he marveled at each time he witnessed one. Be it the first time or the thousandth, it never ceased to amaze him. He thought about how the tracks were laid across the entire length of the continent, from the northernmost point to the southernmost, easternmost to westernmost. He often imagined jumping aboard one and seeing where it would take him.

The sun had set by the time Richard made it home. He walked alongside Ned the entire way back, since the poor mule already had a big enough burden to drag behind him---the elk was tied to a sled that was in turn attached to Ned's saddle. Richard was quite proud of his catch that day. It would be nice to have a good hearty meal, he thought. The squirrel stew he'd been living off the last two weeks just wouldn't suffice anymore. The broth from the elk's bones would make a nutritious meal for his mother. Rose was sick and elderly---she needed all the strength she could muster to make it through winter, and this elk could very well be her saving grace.

Once back at the cabin, Richard took the elk into the shed out back to skin and butcher it. He took just enough to last him through the week then hung the rest, seasoning a portion to make jerky for the winter. He threw the rest in the icebox, turning on the generator to make sure it kept cold. It wasn't awfully hard for him to find fuel for the generator. The ghost town about 20 miles west had an old storage basement packed full of Government supplies. But soon the weather would be cold enough that he wouldn't need the icebox.

He cut up some potatoes and some good chunks of meat, then made a broth and threw it all into a pot. Then he hung it over the fire to let it cook. He sat in the rocking chair his father had crafted while he occasionally stirred the pot. His mother's bed was in the main room right by the fire and adjacent to his rocking chair, where she'd sleep for most of the day. Richard worried that he would come home from a hunt and she wouldn't wake up. He held her hand as he sat beside her, rocking back and forth. He was happy that when he grabbed it, her hand was warm.

Rose squeezed Richard's thumb. She turned over in bed and slowly opened her eyes. "Smells good," she said as a wide smile grew upon her face, revealing her nearly toothless mouth.

"Caught a big one today."

"Mmm, ain't that nice," she said, rolling over and rubbing his arm up and down.

"Sit up, Ma. It'll be ready soon, and I got a little surprise for after you're done eating."

Richard pulled his mother up so that her back rested against the wall. He filled a bowl with the broth and a few chunks of potatoes. He'd take a spoonful and blow it, take a taste test, then give it to Rose. The potatoes were mushy enough that she didn't need teeth to eat them. He always waited for her to finish before fixing himself a plate. It had been like that since he was a boy; since his father disappeared when Richard was just twelve years old. They didn't know exactly what happened, but they didn't believe that he'd abandoned them---he was a loving father and husband, and cared deeply for them both. But they lived in a dangerous world. One where death's head crept around every corner. It might have been bandits, maybe a bear, or he could have even been hit by a train. Richard knew all too well how easily that could happen. Ever since his disappearance, Richard took up his position as man of the house. Without question or fuss, he would hunt, tend the crops, and most importantly, take care of his mother. He knew if his father was still around, Rose would be his number one priority, and Richard respected that sentiment.

When his father disappeared, Richard found his personal journal. He would read it to his mother when she missed his father more than usual. His father worked for the Government when he was a younger man, and anyone who worked for them was taught to read and write. One day, he decided to run away from that life, taking with him that sacred knowledge. Whatever was left of the Government was so small and powerless that running away from that life posed very little threat to one's fortunes. Even so, his father made sure that his family settled where they could never be found. He built their cabin himself, planted the potatoes, and cleared the trees to make room for the horses and donkeys to graze. This plot of land was his legacy, along with his wife and son.

Richard fed his mother her last spoonful of broth and watched her slurp it down. A few drops ran down her chin, and Richard used his rag to wipe them off.

"Ahh!" she exclaimed. "That was wonderful, Richard. Now, what is my surprise?"

"Don't you want to let me eat first?"

"Oh, but I'm a tired old woman, don't know if I can stay up that long."

Richard laughed and kissed her forehead. He walked into the other room and rummaged through the cupboards. He came back holding some small papers and a little box. "Met a Sioux man traveling near the tracks last week. He had some tobacco that he traded with me. Grew it himself." He opened the box and sprinkled the tobacco over a little paper and neatly rolled it up. "I know how you and Pa used to smoke out on the porch together when I was little, thought you might like it."

The look of joy on Rose's face was a sight for sore eyes. Tobacco was a rare delicacy, with only a small number of natives knowing how to grow it. The Government had purged and confiscated all cigarettes a long time ago, and kept them stored in old warehouses. Richard's father worked in one of the warehouses and stole a few boxes before he ran away. He and Rose would sit on the porch and smoke a pack together almost every night. It had been more than ten years since they ran out, and Richard knew that his mother had been dying to have one ever since.

He rolled one for his mother and one for himself. He bent down by the fire and stuck in their tips until they started to smoke. He popped one in between his lips and gently placed the other between his mother's. The two sat and filled the room with the sweet tobacco's fumes.

"How 'bout I read you a bit from Pa's journal before you go to sleep?" asked Richard.

Rose nodded her head and took a big inhale from her cigarette. Richard walked over to his bed and took the journal off his nightstand. It was titled with his father's name, *John Deacon*. Sitting back down beside his mother, he flipped through the pages until he found one he hadn't yet read to her. He had read the whole thing himself just about every night for the last 15 years.

"Ah, here's a nice one, Ma."

I found it today, everything I have been searching for my whole life. Not just a piece of the pie, but the whole bakery. As I sit here atop this hill looking over these open lands in front of me, with the crowded woods to my back, I know I have found my home. If that wasn't good enough, I also met her today. I don't know her name or the color of her eyes or the sound of her voice, but I know she is the one. She was so far away that I couldn't make out any details, but I could tell right away that she was beautiful, and what could be better than having a wife that is as beautiful as the land our home will be built on.

I have had enough with my life as it is. I choose today to end it, start anew and never look back, let alone return. I rode 20 miles today until I found this spot, so deep in the hills and so hidden in the trees that no one will ever come looking. Those fools are so complacent they wouldn't come looking anyway, but I don't care. I don't ever want to see that place again. Tomorrow I'm going to pack all that I have and ride out here. I'll start chopping down trees and clearing room for foundation. This is where my life begins and this is where I plan on having it end. Right here in this spot with her. I will go to the same spot that I saw her, every day and wait for her, and when she returns I will ask her for her hand. And if she refuses, I will come back and ask again and again and again. For I would rather live alone in pursuit of her than settle for anything less. My mind is made up.

He closed the journal and looked over at his mother. She had fallen asleep, her cigarette still burning in her mouth. He pulled it out of her lips, laid her down, and propped her head up on her pillows. He grabbed a blanket off his bed and sat back in the rocker, wrapped himself up, and closed his eyes.

Winter finally arrived, and the fresh meat from the elk was all but gone now. There was plenty of jerky for Richard to make it to spring, but it was far too tough for his mother to eat. He had to ride to the old ghost town with the abandoned warehouse, in hopes of finding enough canned food to make it through the winter. It was a 20-mile ride that would take him longer than he cared for there in the current weather---but the worst was yet to come so it was now or never. He packed his saddle bag full of jerky, threw a rifle over his shoulder, and holstered a pistol to his thigh. It was always a dangerous journey into town; he'd have to follow the tracks most of the way, leaving him exposed to numerous threats.

He hopped on Ned and rode out toward the tracks. Ned galloped swiftly---most of the bears in the area had already started their hibernation and wouldn't be a threat. As they made it out of the woods, he saw the plains. Where before they were green and lush, now they were white and barren. There was no sign of bandits or deer or bison or trains, just white snow blanketing the ground. They rode down the hill until they reached the side of the tracks. Alongside the tracks was clear of snow---a train must've come through not long before. One good thing about riding near the tracks was that cargo would often fall off the shipments; valuable or interesting goods were bound to be discovered.

The sky was clear that day, but the air was still freezing cold. Richard was wrapped up in a large fur coat he had crafted from the hide of the giant elk. He had a large scarf wrapped around his face and neck, thick enough to keep his ears and nose from freezing. He decided to walk beside Ned for a while, even though the mule was bred for hard work, Richard didn't want to overburden him too quickly. As he hopped off Ned, Richard's feet planted deep in the snow. His left foot struck something hard. It couldn't have been the tracks though, he was too far away. Kneeling down, he dug through the snow; perhaps he had found a little treasure that escaped from the mysterious train cars.

After digging a foot or so through the snow, he felt the

object his foot had struck. He removed his gloves and wrapped his fingers around treasure as he ripped it from frozen tundra's grasp. It was a book, the only one he had ever seen besides his father's journal. The cover was leather that had been dyed navy-blue, and the title was worn so that he couldn't make out what it said. He turned it over and examined the spine, only making out the words *King James* printed in golden ink. He wasn't sure what it was, but he was happy to have something new to read.

He remembered stories his father told him about his time as a government worker. He told him that books were the first thing they confiscated from the people, even before they took their cigarettes. No one knew where they stored them, not even Richard's father---he guessed they didn't keep them in one place too long. Like how they transported weapons, keeping them on the move to stay out of people's hands.

One day, Richard had asked his father why the Government didn't burn the books or throw them into the sea. His father agreed that it would have been the smartest course of action, but explained that they had set laws to protect the already destroyed environment---dumping and burning goods were the first two things on the list of what not to do. "They're bad people, Richard," his father would say, "mighty bad, and mighty stupid."

Richard opened his coat and placed the book in a pocket, figuring he better hurry to the town---a beautiful day could turn nasty quite fast in the winter. He hopped on Ned, and they galloped down the tracks toward the town.

As they approached the town, Ned began acting skittish, tugging against the reins Richard held and nipping at Richard's leg as they walked. Richard empathized with the mule---an ominous cloud of uncertainty seemed to follow them as they entered the ghost town.

His father told stories of deserted towns, just beyond the Sioux Nation, places where monsters lived. They were once human, but over time they changed into something else. He said the Government had stored giant weapons, powerful enough to level entire countries, underground in the open lands. But once the nations of the old world joined as one, there was no longer a need for such weapons. The people living in those areas were ordered to dismantle the weapons, but the work wasn't something just anyone could do. Eventually the whole area became contaminated---the crops, the water, even the people. The lands were quarantined and the people living there were abandoned, left to survive on their own. The land became known as the Rotten Plains. He told Richard that whatever was in those weapons had changed the people living there; they mutated until they barely resembled humans. He called them *Outlings*, and said they were a cursed people, to be pitied and feared all the same. Richard didn't know if what his father told him was truth or fantasy, but if it were true, he hoped to never come face to face with one.

Once at the ghost town, Richard tied the mule to an old light post. He grabbed his empty backpack and made his way toward the abandoned warehouse. He mulled over what he needed to find, so to not forget anything. The warehouse basement ran beneath the entirety of the town and had many different rooms with various goods and contraband stored within. Richard stuck to the rooms he was familiar with, but there were hundreds of others scattered about. He didn't like spending any more time there than necessary; the place gave him the creeps, and something about that day gave him an even worse feeling than normal. He gathered all the canned beans and soup he could carry then moved to the room where old medicines were stored. They were usually expired, but the painkillers still did the job if Rose was having a bad night.

After finding some bottles, and preparing to leave, he heard a crash echo down the hallway. He didn't care to find out what it was, so he hurried up the stairs and out of the building.

He ran down the street, back toward the light post where Ned was tied. He could hear the mule from blocks away, crying and yammering. He unstrapped his rifle and pressed it against his shoulder. He prepared to round the corner where he'd be able to see Ned. At first, he thought there would be a gang of bandits surrounding the mule. If not that, then perhaps a bear that hadn't yet gone into hibernation. Neither option sounded ideal.

He rounded the corner with the stock pressed against his shoulder, looked down the sights, and prepared to fire at whatever he saw. He scanned to the left then to the right, but all he saw was an empty road, a lonely mule, a light post that no longer worked, and light snowfall. He lowered the barrel of the rifle and watched as the mule continued to holler and neigh. Richard walked toward Ned and placed the rifle on the ground beside him. He stroked Ned's mane and patted his face to calm him down, but nothing seemed to work.

"What is it buddy, what's got you spooked?" he asked.

He looked into Ned's eye and could see the fear bubbling up within the mule, along with the outline of an approaching figure. Richard turned and saw a giant creature, nearly eight feet tall. It was hairless, except for three long strands that fell from its head. Its bottom jaw hung down to its chest, and its long arms had massive hands that swung past its knees. Its face was built for two eyes but only held one, and it was covered in blistered skin that looked like it had been boiled.

"What in the world?" Richard exclaimed.

The creature made a low gurgling growl and stepped

toward Ned and Richard. Richard froze; his feet were trapped in the thick snow that lined the road. He couldn't begin to imagine what he was looking at, and the creature's wicked strut left him no time to ponder. He pulled back his coat and reached for his pistol. Pulling it out of its holster, he pointed the revolver at the monster and fired a shot into the monster's chest. The gunshot echoed through the ghost town, but the monster did not fall. It stood a bit shorter though, holding its massive hands over its ears and tightly shutting its eye.

Richard's heart was beating out of his chest, pounding against the blue leather cover of the book in his pocket. Fearing for his life, he stepped away from the creature. When his boot hit the ground, the snow and gravel crunched together in the most hideous sound. A sound hideous enough to grab the creature's attention. It removed its hands from its ears and opened its eye, locking onto Richard. Its gurgling growl mutated into a haunting snarl, then into a gargantuan roar! The creature then leapt at Richard, moving its massive body at an incredible speed. Richard turned to run but tripped over his rifle. As he fell to the ground, he dropped his pistol in the snow. Frantically digging through the icy ground, he searched for the gun. He felt the monster right above him as his finally gripped the hidden pistol. The creature raised its hand, a hand that possessed long thick nails that were pointed like claws, and it moved to strike. Richard quickly turned around and fired the five remaining rounds into the creature.

The monster fell on top of Richard, lying there heavy and limp, its claws pressed against Richard's chest. He used nearly all his strength to push the creature off him. He hadn't used so much strength since he dragged the elk off the tracks. He tried lifting the monster's hand off his chest, but its claws were lodged deep into his body. Two of its nails dug into his left shoulder. The others were stuck in the pages of the book, resting in his coat pocket, just in front of his heart. He slowly pulled the two fingers out of his shoulder. Blood spurted out of the wounds staining the snow. He pressed down on the bloody holes to try and stop the bleeding, but the blood continued to spill out.

He managed to get to his feet and untie Ned. He tried riding ahead, but the weather had become quite treacherous. The howling winds and thick snowfall whited out his vision. He already struggled to stay upright as Ned trudged through the snow. Heavy gusts of wind and sleet eventually knocked them both to the ground. As the temperature plummeted, Richard curled up next to Ned and tried to keep warm. His wounds were immensely painful, especially as the frozen wind pierced into the open gashes and penetrated his veins. He feared his eyes would freeze shut if he were to close them. All he could do now was hope the storm would soon pass.

After chanting for several hours, Ashkii concluded the first night of the ritual and sat beside the others near the bonfire. The feathers of his hybrid form began to slowly shed as he morphed into his human form. Hans waddled over to him with a hot bowl of stew.

"Is it working?" Hans asked.

"I think so. I can feel his heart beating when I apply the oils, but I do not want to build up any hopes just yet."

"Two more nights of that, right?" Wyatt inquired as he bit into an old mushy apple he found in the refrigerators.

"Yes."

"It takes three days to get to Fort Young by train," Wyatt started. "Leaving tonight would be our best option. The more time we take, the harder it will be to catch Chance. Can you perform the ritual anywhere, Ashkii? Or does it have to be in this spot?"

Ashkii shrugged his shoulders. "If the song is sung and the oils are applied, it shouldn't matter where it is performed. If there is a kitchen car on the train that should work, I could cook the oils there."

Juan and Wyatt carried Richard aboard the train, walking him through several train cars until they found the kitchen. Ashkii laid out an area for them to place him and started preparing the next set of oils for the ceremony. Juan and the others loaded the horses into an empty car and stocked the train full of supplies from the fort. Shortly before sunrise, the clerk fired the engines and propelled the train off toward Fort Young.

The next thing Richard recalled was a sudden disappearance of the freezing cold---it instead being replaced by a sudden burning that scorched his open wounds. His eyes flashed open, and he let out a loud agonized cry. He writhed in pain, kicking and hollering like a mad animal.

"Whoa there, son! Just calm down," a man with a canteen of whiskey said while trying to restrain Richard. "Gotta try to close up that wound, and we ain't got no fire to cauterize it so this'll have to do, ya' hear?"

A second man delivered another canteen and pressed it up to Richard's lips. "Here ya go, drink some water, kid." Richard took a few large gulps, and while the pain continued, it became more tolerable.

The first man sat back and rested against the wall next to Richard. "Glad to see you're still kickin'," he said. "Ain't many men survive an encounter with a big brute like the one you ran into."

"Who are you two?" Richard asked. He hadn't fully swallowed his last gulp and water came streaming out the corners of his mouth. He scanned the large cement building they were in. His clothes were piled in the corner of the room, and he noticed his chest had been bandaged, presumably by the two men.

"Well, my name is Charles," said the first man, and nodding toward the second man, added "that there is my brother Mac."

"Who the hell'r you?" Mac demanded. He was a large brash man who put little thought behind his words.

Charles gave him a glare and Mac responded with an innocent shrug. Richard pushed himself up so that he sat upright against the wall. "Name is Deacon... Richard Deacon. Thank you both for helping me out back there. Where you from? I didn't think anyone lived in these parts."

"Well," Charles started, "Mac and I ain't really got no home. We roam the open land and take what we can get."

"What brings you to these parts?" Richard asked. He was beginning to feel reluctant about prolonging his stay with the two men.

"Actually, we'd been trackin' that big brute you took down earlier. Ran into it down south a ways away, never seen one been killed before so we thought we'd give it a run for its money, but wouldn't ya know it, some young stud mountain man came and snatched our chance of snaggin' it!" Charles gave Richard a playful punch on the shoulder, hitting him right near his healing wounds, making Richard wince in pain. Mac found the exchange quite comical, falling to the ground as he bellowed with laughter.

Richard stood himself up, reached for his blood-stained shirt, and began to slip it back on. "Well, I want to thank you for what you have done for me. I apologize for stealing your kill there, but believe me, I would've rather had you two taken care of him before me. If you don't mind though, I have a long ride back home and really do need to get going." He bent down to grab his hat off the ground, but before he could, a shiny pistol pressed up under his chin, stopping him in his tracks.

Mac was bent down on one knee, pointing the 9mm at Richard and giving him an angry glare. "Now hold on there, boy... not so fast." His words were long and drawn out; it felt like an eternity had passed by the time all of them left his mouth. "I think you're forgetting a couple things. Number one, you stole us the joy of gunnin' down that ugly fella out there, and that ain't something we gonna' just let slide. Number two, we done saved your life---if it weren't for us you'd be dead in the snow curled up by that dirty ol' mule of yours. Now you got yourself two options, and walkin' out that door ain't one of 'em."

Charles popped the cork on the canteen filled with liquor and took a large gulp. He pushed his hat back on his head and said, "Now I don't know what you learned growin' up, kid, but where we're from if someone saves your life you're in their debt forever, or until they say you ain't."

"What are you trying to say?" Richard asked desperately.

Charles stood up and continued, "Now, like Mac said, you got two options. You can either join our little crew and do whatever it is we need you to do, or Mac can cash in your debt right now with the slightest pull of that trigger... So, what's it gonna' be?"

Mac stood up, keeping the gun under Richard's chin, and Richard stood along with him, realizing he didn't have a choice.

Charles and Mac had spent their entire lives roaming the free open lands and taking whatever they pleased. They hijacked train cars, robbed homes of whatever wealth or supplies they had, and preyed on lowly travelers trying to find their way around the vast lands. Richard never knew why they kept him around; they could have easily killed him and taken all the supplies he had gathered. He thought that maybe it was because he had killed the creature that they saw something in him. Whatever the reason, he wished he'd never met the pair. A part of him would have rather bled out in the snow. It pained Richard to know that he would never go back to see his mother. To think that her body was still lying in her bed, frozen in the winters and thawed in the summers, killed him inside. He often thought about her, how she must have assumed he was dead when he never returned, how he just disappeared without a trace the same way his father had. It saddened him to think that when she finally passed, in her mind, she was completely alone.

Richard traveled with the outlaw bandits for many years, so many that he lost count. The whole time he read the book he'd found by the tracks that day. It was much longer than he originally imagined, and it took him much longer to finish it than he had ever expected. When he first started reading it, the two brothers---never having seen a book---found it quite curious. Richard was flipping through the pages once and Mac asked, "Hey kid, what the hell'r you doin' just starin' at that thing all the time?"

"It's a book," Richard told him, closing the cover, and flipping it around in his hands.

"Well, what're ya' starin' at it for?"

"I'm reading it," Richard said. He was losing his patience, but knew to always keep calm around Mac. He could never be sure when the man's fuse would finally blow, and didn't want to find out.

Mac's face ignited with excitement and he asked, "Where'd you learn how to do that?"

"My Pa taught me when I was young. He worked for the Government. Everyone who worked for them was taught how to read."

"So that's some kind of story book?" Mac asked.

"Honestly, I'm not quite sure what it is," Richard said. He ran his fingers over the large dent in the cover where the creature's claw got stuck. "I don't even know the name of it actually. It seems like a story book and history book, but it's all a bit confusing if I'm being honest."

"Don't know why you'd wanna read some book just to get all confused. It makes sense the Government got rid of 'em all... who needs 'em," Mac said as he rolled over on his side and closed his eyes.

But Richard continued to read the book, learning about the great men who had shaped the world he read about. There was Adam, Noah, Moses, Abraham, David, Joseph and so many more. But the two that stood out the most were Jesus and God. God could create floods and punish man, all while looking down from the heavens. And Jesus would heal the blind and walk on top of water. He was fascinated by the stories, and he found himself learning more and questioning his life as he read. One concept he read about was of Good and Evil. It said that God told his people how to treat their fellow men, while also giving them consequences if they didn't follow his commands. He found the contents of the book so interesting and insightful that he often began to question his own deeds based on what he read. Richard, Charles, and Mac would hijack a train, steal its most valuable contents, and sometimes end a life or two in the process. Charles and Mac would walk away happy to have gotten a score, but Richard always had an inkling of remorse for the men they had killed. Although he was never the one to pull the trigger, he didn't do anything to stop Mac and Charles from pulling it. This process went on for a long time, deed after deed, and each time Richard could feel a little piece of himself being chipped away. There were times he would question what they were doing.

He asked Mac once, "are we evil?"

Mac wasn't an educated man and his response was a simple one. "What's evil?"

"You know, like right and wrong?" Richard tried to explain.

Charles had walked in on the conversation and was furious that it was being had. He grabbed Richard by the collar and pulled him close so their faces nearly touched. "That damn book of yours is going to end up getting us all killed, ya' hear?" He said sternly while shaking Richard. "None of these damn questions you ask are gonna do any of us one drop of good! Don't you think there's a reason there ain't supposed to be none of those damn things around? It's because all the smartest people in the world, hundreds of years ago, realized that them things are dangerous!" He spoke with great ferocity, and if Richard didn't know better, he could have sworn he saw tears building up in Charles' eyes.

"Charles," Richard said, "I was just asking a question. Don't you think it might be wrong? Stealing and killing like we do?"

"I think that if it weren't us doing it, then the next guy would stick a gun right in our face, pull the trigger, and go on doing it even better than we did! That book you got is a damn story and ain't none of it's real. There is no good in this world, no evil, no right, no wrong! You either kill or get killed, and I'm not planning on the latter anytime soon, ya' hear me!"

Richard had never heard Charles say so many words in such a short span of time. In fact, he wasn't sure if he had said this many words in the ten or so years he had known him. Mac just sat and ate cold beans out of the can as he watched the two bicker back and forth.

A few months after that conversation the men had migrated south, where the winters were more wet than icy. They set up camp in an old wooden building. It had colorful broken windows and some cracks in the ceiling, but it worked well enough to hunker down for the winter. Considering Mac had fallen ill, they had to settle for whatever shelter they could find. They were very close to an area that was notoriously inhabited by large groups of outlings, a lost land---one that neither the Government nor the Natives cared to maintain influence over. The contamination wasn't very harmful anymore, so it was a relatively good spot for the three to lay low. The building was large and fairly open inside, other than the rows of benches that were laid out from the front of the building to the back. The benches provided a good space for much needed sleep and privacy; the backs of the seats were high enough so that they couldn't see each other when they'd lie down.

Mac's illness worsened rapidly---he had a hoarse cough and could hardly get off his bench during the day. Richard was scouting one day, and through his binoculars, he saw a herd of deer grazing out by a set of tracks a couple miles away. He went back to the building and grabbed Charles. The two then rode off to try and score a good kill for the winter. Mac desperately needed some soup with meat and nutrients, if he were to have any hope of getting better. Their supply of canned food was running low also, and Mac wasn't the only one who needed to eat.

It was close to sundown as they approached the herd.

The sky was covered in dark clouds that blocked what little light remained. In the clouds, the deep rumbling of the brewing thunder echoed over the plains. The herd was gathered on and around the tracks, grouped together tightly so they appeared as one single mass. They were in a vast and open field---tall grass painted the landscape like a giant green ocean, interrupted only by a lone elm tree standing a few yards away from the tracks. It reminded Richard of the day he had taken down the elk, except that day was much clearer and the grass far longer. Richard could hear the sound of the gurgling thunder growing, like the clouds had an empty stomach and were on the hunt as well. He warned Charles that they shouldn't get too close to the metal tracks. The only problem was that neither of them had a rifle, the only one they had jammed up a while back and they dumped it. Richard's revolver was the only gun powerful enough to take down a deer, but he was too far away to hit one from where they stood.

Charles ordered Richard to move closer and kill one, that his brother's life depended on them bringing back one of those deer. Richard did as the man said and made his way toward the herd, creeping behind the lone elm tree to keep himself hidden. He stopped about 30 yards away from the herd, with the elm halfway between them. In the distance, he could see bolts of lightning shooting down from the clouds, and the thunder that followed boomed so loudly that the cocking of his pistol didn't make a sound. He usually gripped his pistol with one hand, but this time he used two. He had all ten fingers wrapped around the worn wooden grip, stretching his arms out and peering down the metallic sights. He aimed at a large buck standing on the tracks. He rested his finger on the trigger and prepared to pull it. He took slow deep breaths, and noticed the deer's breathing matched his own. Its abdomen expanding and shrinking, slowly and methodically, like it knew what was to come and had found peace in its demise.

Richard's finger trembled as it rested on the trigger, and with each thunderous boom that exploded in the distance his deep breaths became shorter and more violent. He focused on the deer and readied himself to fire. But right before he pulled back on the trigger, he felt the ground tremble beneath his feet. He thought a train was coming and wondered if he really was back home, if he really had gone back to that day that he killed the elk. But then he remembered there was no storm that day, and if he were back, then the sky would be calm and the grass longer.

The ground quaked and rattled harder than if any train was approaching. Richard looked to the sky. Then in an instant a giant bolt of lightning came crashing to the ground and struck the deer that stood on the tracks. The thunder knocked Richard back and the bang from his pistol firing immediately followed. The entire herd bolted off, stampeding away from the tracks. Richard jumped to his feet and fired every last shot in the herd's direction, praying that one would find its target. After his last shot was fired, the ground began to tremble once more. He looked back to the sky. The clouds began to glow and flash as another mighty bolt hurled down, this time striking the elm that stood before him, igniting it in thick hellish flames. The force from the bolt knocked Richard back to the ground, where he sat and watched the tree burn brightly in front of him. He swore he heard his name being called from within the flames. He thought he saw the fire grow lips and mouth his name, saying, "Richard… Richard!"

Then he felt a hand grab him by the collar. He turned around and saw Charles shouting at him---"Richard! C'mon, Richard!" He pulled him up on his feet, then they hurried back to the old building to hide from the thunder and lightning.

When they came tumbling into the old building, the

sound of Mac's coughing was as loud as the thunder. Charles was angry, Mac's coughing seemed to annoy him, making him jump each time he heaved. Charles grabbed Richard and shook him again. "What took you so long to take the shot?" he barked.

"It was too far! I had to take my time!" Richard pleaded.

"Mac needed that deer! He ain't gonna make it now!" Richard thought he saw the tears growing in Charles' eyes again. He stood there silently and let Charles scream at him. "We ain't got enough canned food to get all three of us through the winter. You had one shot, kid, and you blew it! I told you this world is kill or get killed, and we ain't got no room for the weak! This is on you!" Charles hollered, then threw Richard to the ground.

Charles pulled out his pistol. Richard laid on the ground staring at the black muzzle, fearing for his life. Then Charles turned to Mac, lying motionless on the bench, making no noise besides his coughs. Richard couldn't see Mac, all he could see was Charles invade the sick man's space and point his gun at him.

BANG! BANG! BANG! BANG!

The screaming train zoomed west down the tracks. Hans gazed out the windows as the ever-changing landscape swept past his eyes. He could see the light from the rising sun creep over the horizon and realized they had already been riding for a day. He walked through the cars until he made it to the kitchen where he checked in on Ashkii and Richard.

"Is he alive?"

"He is not dead," Ashkii answered, "but he is in pain.

Whatever happens, after tomorrow night the pain will subside."

Hans walked over to Richard and caressed his cheek. He moved his head against Richard's chest and listened for the faint heartbeat.

Ashkii took a sip of hot tea he'd been cooking on the stove and watched Hans with a sense of empathy. "We have all lost those we are close to, it is a part of life. I lost my father when I was young, then lady Kai took me under her wing. Richard is like a father to you, isn't he?"

Hans held Richard's hand and felt his cool skin in his palms. He nodded, then wiped the falling tears from his cheeks.

"Stay strong little Hans---just one more night."

As winter ended and spring came into blossom, the men's rations began to dry up. Charles went scouting one day and found an old town that had plenty of canned goods they could gather. But outlings were running rampant in the town. To get to the supplies would mean having to kill dozens of them, Charles explained---that it would be high risk and high reward. Richard didn't want to kill, but outlings were different, they were monsters that had tried to kill him before. It was hard for him to think of them as anything more than animals. Richard agreed to the task and the two men gathered their munitions and prepared for an extremely dangerous fight.

The town was only half a day's ride from where they stayed. They left at dawn and arrived a little past noon. The town was quiet; weeds grew out of the cracks in the sidewalk and old traffic lights swung back and forth as the wind blew. Richard felt uneasy, if there was one outling running amok it made sense it would be quiet, but if there were as many as Charles said, then they wouldn't be hiding. They were human at one time after all, and tended to work together if they were in a group.

Charles pointed out the building where the supplies were stashed, and he sent Richard to collect them while he went to go look for where the creatures were hiding.

"Wouldn't it be better if we stuck together?" Richard asked. "I wouldn't want to take on a group of those things alone."

"That's why you're the one getting the supplies and I'm the one taking them on," Charles replied with great arrogance.

Charles was never kind to Richard, but he changed after Mac's passing. That night haunted Richard---he didn't have siblings, but couldn't imagine someone killing his own brother the way Charles had. The only family Richard ever had was his mother and father, and he could never have done that to them. Then he remembered how he abandoned his mother, and he thought that perhaps what he had done was no different. Richard knew there wasn't a drop of good within Charles, and he wondered if there was such a thing as a soul---if he even possessed one.

The two men split up, Richard heading to the west end of town, and Charles to the east end. Richard carried two large bags and began filling them up with all the canned foods he could find. As he shoved the cans inside the bag, he thought he heard something rustling around the other room, but it was too quiet to be an outling. Anything that was eight to ten feet tall would be making more noise than what he heard---it must have been a rat or squirrel. But after a while the noises grew louder, like whatever was making them was moving closer toward him.

As he filled the second bag, the noises seemed to be right behind him. There was a tap, then a crackle, then a sniff. He slowly moved his hand to his pistol, wrapped his fingers around the handle and listened carefully to the approaching noise. Drawing the pistol from his hip, he turned around to face the creature! He pointed his gun where he thought the beast would be, but all he saw was the shadow of a small body running back into the darkness of the adjacent room. It must have been the biggest rat he had ever seen---contaminated most likely, he imagined it would have a longer tail. He holstered his gun, and as the iron barrel slipped into the leathery socket, he heard shots being fired from another building, followed by terrified screams.

Richard took off in the direction of the gunshots, leaving the two bags behind so they wouldn't slow him down. He found the building where the shots originated and went crashing through the door, holding out his pistol, ready to fire at whatever monster he saw first. But what he found was unexpected. He saw Charles, standing with his gun drawn, and pointing it at a group of small timid looking beings, huddled together in the corner of the room. The tallest one out of the group stood only four feet tall, and that was being generous. Their faces were deformed and blistered, their backs all hunched forward, and their legs only a fraction of the length they should be.

They were scared, all of them, their wrinkled faces showed shock and terror. They were hideous, but they were far more human looking than the outlings he had encountered before. Their features were distinct. Richard could even tell the difference between the men and women. He heard them whispering words to one another, not grunting or roaring the way the other did.

"What are you doing?" Richard yelled out to Charles

from across the room.

Charles turned around but kept his gun pointed at the group. "Getting rid of these monsters like I told you!" he laughed.

"You said there were going to be dozens of outlings, these things aren't those monsters! They're harmless, look at them!"

Charles pulled his gun away from the group and pointed it at Richard. "When are you going to learn, boy?! I've told you a hundred times, this world is kill or be killed!"

"Those things are petrified! They pose no threat to us! Charles, this is evil!"

A familiar look of rage rifled upon Charles' face, and he began marching across the room toward Richard. He holstered his gun then pushed Richard to the ground and jumped on top of him. As they hit the ground, Richard's pistol fell out of his hand and slid across the floor. Charles grabbed Richard by the shirt and began lifting him up and thrusting him down against the floor. Richards' head crashed against the cement with every thrust and splotches of blood spread across the floor.

"I am so sick and tired of that damn good and evil crap you keep spouting!" Charles yelled. "I should have let you die that day you damned fool!" He stopped his thrusting and began to pound his fists into Richard's face. "You love that damned book so much? You talk about that damned, God! Let's see if he'll save ya' now!" Then Charles pulled a knife out of his belt.

Richard managed to throw a punch and knock Charles off him. He tried crawling for his pistol, but Charles pounced back onto him and thrust the knife down toward Richard's face. Richard threw his hands up and caught Charles by the wrists before the knife could hit him. The two men struggled.

Charles pushed down hard so that the tip of the knife dug into Richard's forehead, just above his left eye. Richard let out a painful cry, and Charles laughed as he dragged the knife down Richard's face. The tip of the blade cut through Richard's eye, and he let out another agonizing scream. Richard struggled to keep it from cutting any deeper, but it continued to drag down past his eye. He let out one last yell, and with all his might, he pushed back on Charles. Richard twisted his body and Charles went tumbling off him, but as he fell his knife cut across Richard's eye once more, perpendicular to the first cut.

Richard mustered the strength to lunge at his pistol, only a few feet from him. He grabbed the gun and quickly turned around to see Charles charging at him once more. He looked just like the giant creature from that day so many years before, and in that moment Richard made the same choice he had made then. He pulled the trigger back and fired the rounds into Charles as he came flying toward him. Charles fell on top of Richard, knocking him back to the ground. His head crashed into the cement once again, then the room went black. Richard lay motionless on the cold cement, his body immersed in a pool of blood that leaked from his head, and the holes in Charles' dead body.

Richard found himself in a dark empty space, accompanied only by the same burning elm that he'd seen the day of the lightning storm. The same elm that had grown lips and called to him. The flames were magnificent, terrifying, and awesome in their own right. A flood of emotions filled his body, and he found himself on his knees, kneeling to the burning tree. As he watched the fire burn, he once again saw the lips form within the flames, and once again, they spoke to him.

"Richard Deacon!" the tree called out, in a deep thunderous voice.

"Who are you?" he pleaded.

The tree did not answer his question but rather continued with its message, "Richard Deacon… you among many have sown the seeds of evil into my garden. You sat back in complacency and followed in the path of the serpent who slithers, unwelcomed, through my sacred garden."

"No, I swear, I never-"

The tree ignored his defensive words. "But today you have changed your path. You have stepped upon the neck of the great serpent and banished it from my garden. You are one of the few who knows my words and now I call upon you to restore life and righteousness into my great creation. Protect and nurture these new seeds in my name, and the penance for your wicked past shall be paid."

Richard stared at the flaming tree in awe and in fear. "How? How do I do it?"

The tree finally answered his question, and its answer was but two words. "Start small."

At that moment Richard awoke from his great dream; the left side of his face was bandaged and in great pain. He wasn't clothed, but he was covered in a blanket, and his beard had grown out longer than he remembered. He heard the same rustling from when he was gathering supplies. He popped his head up to see what it was, then from the doorway he saw a small man and woman walking toward him on all fours. It was more of a waddle than a walk, their backs were hunched and their faces were blistered and covered in boils. The woman was holding a bowl filled with water, and the man walked in front of her cautiously.

"You are awake," the man said.

Richard had no response. He could not believe it, never before had he seen an outling speak, and one had certainly never *spoken to him*. He lifted himself up to get a better look. Then, after taking a moment to examine them, he asked, "How long have I been out for?"

"Four days!" the woman called out, eager to talk with him, but the man looked back at her as if she had answered too quickly.

"You have been looking after me all that time?" Richard asked. The two of them nodded their heads. "Thank you," he said.

"You saved all of our lives," the man said. "No straight-back has ever helped our kind, let alone almost died for us." His voice was quiet and raspy, it sounded a lot like his parents' voices---he wondered if these little people smoked cigarettes as well.

"What about the other man?" Richard asked.

"Dead!" said the woman. She hobbled over and handed Richard the bowl, pressing it up to his lips, and pushing it back so he could drink from it. A wide smile lit up her scrunched-up face.

"If I were you, I would rest for another day. We can change the bandages, then you can go where you please," said the man.

Richard stayed for a couple more days. He met all the outlings that resided in the town and realized that their tribe was not much different from normal men. If anything, they were more peaceful---they were a community and worked together for the benefit of the group. They were kind to Richard and assured him that he would be welcomed back with open arms whenever he pleased. They considered him a friend, and just knowing that filled Richard with much joy.

Richard thought constantly about his dream and how the tree asked him to teach others what he knew. He pondered that the only answer the tree gave him was to "start small". He traveled for the next year, north and south, east and west. He spoke to natives and non-natives, and tried to teach them about the book and its contents, but everywhere he went his words were rejected. After the night he killed Charles, Richard wasn't quite the same. He had to wear a patch over his left eye, and the repeated blows to his head had affected his speech. He talked much slower than he had before and would often slur some words. Everyone he spoke to simply wrote him off as a drunkard or a nut who thought he could talk to trees. After some time he eventually made his way back to the old wooden house where he and Charles and Mac had stayed.

He walked around and thought about the many nights he spent there. The bench where Mac slept still had the four holes in it from where Charles shot him. He sat on that bench and looked toward the back of the room. He saw something that he hadn't noticed before; there was a door behind the big table that stood in the back of the room. The handle had fallen off, and the rotted wood blended in with the rest of the wall, so you didn't see it if you weren't looking hard enough. He opened the rotted wooden door and walked into the small room hidden behind it. There was a desk in the room, and on top of it was a small wooden cross with a man on it. There was a story in his book about the man named Jesus who had been nailed to a cross; he had a crown of thorns, a gash in his side, and holes through his hands and feet. Richard picked up the small cross and observed the figure on it. The little man had the same crown and a gash carved into his ribs, and there were nails through his hands and feet.

He saw a small mirror on the wall. He picked it up and stared into it. It had been a long time since he saw his reflection. His face had grown much older than he remembered---he reminded him of his father. He hadn't seen himself with the eye-patch before; the sight of it saddened him. He took the small piece of leather off his face and observed what his eye looked like without it. The scars from the two cuts on his eye had closed up---one ran down the middle from his eyebrow to his cheek, and the other had cut right across his eyelid. The scar was the same shape as the cross he held in his hand, and as he looked at himself he was assured that the path he had chosen to pay his penance was the right one. He looked around the room and found a few books hidden away. He skimmed through them quickly and saw that they were all about the same things as his book with the blue leather cover. He took the books and stuffed them in his bag.

As he left the building he realized that he was close to the town with the outlings. It had been a little over a year since he'd been there and decided that he would go visit them. He went on a hunt on his way there and killed a large buck. He thought it would be nice to bring it to them as a gift and prepare a feast. As they had promised, he was welcomed into the town with open arms. Some newborns had popped up since he'd been there last. It amazed him to see that the little things could still breed, but to each other they must have not seemed so ugly. He butchered the deer and cooked up the entire thing, making a stew for them just like he used to make for his mother.

After the meal, Richard sat around with the group and told them stories of when he was growing up. Stories of danger and adventure, and the love stories of his mother and father. While he was talking, one of the young children was looking through his bag and pulled out the book. She brought it over to him and asked him what it was. Richard took the book and brushed his hand over the cover and the spine. Running his fingers down the length of the golden lettering, he felt the warmth of the navy-stained leather, and the hole that punctured the cover. He looked at all the little outlings gathered around him, listening to his stories, and he remembered the burning elm's words, *Start small.*

Richard took the little girl and sat her on his lap. She looked up at him in awe as she rested her ugly, yet charming face against his burly chest.

"Now if you thought the stories I told you all before were good, wait until I tell you this one," he said. The whole group started clapping their hands and Richard began to read.

"In the beginning, God created the heavens and the earth..."

Richard gasped as he breathed in a deep cool gulp of air. His right eye shot open and scanned back and forth across the room until it focused on the bright overhead light. "Has it happened?" he thought to himself. "Am I dead?" But little did he know his thoughts were not so silent. Ashkii heard his mumbling from the other side of the kitchen and scurried over to him, dropping his soup on the way.

"Deacon? Deacon, can you hear me?" he asked as he patted Richard's bearded cheeks with his taloned hands. Richard lay there moaning and groaning; every so often his eye would flicker open, only to shut again. Ashkii ran over to the sink and poured some water into a bowl. He brought it over and let the water spill into Richard's mouth. He could see his tongue fighting for the droplets, then his lips began to smack together.

Hans waddled into the kitchen and hollered out, "Ashkii! Any sign of Richard waking-" Before he finished, he saw Ashkii holding Richard's head as he helped him drink. "Richard!" Hans scurried across the kitchen as quickly as he could, nearly knocking over all the pots and pans en route. He moved his face so close to Richard's that his swollen bulging eye nearly touched Richard's only good one.

"Hans?" Richard mumbled, "Hans, my boy?"

"Yes, Deacon, it's me!"

"Did you die as well?"

"Die? No, no! No one is dead. You… you're alive. And Juan and Ashkii and Wyatt!"

Juan and Wyatt entered the room next, and the door slammed behind them, drawing the attention of the others, including Richard. He could finally see clearly now, and the clearest figure he saw was that of Wyatt Cole, standing over him just like he had been after shooting him. Richard began to shake, an unnerving fear ran through his veins, and he began spitting up some water he'd been trying to swallow. "What is he doing here? Has he captured us all?"

All eyes turned to Wyatt, who pushed his hat down over his eyes to hide his embarrassment. Juan couldn't help but chuckle. He knelt beside Richard, patting his bare chest. "Turns out the Marshal and I are old friends---I must have forgotten that I saved his life some time ago. He is with us now, and we are almost to Fort Young. Then soon we will be at Geronimo Park to save Felina. We are really going to do it, Richard."

Wyatt took a few cool steps over to Richard and leaned back against the wall. He crossed his legs, then his arms, but kept his brim covering his eyes. "Hope there's no hard feelings, Mr. Deacon. It seems all we had was a bit of a misunderstanding." He reached into his back pocket and pulled out a little white paper box. He tossed the box to Juan, and Juan handed the box to Richard. "Found an old pack of confiscated cigarettes back at Fort Thompson. The little guy told me you liked them. Consider it a gift of gratitude for keeping Juan safe all this time. He and his family mean a lot to me… Thank you. And I hope you can forgive me for our little… misunderstanding earlier."

Richard pinched the end of the box with two fingers and opened it. He pulled out a single stick and placed it between his lips. Ashkii grabbed a match that he found in the kitchen and quickly lit the cigarette for Richard. He breathed in a large lungful of smoke and slowly let it release out of his mouth and his nostrils. Then he let out a long, satisfied, "Aahhhhhhh."

Chapter 13

THE CLERKS OF FORT YOUNG

The clerk pulled a lever, and the brakes began to scream, spitting out sparks as the train slowed into the station at Fort Young. Wyatt stared at the fort through the window---it was drenched in sunlight, and the morning dew looked more like a nervous sweat. He tapped on the clerk's shoulder then made his way out of the engine room and over to the next car. Juan was cleaning off the shining barrel of his pistol, Ashkii was wrapped in his blanket asleep on the floor, and Hans was looking in a mirror adjusting his shawl. There was a small tomahawk on the table beside Hans. "That yours?" Wyatt asked.

"Ashkii made it for me, fine craftsmanship don't you think?" Hans stated. He clearly took much pride in his newly gifted weapon, as he did in his shawl.

"I've never seen a Mexican-Navajo before," Wyatt laughed, "I think you fit the part."

Hans smiled then hopped off the table and walked over to wake up Ashkii. The door to the next car opened, and Richard walked in, buttoning up his shirt and slipping on his thick coat. He had trimmed and washed his beard. For someone who recently escaped death, he looked the most put-together of the whole bunch. Juan's dirty face and juvenile mustache looked as dirty as his worn-out shawl. Wyatt's scruff had grown into a thin yet full beard, and his tan had slightly faded over the past weeks.

"Feeling alright, Deacon?" Wyatt asked.

"Like a new man," Richard laughed. He tossed his large hat back on his head, attached his holster to his hip, and slung Falkner's old shotgun over his shoulder.

"Good, it looks like we're here. What do you say we go check it out?"

"Just the two of you?" Juan interjected. "Last time I was meant to stay behind Richard almost died. I'm coming with you."

"Well, no telling how many outlaws we're going to run into, one more can't hurt," Wyatt conceded. "But Hans and Ashkii need to stay behind to guard the train. I'll go grab the clerk."

So, they left the train and stepped onto the grounds of Fort Young. A cool breeze pushed them toward the entrance as they cautiously approached the doors. It looked quite similar to Fort Thompson, except the surrounding area seemed less littered with toxic dust. Perhaps because the fort had been occupied for a while. One similarity Wyatt caught onto rather quickly was the lack of commotion. Fort Thompson was dead quiet, and from what he could tell, Fort Young was the same. Even before they entered, Wyatt had his pistol drawn, and Richard's shotgun was readied at his hip.

"Awfully quiet for the hub of a notorious gang," Wyatt smirked. "Quick, let's get to the control room of the station."

Wyatt led the way; the layout of Young was nearly identical to that of Thompson, and he had studied the maps quite closely on their ride over. With every room they passed the only sound they heard was the echoing of their own footsteps. The silence worried Juan, things were not going as planned. He would have rather had a blazing shootout right from the get-go---anything other than this.

"Are we close?" Juan asked.

"The control room should be just at the end of that hall," Wyatt explained as he pointed his gun forward, "we'll check the logs once we get there."

After a few more steps in silence they reached the end of the hallway and pushed open the door to the control room. Wyatt silently slipped in first, then Juan behind him with his pistol drawn, and Richard last with the clerk at his side. Alone in the room was a single seat, with what appeared to be a man sitting in it, but all they could see was a white cloth tied into a bow at the top of his head.

"Chance…" Wyatt whispered while cocking back his pistol.

The chair began to spin around, as it turned, the barrel of a pistol appeared in the pasty white skin of the seated man's hand. The chair spun all the way around, and what Wyatt saw was not the face of Chance Havoc, but a face nearly identical to the clerk who was with them. He had the same lifeless eyes and same necrotic-white skin. His wrists were tied to the arms of the chair, his jaw tied shut by the cloth wrapped around his head, and tears fell from his panicking face. Wyatt began lowering his pistol, and as he did, Juan noticed the clerk's finger tightening around the trigger. The hammer of the pistol locked into position, but before he could get a shot off Juan fired his own pistol, sending a round right into the clerk's heart

Wyatt turned to Juan in shock. "What's going on, Wyatt?" Juan asked.

Wyatt walked up to the clerk's body and began patting him down, feeling around for anything. Then he saw a piece of paper sticking out of his shirt pocket. He pulled it out and unfolded it.

"What does it say?" Juan asked.

Wyatt skimmed his eyes over it then began to read.

"Falkner is dead. Marshal Cole headed for Fort Young. Depart for Geronimo Park immediately."

Richard turned his attention to the clerk who stood beside him. He looked down and saw the clerk's hand hovering over his holstered pistol. The clerk grabbed the gun off Richard's hip then pushed him aside and pointed it at Wyatt.

BANG! BANG! BANG!

Smoke arose from Juan's pistol, and the clerk fell to the ground with three bullets lodged in his chest. Juan kicked the pistol out of the clerk's hand and jumped on top of him. "Hans was right. We should have never trusted you!" Juan yelled as he began punching the clerk in the face.

Richard got to his feet and pulled Juan off the clerk. Wyatt picked the clerk off the ground and dragged him over to the control desk. "Where are they?" he yelled. "When did you send that message?

The clerk coughed up blood as he began laughing maniacally. "I sent the message before the Navajo man even started the ceremony! They are already done with the Apache and on their way north to Little Raven! Soon we'll all be free, Marshal! Oh, and that wasn't the whole message. I told them about the Mexican's sister... they said... they... were..." Blood spilled from the clerk's mouth and he spoke no more.

Wyatt dropped the clerk. He heard a commotion happening in the corner of the room---it was Juan, crying. He pulled up the map on the navigational computer and saw a bright flashing light moving away from Geronimo Park. He skimmed through the logs and noticed the clerks in Chance's crew were communicating through them.

The newest message read:
Mission accomplished at GP. Precious cargo headed north to LR.

"Juan! They're headed north. They're on their way to Little Raven."

Juan pushed Richard aside and stormed across the room to Wyatt then slugged him in the chin with a wicked punch. It was enough to make Wyatt stumble, and not just from being caught off guard. "What the hell do I care about Little Raven!?" Juan snapped at him. "You are the Marshal, not me! The only damn thing I care about is getting Felina back! And because of you she is dead now!"

Wyatt grabbed Juan by the shoulders and shook him. "I know, damn it! But she might not be dead! I know you don't think this shit with Chance is your problem, but let me tell you it is! If you thought what the Apache did was bad, then just you wait. Now the last message they sent said they have precious cargo and that means people, probably girls. They might have Felina and that means while she isn't safe she might be alive."

"He is right, Juan," Richard started. "Outlaws are creatures of desire. It's likely they would have taken the girls from the casino."

"And what if she is still at Geronimo? What if she is already dead? What is the point of it all?" Juan cried. He couldn't help but imagine his father's face as he died in his arms, and he felt the shame from what he had done. "None of this was part of what Kai showed me… I did everything she said."

Richard took Juan from Wyatt's grasp and embraced him, like a father would his crying child. "Remember the last thing you told me Kai showed you," he whispered to Juan, "about the rat's bite, and the disease it carries? Maybe the path she sent you on wasn't to save Felina, but for something much greater."

"But… I don't care about anything greater… I just

want my hermana back."

"And maybe you will still get her back. But not if you lose faith now. Now is when you need it most."

"We should go back to the train and plot out our next move," Wyatt instructed, then hurried back down the halls.

Richard pulled Juan's hat off and placed his hand on his cheek. "You didn't give up on me, Juan. Don't give up on Felina just yet."

Juan gazed into Richard's eye. He crept his fingers up Richard's face and pulled down his eyepatch. Running his thumb over Richard's scar, he felt the risen flesh. "Alright… let us go."

The crew discussed the situation and decided to head to Little Raven to warn Chief Cheyanne of the Arapaho. Wyatt plugged in the coordinates for the depot nearest Little Raven and sent the train north.

Chapter 14

GERONIMO!

Four men and a woman sat around the blackjack table while a large Apache man dealt cards. The dealer was tall with a firm square jaw, a strong nose, and a ponytail that fell to his lower back. He dealt two cards to each of the patrons---first to the woman who sat to his left, also an Apache, old and wrinkled and smoking from a pipe she had packed with fresh tobacco. The man next to her possessed the face of an experienced ruffian, with a scar across his right cheek and his denim jacket torn at the shoulder and ripped in a few other spots. His patchy black beard was only slightly darker than his skin, or at least the layer of dirt that covered it. The dealer scowled at the ruffian as he placed the cards in front of him, but the filth-covered man paid no attention to the dealer's expression; he was too affixed on the sweet smell of the old woman's tobacco.

While the dealer dealt, the man leaned over to the old woman and took a strong sniff. "Mmm," he sighed, "that's some crop ya' got there."

"Hit," the woman said. The dealer placed another card then she waved her hand over it and said, "Stay."

The ruffian leaned in closer to the woman. "I said, that sure is some nice crop ya' got there, old lady."

"Hit or stay?" the dealer asked him.

"Why don't you give me a little puff of that?"

"Hit or stay?"

He ignored the dealer and grabbed onto the woman's forearm. She finally turned to him then looked down at his cards. "This pipe is for Apache," she said coldly. "It is not meant for pale-faces."

"Hit or stay?"

The ruffian growled at the dealer then hollered out, "Hit me!"

The dealer leaned in and threw his large fist into the jaw of the ruffian, knocking him to the floor and causing him to bellow in agony. Then a guard, even larger than the dealer, grabbed the man by his jacket and dragged him across the casino floor. He kicked open the doors and tossed him out into the dirt. Then two guards outside began kicking and beating him until his bellowing subsided.

John Doe watched from across the casino as he made his way to the showroom. He shook his head in frustration at the spectacle. They can't sit still for five minutes, he thought to himself. He was carrying a hat with him, black with a short brim and a round top, and a turquoise band wrapped around it. Although he was slightly distressed by his peer's exodus from the casino, he walked with a certain hop in his step, tossing the hat in the air playfully and watching it flip. He pushed his black leather boot against the door to the showroom, letting it swing open violently. Chance sat alone at a table in the middle of the room. The slamming door drew his attention. He leaned his neck back and saw John standing upside-down in the doorway. John walked in and plopped the new hat atop Chance's head, covering the neat bow of the handkerchief.

"I hope you like it," John said as sat down beside Chance.

"Looks expensive, what'd it cost ya'?"

"Traded one of those packs of cigarettes we got from

237

Fort Young. It's more of a pawn really---I imagine we will get them back soon."

Chance laughed and leaned back in his chair. He pulled off the hat and gave it a thorough inspection. A small girl walked over to the table and set down two glasses filled to the brim with whiskey. As she turned to walk off, Chance hunched forward and wrapped his skeletal fingers around her arm, stopping her departure. "What's your name, little girl?" he hissed.

"Doli," she whimpered.

John watched in silence, unsure of what Chance was planning, but most curious. Chance pulled Doli in closer, took a whiff of her long black hair and tried his best to paint a smile upon his slacked jaw. "Is there going to be a performance anytime soon?" he asked, nodding his head toward the stage.

"Yes, sir. Her name is Felina, she's a beautiful dancer."

Chance ran his eyes over to John, who caught his glance immediately. "Now that ain't a name ya' hear every day, is it?"

"One of a kind, I would say," John agreed.

Chance reached deep into the pocket of his slacks and pulled out a long string with a medallion hanging from it. He pulled Doli's hand closer, then gently placed the necklace in her palm. The medallion was a carved piece of turquoise that resembled the head of a stallion, and it was encompassed in a golden ring. Chance leaned forward and whispered into Doli's ear. "Be a doll, Doli---Go bring that to the chief and tell him I have a business deal I would like to discuss with him."

Doli stared at the necklace, completely entranced by it. She looked into the cold empty eyes of Chance Havoc and wondered who he might be to have such a splendid gift for Lipan. After pausing for a few moments, she nodded her head and scurried off toward the showroom exit.

The curtains opened up on the stage, and the lights within the showroom dimmed. A brief moment of silence settled across the nearly empty room; even the distant shouts of the gamblers and drunkards seemed to fade away. Heavy thumping footsteps resounded on the stage and were followed by much lighter clicking footsteps just behind. Chance's attention was sharply fixed on the pitch-black stage that sang out with echoing footsteps. John was amazed by Chance's tranquil concentration---it certainly was not his forte. John leaned over and whispered carefully to not disturb the silence, "Is this our girl? The one Falkner's clerk told us about?" Chance responded by nodding his head up and down in a rhythmic bobbing that matched the distant footsteps.

"HaaaaaaAaa!" a voice called out from the back of the stage. Then the quick and continuous strumming of a guitar cut through the silence and filled the room with nervous vibrations. The lamps above the stage exploded with light and revealed the beautiful silhouette of Felina, her arms raised above her head like vines wrapped around an ivory pillar. She had a long flowing crimson dress with sleeves that covered her arms and flared out at her wrists. Her hair was pulled back into a refined ponytail, except for two long locks that fell over her eyes. She picked up the bottom of her dress and stomped the floor with her black-heeled boot, and the guitarist ceased to strum. She spun around the stage and dragged her dress with her, then the voice called out again. "HaaaaaaAaa!" She stomped once again, queuing the guitarist to resume. Her tapping and stomping set the pace and led the melody. She flowed and spun across the stage with such grace that it was inconceivable such violent stomping was coming from her feet. Her arms slithered out and around her body, while her dress seemed to lift and fall on its own.

John watched Chance fall under the enchantress' spell. Between her movements and the guitarist's strumming, the room had become more captivating than during a Navajo healing song. When Felina spun, her eyes would connect with Chance's for just an instant, and when they did he saw something cold and empty within them---an element that he liked very much. It infuriated him that he could only look for an instant at a time. He felt himself longing for more and becoming angrier that he did not already have it. Without thinking, he arose to his feet with full intention of marching across the showroom and onto the stage, to look into her eyes for as long as he pleased. But before he could take his first step, someone grasped his arm and stopped him in his tracks. He turned his head away from Felina and stared into the angry eyes of Diablo.

"Let go of me," Chance snarled.

Diablo slammed his free hand against the table. He moved it away and revealed the turquoise medallion. "My father will see you. Follow me, pale-face." He released his grip and started for the exit. John got out of his seat, grabbed the medallion off the table, and followed behind Diablo. Chance took one last look at the dancer then reluctantly followed the others.

Lipan sat behind his desk and played with his turquoise medallion, running his fingers over the expertly carved stone. His medallion was nearly identical to the one Chance had brought; it had the same golden ring encompassing the stone, but instead of a horse, his was carved into the shape of an ancient warrior's face. His wrinkled fingers made a sharp contrast with the smooth gem and gold. His emotions could not be read by looking at his face alone---the way his skin slumped and his eyes barely opened revealed nothing at all. How can one tell the emotions of a sleeping man? But when the doors to his office crashed open, his eyes opened wider than they had in many years.

"These are the men who brought us Nakota's jewel," Diablo announced as he strutted into the room.

Lipan's third son, Kuruk, stood beside the chief. Lipan waved his hand, and Kuruk hurried to the corner of the room, grabbing a second chair to place beside the one in front of Lipan's desk. "Sit down, you two," the chief ordered.

"Don't mind if we do!" Chance said, happily skipping across the office and plopping himself into the chair. On the contrary, John walked calmly behind him and sat down just after.

Diablo closed the doors behind them and turned the lock, making a loud CLICK. Chance looked back at the exit and smiled at Diablo. "Thanks for that. It's a little drafty in this place. I'm sure that will help keep the heat in."

Diablo sneered in Chance's direction, but did not bother to entertain him with a response. His serious nature made Chance giggle. He got far more enjoyment out of the large man's caution than he would've from a snide remark.

"This medallion belonged to Chief Nakota of the Sioux... the Apache gifted it to his tribe many generations ago," Lipan started. "There has been word of a gang throwing the Heart into turmoil. You are those men, are you not?"

Chance shrugged as he gleefully turned to John, "I guess we're famous!" He cleared his throat and turned back to the chief. "You sure are sharp, Chief. The name is Chance Havoc, pleased to meet ya'!" He shot out his hand for Lipan to shake, but the distance between them was 15 feet, so no shaking followed.

A look of disgust and bewilderment were plastered upon Diablo's face. He was truly disturbed by Chance, and almost more so by John, who was as silent as a desert midnight.

"You attacked the Sioux and the Comanche, and now you have come for us Apache," Lipan said, "but don't be so naive to think that two men can disrupt Apache order that easily."

".... Ha... Hahahaha! Chief, chief, chief! I'm offended, you think so little of me," Chance bellowed.

"Don't take it personally, pale-face," Diablo butted in. "We don't think much of any of your kind."

"Fair enough," Chance said, tipping his hat to Diablo. Chance pushed himself out of his chair. All the Apache men moved for their pistols, but Chance raised his hands and shook his open palms at them. "Easy, easy! I only wish to explain. Chief, did ya' really think I would try to storm the glorious gates of Geronimo Park the way I did with the others? Do I truly come off as that predictable? Ya' see, I know that the Apache are a different breed---you're a unit, a strong connected tribe, and I happen to know what it is that ya' want, and I think I can help ya' get it."

Diablo marched across the room to Lipan. "We do not need anything from this man!"

Lipan raised his hand to hush his eldest son. "Perhaps, but let's hear the man out. Continue."

Chance tiptoed closer to Lipan and lowered his hands onto the chief's desk. He stared into Lipan's baggy eyes and smiled. "I know about the wild goose chase you sent that Marshal on. I know you're worried about him getting in your way of taking over the Arapaho territory. But I also know a few things you don't know. Firstly, Wyatt Cole not only hasn't killed that Coyote you sent him off to find, but he's joined up with him---turns out the two of them are old friends. And the next place they're headed is right here to take back a little someone they feel you took from them." He turned around and pointed to the doors. "That pretty little dancer ya' got out there!"

"Now this is where I come in," Chance continued. "You let me take the girl. I can lure the Marshal away from the Arapaho and take him out---Then we take over the land together."

Lipan waved his hand and Diablo helped him to his feet. He shuffled his way around the table until he stood in front of Chance. "We do not need a lying pale-face to help us take what is ours. While your hateful acts against the Sioux and Comanche have worked out in our favor, you have still tarnished the pride of our native cousins. Now leave! And if you return, you will not be met with such grace."

Diablo and Kuruk grabbed Chance and John, then tossed them through the office doors. They landed with a loud crash that sent a buzz reverberating throughout the casino. The gamblers turned from their cards, the musicians paused their playing, the waitresses dropped their drinks, and Felina ceased her stomping.

Chance pounded his fist against the carpeted floor and frantically pushed himself up. "Now wait just one damn second, Lipan!" He ran back through the office doors, pushing Diablo and Kuruk aside. "Everything I've been through has brought me right here in front of you! Now I'm here and I've taken a different approach with you than I have with the others and that ain't for no reason. 3 Red!"

"What are you saying?" Diablo demanded.

"One spin of the roulette! If it lands on 3 Red, then you reconsider. It's my lucky number, Chief, and when it lands on that 3 you'll see my coming here wasn't for no reason!"

"Father, we should kill him now. The man is insane!"

Lipan examined the casino floor from outside his office. Everyone in the casino stared back at him--the tension of the moment was a magnet pulling the crowd's attention to his next words. "You dare mock the Apache?" he said angrily. "You dare step into my home and defy my word? The warriors of old had hardened spirits, they were willing to risk everything for victory. If it lands on 3 then I will reconsider, but if it does not, you die here and now. What do you say?"

"Oh, what a wonderful idea, Chief! I accept!"

They walked out of the office toward the roulette table. As Chance passed by John, he reached down and gave him a hand. "Let the show begin," Chance whispered. John brushed himself off and followed behind Chance.

Lipan placed Nakota's medallion on the table and covered the red number 3. He turned to the dealer and motioned for him to spin. The dealer spun the wheel and the numbers were lost in a spiraling blur. He placed the ball at the edge and rolled it in the opposite direction of the spin. The only noise that permeated through the air was that of the ball rolling round and around the spinning wheel. It passed once, then twice, then again and again as it seemed the rolling would never cease. The whole of Geronimo Park was fixed on the future destination of the little white ball. After five passes Chance could hear the hammer of Diablo's pistol clicking back into place. The ball began to move away from the edge of the wheel, approaching nearer and nearer to the center, where it would soon snag a number. After a few more passes the ball clipped one of the squares and began bouncing around as the wheel spun beneath it. It bounced and bounced until it did not. It settled into a slot, a red slot, but the number was still blurred as the wheel continued to spin.

The dealer reached for the wheel, but before he stopped it, he looked across the room as a loud crash at the front doors disrupted the silence. One of the guards wobbled backwards into the casino and fell to the floor. His face was bloodied and beaten, and he had two stab wounds in his chest that were leaking blood. Diablo turned to look, as did Lipan, and everyone else in the casino, except Chance---who was still gazing at the spinning wheel. Through the doors walked the bearded ruffian, who'd been ejected earlier---brandishing a large knife covered in the guard's blood. He marched over the guard's body, straight toward the table where he had been gambling---to the old woman still puffing on her cigarette. Each step he took seemed to last an eternity as everyone watched him. The ruffian stood above the old woman and growled at her through his dirty beard. He lifted his knife into the air then drove it downward into the woman's chest.

BANG! A gunshot rang out from the other side of the casino.

Diablo turned toward the shot and saw another man, who looked much like the ruffian, holding a smoking pistol, and standing over one of the dealers with a fresh bullet hole through his head.

BANG! Another shot fired from the far corner of the casino. BANG! BANG! BANG! BANG! All across the floor of Geronimo Park a symphony of gunshots sang in harmony as outlaws fired at will.

Diablo turned around and saw Kuruk face down on the table. Standing above Kuruk, John held the gun that was pointed at his own head just moments before. Chance was no longer in front of Diablo, but behind Lipan, holding the little white ball in his fingers, flashing it in front of the chief's eyes.

Diablo pointed his gun at Chance, but before he could fire, John sent a shot plummeting straight through Diablo's neck. He dropped his pistol and fell to the floor as he drowned on the blood leaking from his neck.

Lipan watched his son flailing on the floor, then turned to Kuruk who laid motionless on the table. Then Chance grabbed him from behind and slammed the old man's face into the roulette wheel. He pulled him off the table and threw him to the ground. Chance knelt down and picked up Diablo's pistol. "On second thought, I think I'll keep the North for myself, Chief!"

He cocked the pistol and pulled the trigger.

Felina watched through a crack in the showroom doors as gunshots peppered the casino floor. She watched numerous Apache bodies fall lifeless and looked on as the crazed outlaws scurried around the gambling floor like a pack of rats. They ran upstairs through the brothels and smashed up the bars below. What's happening? She wondered, where do I go, what do I do?

One of the men who was looting the bar turned his gaze to the crack in the showroom doors and caught Felina's stare through the small slit. She saw him toss his bottle across the room and bolt toward the door. Felina stumbled back then sped toward the stage; there was a hall behind the curtains that led upstairs. She hopped onto the stage and ran through the curtains. As she pushed the thick drapes aside, she was abruptly stopped. Nitis stood stoically as Felina ran into him. He held her face, trying to get her attention without frightening her. "Come, we must get you out of here!"

"Doli!" she pleaded, "we need to get Doli."

Nitis grabbed her by the forearm and started down the back hall toward Lipan's office. They entered the back of the office and scanned the room. Suddenly, Lipan's chair spun around with one of the outlaws lounging in it, drinking from a bottle of whiskey. He spotted Felina, jumped out of his seat, and lunged at her. Nitis pulled his tomahawk from his belt and struck the man in the back of the head with the blunt stone end of the weapon. The outlaw's body hit the floor and was followed by a high-pitched scream.

Felina bent down beneath the desk and found Doli, curled up in a ball with tears streaming down her face. Felina grabbed her and dragged her out from under the desk. "Come on, Doli---We need to go!"

"What's happening, Felina?" Doli cried.

Felina ignored her question and pulled her back to the hallway. Nitis followed them down the hall. Felina started up the staircase to the second floor, but Nitis quickly stopped her and pulled her back down. "Where are you going?"

"Misa and Dakota are up there!" Doli said.

"You two need to leave now. They are after you, Felina!"

The door at the top of the staircase swung open. One of Chance's men stood in the doorway, and he raised his pistol at Felina and the others then fired a shot. The bullet whizzed over their heads as Felina and Doli dropped to the ground. Nitis adjusted his grip then hurled the tomahawk at the man. The sharpened edge stuck into the outlaw's chest, and he came rolling down the stairs. Another man entered the hall from the far end, where Felina and Doli hoped to exit, and started toward them. Nitis pulled the tomahawk out of the man's chest, then he kicked open the door beside them. Leading them back to the showroom stage, Nitis pulled the girls behind him.

The three then hopped off the stage and hurried toward

the showroom exit, that led back to the main gambling floor. Nitis reached out his arm to push open the doors, but before he could touch the warm wood, the door swung open from the other side. He looked across the open room at countless Apache bodies lying dead. In front of him were five men, including Chance and John, all pointing their pistols at him. Nitis turned to Felina and Doli, who both frantically backed away as they noticed the gunmen. His lips mouthed the words *I'm sorry*, but no noise seemed to project from them. He turned back to face the men and hurled his tomahawk in one final effort to save the girls, but just as the wooden grip left his fingertips, five bullets from the men's guns tore through his chest. Felina's screams were drowned out by the continuous gunshots, not ceasing even after his body lay dead on the floor. Then the man from the hall grabbed Felina and Doli, restraining them in his arms, and muting their screams as he covered their mouths.

Smoke from the gunshots filled the room and hovered over Nitis' body. Chance stepped over his corpse toward the girls. His boots trudged through the pooled blood that had gushed out of Nitis' chest---they made a *splish-splash* as the pool rippled with each step. Felina watched, with tears in her eyes, as Chance crept closer. He had a closed-mouth smile on his face that stretched from sunken cheek to cheek. He put his hands on his knees and leaned forward so that he stared directly into Felina's black eyes. "What are you crying for, Señorita?" Chance whimpered, "What? Do you think I'd hurt ya'? C'mon on now, don't you know I'm here to save ya'? Yeah! Your dear friend the Marshal sent me to come pick ya' up!"

Felina struggled in the man's arms, trying to shout and kick, but the muffled noises stayed trapped behind the man's hand. Chance continued as though he could understand her indiscernible noises. "Well, no--you have a point. We aren't really friends, Wyatt and me. But I'm doing this as a courtesy to him. Now he really wants to see ya', and I really want to see him and have another chat. So you comin' with me just kills two birds with the same rock---It's what we call a win-win." Felina tried again to speak but her words were still stifled. Chance gave her a look of disdain and turned away feeling truly offended. "Now I don't need to hear one more nagging word out of you, little lady!" he snapped. Then, waving his hand, he called out to his men, "C'mon boys, round up the rest of the gals and load 'em into the train, they'll make good company once we get settled in up north!"

The man holding Felina and Doli moved forward and pushed the girls along with him. They marched through the corpse-laden grounds of the casino, stumbling over countless bodies, some of them still moaning in agony. Felina looked over to Doli and noticed she had fainted, her feet knocking against the bodies as the man dragged her along. She looked up to the second-floor balcony and watched as the other girls were led down the stairs and out of the casino. They all looked like Dakota, with pale skin and light blonde hair, it was hard to tell if any of the girls were actually her. Their arms were deeply bruised, their hair was messy and tangled, and their thin gowns were tattered. She also saw the floor girls being led out, and immediately spotted Misa, who seemed to be as shocked as the rest of the girls but made no fuss as the men pushed her along.

They were led to the tracks near the casino, where they saw an empty train ready to be loaded. Chance's outlaws shoved the girls into a few empty train cars. Felina was huddled together with Doli, just as they had been back when they were on the way to Geronimo Park. Doli lay asleep in Felina's lap, and it comforted the young woman---It felt good to be holding Doli and share her warmth. But the warmth of her friend was not needed; the car was already hot, and it began to smell of thick smoke. As the train began rolling along the tracks, Felina stood up to look out the small open window. The train sped off, and she watched as flames engulfed Geronimo Park, quickly swallowing it whole.

Chapter 15

SO LONG, MARSHAL

The nearest depot stood a mile away from Little Raven, on the crest of a hill, giving Juan and Wyatt a clear view of the complex below. They had just arrived at the depot, and from the looks of the camp below, Chance and his gang had already made themselves comfortable. They watched the steam rising from the gang's train just outside the camp. Little Raven was unlike the casinos of the Apache, Comanche, or Sioux. Chief Cheyenne didn't believe in such hedonistic facilities; she honored the ways of old and her camp was a testament to that. Behind the large log walls, countless teepees were scattered across the grounds, all arrayed around a massive teepee at the center of the complex. The main structure consumed the same space that 20 of the smaller teepees would; it stood nearly 40 feet tall and had a thick cloud of smoke rising out of the top.

"Ashkii," Wyatt hollered, "are you ready?"

Ashkii sat on the steps of the train, wrapped in his blanket. The woven linen began morphing into layers of feathers on his back, while his hair wrapped over his face and formed into his beak shaped cowl. His nails slowly extended into sharp talons, and his tan skin hardened into a wrinkled black leather. "I am... *kaww!* Ready." Running from the train to the edge of the hill, Ashkii jumped into the air. In the blink of an eye his body shrunk, and flapping his raven wings, he soared off toward the camp.

251

As a raven, Ashkii's vision was much sharper. He could see Chance's men strutting around the camp, drinking liquor, and getting into drunken fights with one another. It only took him a couple of minutes to land on top of the camp's large wooden gates. He scanned the terrain and listened carefully. He heard men laughing, some shouting about losing a hand of cards, others coughing as they took too large of a sip of booze. None of it was what he searched for. He hopped off the wall and glided to the other end of the camp. He hopped between the teepees until he heard the faint sound of a crying girl. He tilted his head from side to side, watching the teepee. He grabbed the bottom of the thick hide wall with his beak and lifted it over his head, then he crawled into the tent.

There were four girls huddled together---one that Ashkii immediately recognized. "*Kaww!*" he blurted out. The girls jumped back when they saw a bird had made its way into the tent. "Doli," he cried. Then, hopping over until he was right beside the girl's feet, he cawed her name again, "Doli!" It had been longer than a year since he had laid eyes on the girl, since before he was kicked out of the Navajo camp.

Doli cowered back into Felina's arms. "Felina?" she whimpered, "did you hear that?"

Ashkii twitched his head and looked up, "Felina?" he said.

"What?" she looked down in surprise, not believing her own ears.

"*Kaww! Kaww!* Felina! Doli!" he cheered, jumping up and down, flapping his wings, and startling all the girls.

A man ripped open the drapes that enclosed the teepee and shouted, "What's all the racket about in here?" Looking in, he saw the girls backing away from the flailing raven. Then Ashkii turned around, looked the man in the eyes, and flew past him.

252

He sped through the camp, listening carefully. He could hear the whispering of more girls packed together inside their small teepees. He watched as some of the girls were dragged out of the huts and forced to the ground by the men. Though he wished to act, he had promised Juan that he would stick to their plan. He continued to hop around the camp, listening for a specific voice, one he eventually heard coming from inside the large main teepee. He jumped up and flew into one of the four entrances at the end of the tent. He was surprised at how large it was inside; there was enough room to fly around freely. He took a perch on top of one of the beams that held the structure up.

There were ten men and three women inside. Two of the women danced around the large fire burning in the middle of the tent. Some of the men would occasionally grab them and kiss up and down their necks. Others would throw the final drops of their drinks on them when they passed by. Two of the men sat further back from the fire; one of them with the third woman sitting next to him, restrained to a chair. She was the one Ashkii searched for. Beneath her bruised skin, ruffled hair, and ripped clothes was one of the most beautiful women he had ever seen. Stories had been told throughout the Western Heart about the beauty of the Arapaho Chief Cheyanne. Her hair was long and brown, falling past her back and almost touching the ground. She had a tan dress with fringe cut along the sleeves and bottom of the skirt, and wore a tight necklace with a large turquoise medallion carved into the shape of a raven.

The man beside her was just as Wyatt had described to him---thin, crude, with a cloth wrapped around his head, only now the bow was hidden by the hat he wore. Chance Havoc, the man who was responsible for the deaths of three Native chiefs and countless other Native men and women. He was sitting close to Cheyanne, whispering in her ear, but even Ashkii's hearing was not sharp enough to make out what he said. He swooped down from the beam and landed a few feet from Cheyanne.

"C'mon now, Chief. You should be grateful for the mercy I've shown you and your people," Ashkii heard Chance whisper. "I've dreamed a long time about making this land my home. There's no reason we can't share it together."

Ashkii hopped closer to Cheyanne, then lightly pecked at her toes. She looked down at the raven, and Ashkii stared back at her. "*KAWWW!*" he cried. He looked to his right where he saw a man dressed all in black aiming a pistol at him. He hopped back then took off into the air toward the nearest exit.

John fired a shot that whizzed past Ashkii as he soared out of the camp. John pushed his pistol back into his holster then looked down at Cheyanne. "A friend of yours?" he asked.

"The raven is a friend to all of my people, they bring messages from the stars," she said.

"And what message did this one bring you?" Chance mocked.

Cheyanne glared at her captor with great disdain. "I don't know... I don't speak raven."

"HA-HA-HA!" Chance bellowed, "Wow, ya' sure are a mysterious woman, Chief. I already like ya' more than those damn Apache." He turned around and waved to John. "I'm tired of these girls. Go bring me the Mexican. Now, she knows how to dance! Oh, Chief, you'll love this girl! Ya' ain't never seen anything like her before! That's a promise!" He grabbed Cheyanne by her cheeks and laid a wet smooch on her lips. Then he jumped up and started dancing with one of the Arapaho girls around the fire.

John left the teepee and headed for the back of the

camp to find Felina. He stormed into her teepee and dragged her to the main structure. Ashkii was perched on top of the wall and watched as John led her to the giant teepee. Before they made it to the entrance, John turned his head and stared at Ashkii. He only gave him a momentary glimpse before entering the tent, then the drapes closed behind him. Ashkii jumped off the gate and soared back to the depot.

While Juan and Hans rested inside the depot, Wyatt and Richard unloaded the horses from the train. Wyatt led Peaches and one of the others by the reins while Richard took the third. The music from Little Raven couldn't be heard from atop the hill---in fact, no sound could be heard other than the light tramping of the horses' hooves. The air was cold, but the night sky was clear and littered with bright stars. Wyatt didn't remember the last time he'd looked at the stars and appreciated them. He wondered why tonight, of all nights, that had changed.

"What's on your mind, son?" Richard asked.

"It seems like everything has changed," Wyatt started. "For the longest time all I cared about was keeping order, and being a marshal. Now look at me, there's no order to keep anymore. I've killed another marshal, and nearly took the life of an innocent man. Not to mention I promised that girl I would come back to her one day---now she may not even be alive. Even if we stop Chance and his gang, the damage has been done; the whole Western Heart has fallen into chaos."

"I hate to break it to you, Marshal, but you think too highly of me. I am far from innocent. In fact, I used to be fairly close to a man not unlike Mr. Havoc." Richard stopped walking and turned to Wyatt, pulled off his eye-patch and revealed his scar. "If there is anything I have learned in my time, it's that nothing turns out the way we think it will at first, but it ends up the way it was always meant to. You need to change your thinking. What would have happened if you didn't kill that marshal? What would the Apache do to you if they found out you helped the man you were sent to kill? You say the world is in chaos… Well, the world was created from within a void of eternal chaos. Whatever you think doesn't matter right now. What matters is that that young man and his sister are relying on you, and you can't afford to show them any doubt."

Wyatt looked closely at Richard's scar, then he turned back to the sky. The cross shaped scar was reflected in the starry galaxies. Wyatt knew he was right, he knew that Bill would have told him the same thing had he still been around. He believed there must have been a reason that he and Juan were reunited---Felina must be alive. None of his doubts mattered anymore; he still had a chance to keep his promise to Felina, and that was all he needed.

"Thank you, Deacon," Wyatt nodded.

"It's Ashkii," Richard said as he pointed into the distance.

The raven came swooping down from the sky and landed on Peaches' saddle. "*Kaww!* They have Chief Cheyanne. Felina is there too, as well as a Navajo girl I remember. There are a couple dozen other girls from what I could tell. Chance's men are all around the camp, and don't seem to be in the sharpest state of mind. I say we-*Kaww*-hurry."

"I'll go get Juan and Hans," Wyatt said, and ran off toward the depot.

When he got to the depot, Juan and Hans were already outside. "We heard Ashkii's cawing," Juan explained. "What did he say, Wyatt? Is Felina there?"

Wyatt couldn't help but grin. "I told you she would be. Didn't I?"

Hans jumped up onto Juan's back and embraced him, "That is wonderful, Juan!"

"From what Ashkii told us, Chance's men seem to be off-guard, and perhaps a bit drunk. He thinks we should leave as soon as possible, and I agree."

"Well, what are we waiting for?" Juan and Hans said in unison.

Ashkii explained the layout of the camp and where the girls and outlaws were located. After a short discussion, the men all mounted their horses. Wyatt hopped on Peaches, Richard on his horse, with Ashkii perched on his shoulder, and Juan and Hans riding together on their own horse.

Fixing his hat firmly on his head, Wyatt turned to the others and asked, "We all know what to do?" The others nodded in confirmation. Wyatt kicked Peaches' sides and she raised up on her hind legs, then sped off down the hill with the rest of the team following close behind.

Two of Chance's men sat outside the gates, supposedly keeping watch. The first man raised his bottle of whiskey, turning it upside down and giving it a little shake. He looked through the opening with one squinty eye and waited for more liquor to appear, but after a few long seconds of staring at the empty bottle, he chucked it into the darkness. "Well shit, Earl, I guess we're dry," he pouted.

"It sure sounds like they're having a good time in there. How did we get stuck on guard duty? We already had to pile up all those dead Natives from earlier. I didn't sign up to be no chore boy," said Earl.

The drums pounded from inside the camp and the hollering of drunk outlaws blasted out into the empty northern plains. The festivities distracted the men; Earl tried hard not to tap his feet to the rhythm. "C'mon, Ralph," Earl grunted as he pushed himself out of the dirt, "Let's go scratch our itch---ain't nothin' gonna happen tonight."

"Ehh, just go get me another bottle," Ralph said, "I'm just thirsty."

Kaww! Kaww!

A raven swooped down from the night sky and landed by Ralph's feet. It started to peck at the ground where the last drops of whiskey had landed. Ralph bent forward and inspected the large bird. He smiled and said, "Looks like I ain't the only thirsty one."

Earl watched as Ralph admired the bird. "Curious little fellow," he said.

The raven turned its head to Earl, then hopped over in his direction. Earl backed away at first, surprised at how comfortable the animal was around them, then he squatted down and let the raven approach him. The bird hopped closer and closer, then Earl reached out his hand and the raven jumped onto his palm. "It sure is heavy," Earl laughed.

"Hey, be careful!" Ralph exclaimed. "You don't know what kind of diseases that thing's carrying."

"Oh shut it, I know what I'm doing," Earl barked. He stood up and lifted his hand so that he and the raven looked directly into each other's eyes.

The raven tilted its head from side to side, then it opened its beak and said, "Run."

Earl looked over to Ralph. "Did you hear that?" he asked. He looked back at the raven in utter fascination. It moved its head closer to Earl's face, and Earl leaned closer to it. The raven opened its beak once again and Earl waited for more words to come out of its mouth. Then the raven snapped its beak shut and pecked Earl in the eye. "ARGHH!" he cried, falling back, and dropping the raven.

The bird landed in the dirt, and Earl pulled his pistol out and fired a shot at it. The raven flapped its wings and flew through the gates. Ralph ran over to Earl and picked him off the ground. "You damn idiot! I told you to be careful! You could've shot me just then!"

"That… that bird. Did you hear what it said? It… it told us to run," Earl mumbled.

"I didn't hear nothin'!" Ralph responded.

"Shhh! Listen, do you hear that?" Earl whispered.

Ralph settled down and listened. He thought Earl was losing his mind, until he heard a soft distant thumping. It was like hearing his own heartbeat, but it was off-rhythm and not coming from his chest. It was coming from the soles of his feet, and it was growing louder. The thumping grew and grew, like it was getting closer. He looked into the distance but all he saw was black---the torch that lit the gateway only shone a short few meters, doing nothing to light the dark void in front of him. Although he could see nothing, he couldn't turn his gaze away from the approaching noise, and after a few long moments he saw something. It looked like a new star had ignited just over the horizon, only it was not still, it was like a shooting star moving right for him.

The noise grew until it was right on top of them. They watched as a horse, as black as the night sky, ran into the revealing light of the torch. Atop the horse rode a man with a black leather hat and a dark brown shawl who pointed a silver revolver directly at Ralph's heart.

BANG! Juan's shot exploded into Ralph's chest. Earl lifted his pistol, but before he could pull back the hammer Juan shot again, his bullet tearing through Earl's hand. "Vamos!" Juan hollered. He kicked the sides of his horse and galloped through the gates. Hans held on tightly to Juan's waist as they rode through the camp.

"Great shooting, amigo!" Hans exclaimed.

"Gracias," Juan replied. He scanned the distance then pulled on the horse's reins, turning him slightly. "We need to get to the back of the camp. Once we find the girls I will leave them with you, then I'll meet the others in the main teepee."

"Right!"

On hearing the gunshots, the outlaws left their tents and ran toward the gates. Some of them checked out the bodies, others followed the tracks Juan left behind, and some wandered around drunkenly trying to get their heads straight. Before they could get a fix on what happened, Peaches sped through the gates and trampled three men. From her back, Wyatt drew his pistol and shot one of the outlaws already aiming a rifle at him. Richard followed in behind him, swung the stock of his rifle and bludgeoned the man outside the gate.

"Two of them are after Juan!" Wyatt shouted.

Richard aimed his rifle at the men chasing Juan. His first shot hit the man on the left, but before he could shoot again, a man popped out of a teepee and shot Richard's horse in the neck. Richard was thrown from his saddle as his horse crashed to the ground. As he rolled through the dirt his rifle skidded away from him. Wyatt aimed at the man in the tent and shot him dead. Turning to the man following the tracks, he fired a stray shot that completely missed; it was too far out of range for Wyatt's pistol.

"I've got it!" Ashkii called out as he swooped down from the skies, speeding toward the running man. Furiously flapping his wings, he sped past the man. Once in front of him, Ashkii quickly flipped around, while morphing into his cowled hybrid form, and threw a knife into the man's thigh. Then in the blink of an eye he shifted back into a raven and swooped over to Wyatt.

Hearing the gunshots ringing about, Hans looked behind him. "Do you think they are okay, Juan?"

"We cannot worry about them right now, we have to focus," he replied. They made it to the far end of the camp and Juan tugged hard on the reins. The horse came to an abrupt stop and the two hopped off the saddle. Juan stayed low as they shuffled in between the teepees, listening for the girls' whispers. "Hand me your hatchet," Juan whispered.

"It's a tomahawk," Hans corrected, "and what do you need it for? You have a gun."

"It's too risky, if I miss a shot it could go straying into a tent and hit one of the girls." Hans agreed and handed Juan the weapon. "I will give it back to you once we find the girls."

They walked to the nearest teepee and tugged at the opening; it was empty except for some canteens spread along the ground. Hans pulled on Juan's shawl and pointed to one of the other tents. "I think I hear something over there," he said.

Juan closed the drape and started in the direction Hans was pointing. He walked up to the drape and pulled it back. He felt a heavy force crash against his abdomen, and he found himself falling to the ground with a large man on top of him. The man's shoulder dug deep into Juan's lungs as he tackled him, knocking the breath out of the boy, and sending the tomahawk flying from grasp. The man pinned Juan to the ground and sent a punch soaring into his left cheek. It hurt, but all the noise Juan could get out was a muted grunt. He could feel the blood rush to his face as his cheek immediately started to bruise.

"Who the hell'r you?" the man roared. He clenched his other fist and punched Juan's other cheek. Juan tried desperately to reach for his holstered pistol, but the man's knee was blocking it. He raised his right fist once again and threw a third punch, but to Juan's surprise this one didn't hurt---in fact, the punch had not even connected. All he felt were droplets splashing on his chin, then he heard a quiet thump as something fell next to his ear. Juan turned his head to find Hans standing above him, holding the tomahawk, now covered in blood. Juan looked up at his attacker and saw him screaming and holding his wrist, which appeared to be missing a hand. Juan looked at the ground beside him and saw the stray fist lying in the dirt, still clenched, and spewing out blood.

Hans took a mighty swing with the tomahawk, and the sharpened edge tore into the man's chest, which sent him falling off Juan. The hunchback quickly inspected Juan's bruises and asked him, "Are you hurt?"

"Just a little shaken up, but I'm fine," said Juan. After Hans helped him to his feet, he pulled the weapon out of the man's chest. Hans gazed sullenly at his victim's body. He had never taken a man's life before---he surprised himself when he acted so quickly and without thought. Juan tugged at Hans' shawl and whispered, "Are you alright?"

"I... I feel... dangerous. It feels quite nice actually," Hans grinned.

"You're a real monster, my friend. We will tell tales of your terrors when this is all over, but we have to keep searching."

"Right. I'll let you pick the next tent. I am quite obviously no good at it," Hans chuckled.

Juan was startled by Hans' apparent light-heartedness---he hadn't a clue where this newfound confidence had come from. Perhaps Wyatt had filled his head with stories of brave marshals fighting off dastardly outlaws. But he didn't let the hunchback's heroics perplex him for long. He quickly shuffled along, listening for cries or other noises little girls made.

They made their way past three or four teepees, with not so much as the chirp of a blackbird coming from within. At last, Juan heard the faintest cough echo out of the next tent. He saw a fire burning behind the drapes, and the vague silhouettes of a group of girls painted in shadows. He moved to the front of the teepee, but he stopped when saw an outlaw just around the corner, relieving himself. Juan crept back to the side of the teepee and raised up the tomahawk, thrusting the sharp end into the side of the tent and pulling down---the fibers ripped and a large slit opened in their wake. He poked his head through and found himself face to face with a dozen girls, some younger than him, others right around his age. He pressed his finger to his lips and let out a calming, "Shhhhh." Then he opened his hand and extended it for the nearest girl to take. "We're going to get you out of here," he told them.

It was dark within the teepee, not much was illuminated by the faint fire, making all the girls in the cluster blend together. He couldn't tell what emotions were showing on their faces. He assumed they wouldn't trust him but desperately hoped they would. He was amazed when one of the girls' hands crept out of the shadows and grabbed onto his. Pulling her away from the others, he led the girl through the slit. When she exited the tent's dimness, the light from the stars and the moon touched her face. It was a face that Juan had seen once before. Her eyes were as blue as the sky on a hot desert day, her skin resembled the petals of a white rose, and her hair was the color of the southwest plateaus' red earth.

"You're the boy from the train," said the girl.

Up until that moment, he had forgotten about that girl from the train, but as she knelt in front of him it was clear that she was indeed the girl from that day. That day, when he did nothing to help her, felt like a lifetime ago…but today was not that day. He knew that things would end far differently than they had that day---he had faith that they would. He felt it in his heart and knew that seeing her was a sign from the one Deacon had told him about.

"That's right," Juan said confidently. "Now you and the others need to follow my friend, and he'll lead you to safety."

The girl nodded her head then fetched the rest of the girls from inside the tent.

"Alright, Hans," Juan started, "you know what to do?"

"Get them to the gates while you and the others draw the outlaws to the main teepee."

"Bueno." Juan flipped the tomahawk around and handed it to Hans. "Be safe."

"You too, amigo!"

Juan ran back to his horse and kicked him into a gallop, straight for the main teepee.

Richard crawled toward his rifle as an outlaw pointed his cocked revolver at him. He reached for the rifle but was stopped by a loud bang, then he watched the outlaw's body drop to the ground. Wyatt rode up behind the fallen body, the barrel of his pistol still smoking. He flipped open his revolver, flinging out the shells then filling the empty chambers with fresh bullets. He hopped off Peaches and helped Richard to his feet.

"You hurt?" Wyatt asked.

"I'm an old man who recently danced with death. I'm always hurting."

Wyatt chuckled. He scanned the camp, and Ashkii swooped over and perched on Peaches' saddle. "What's the plan, Marshal," the raven asked.

"We have to assume Juan and Hans did their part. If that's the case, then Juan should be headed for Chance and the others right now, and Hans should be leading the girls back this way. Hans is smart, but if he runs into any of Chance's men he's going to be a sitting duck."

"I'll go help him," Richard suggested. "I'll take Peaches and get the girls out of the camp. The horse can probably hold a few of them at a time. I'll just get in the way if things go south with Havoc anyway."

Wyatt nodded in agreement and turned to Ashkii. "Go with him to make sure the path is safe. Then group up with Juan and me when you can."

"*Kaww*! Right." He jumped off the saddle and took flight toward the back of the camp.

Wyatt helped Richard on top of the bald mare then whispered in her ear, "Keep them safe girl." He slapped her rear end then they took off behind Ashkii.

Richard turned and watched Wyatt start toward the center of the camp, toward the giant teepee. He desperately wished that he could have been more help, but knew that his duty was just as important as the others, and he worried for Hans. He kicked Peaches' sides and felt her accelerate through the darkness.

"Ashkii!" Richard called. "Do you see them?"

"*Kaww!* There! Just ahead!"

Hans was surrounded by four of Chance's men. Holding up his bloodstained tomahawk, he waved it furiously at the pack. "Stay back!" Hans growled.

"What the hell is that thing?" asked the man in front.

"It's hideous. Must be some Native monster that snatches up little girls," said the second man.

Hans was unsure whether it was anger or fear he felt

coursing through his veins. He watched as the men drew large knives out from the back of their belts and pointed them at him. The girl's cries from behind him were faint in reality, but to his ears they sounded like deafening howls. His fist clenched around the grip of his tomahawk and he let out an adrenaline-filled roar. "You should cower in fear! For God has sent me to expel you from his garden and I fight with the force of his mighty fist!" Then without a second thought Hans lunged at the nearest outlaw. His movement was swift, catching the men off guard. Hans drove the tomahawk into the man's shoulder, but soon after, the outlaw grabbed a hold of Hans and slammed him into the dirt. The breath evacuated from Hans' lungs, and all he could do was watch as the four outlaws, with their long knives, surrounded him.

"Dirty little monster," hissed the man he had attacked, pulling the tomahawk out of his shoulder.

Richard watched the man raise his knife, preparing to drive it through Hans' heart. He wished to shoot at him but knew he couldn't risk hitting the girls behind them. He looked up to the night sky and watched as Ashkii plunged down from the stars toward the outlaws.

"*Kaww!!*" Ashkii gripped the man's hand in his talons and tore the knife from his fingers. The four men backed away from Hans, turning their attention to the raven. In the blink of an eye Ashkii spun around, now griping the knife with his human hand. While still in the air, he hurled the knife at the first man, and it pierced through his heart. Ashkii blinked back into a raven and swooped over to the second outlaw. He dug his claws into the man's chest then repeatedly pecked at his eyes until blood flooded down his cheeks. Pushing himself off the newly blinded man, he blinked back into his hybrid form and lunged at the third. Ashkii snatched the knife out of his hand and stabbed him repeatedly in the chest.

"Look out!" Hans hollered, as he spotted the last preparing to throw his knife at Ashkii. He ducked, then he hid under his feathered cowl as the knife flew over him. He hurled his knife back at the man, and the blade sliced right through his throat.

Richard pulled on the reins, slowing Peaches as he neared Hans and the girls. "Is anyone hurt?" he asked. The girls shook their heads and so did Hans. "I'll take them from here. Hans, Ashkii, you should go help the others."

"Ashkii?" a quiet voice asked from within the group of girls.

The birdman turned his head to the group. "Doli?" Ashkii ambled over to the group, scaring almost all of them except for one of the smallest, a Navajo girl. The feathers fell from his cowl, and his beaked hood disappeared, revealing his painted face and braided black hair. Doli saw his face and tears fell from her eyes. He reached out for her, and she ran into his arms.

"Brother Ashkii," she cried, "when Lady Kai exiled you from the camp, I thought I'd never see you again!"

"Fear not, little Doli. I am here, and soon we will be back with our family." He held her soft face against his bare chest and let her tears drip down on him. "I need you to listen to me now. You and the others must stay close to my friend Richard. He will lead you to safety."

Doli nodded and rounded up the girls to follow behind Richard. Ashkii picked up Hans' tomahawk and handed it to him. "Come now, friend. We must assist the others. I will fly there, and you get there as quickly as possible."

"Right," Hans nodded.

A thick cloud of smoke hovered above the giant teepee, blocking out the starlight and casting a dark shadow over the structure. Loud drums were beating within, and their rhythm was echoed in the beat of Wyatt's heart. The entrances to the teepee were tall, and the drapes hung wide open, inviting him in. He gripped his revolver and pulled it from the holster, then he strode into the teepee. A thick bonfire burned in the center of the structure, and around the fire danced three women. Wyatt looked to the left of the fire and saw a handful of Chance's men, then to the right and saw a mound of native bodies piled together. Then he looked past the fire to the far end of the structure. He saw a group of faces he had seen before, and one he did not recognize. The first face had sunken cheeks, dead eyes, and a goofy cloth wrapped around his head. Beside him was his friend, the beautiful Chief Cheyanne, on her knees beside his chair with her wrists tied together. Next was the face he had never seen---a man in a black hat, black glasses, and a long black coat. But the face next to his was the face Wyatt would recognize until the end of time; she had long black hair, matching black eyes, and was wearing a crimson dress.

"Felina," he whispered to himself. He took another step into the room, knowing he would now be in plain sight. His boot hit the ground, and he immediately watched the man in black raise his pistol. Before Wyatt could react, a shot was fired. One of the three dancing girls collapsed as the bullet blew through her chest. The girls beside her scurried away but were quickly caught by the group of men to Wyatt's left. The drums ceased to play and Chance pushed himself out of his seat.

"Marshal!" he hollered, "Oh, how wonderful! Our guest of honor has finally arrived! Say hello, ladies." Chance turned to Cheyanne and Felina and gave them a wicked stare.

"Hello, Marshal," they both mumbled.

"Marshal, why don't you throw down your pistol. It ain't gonna help ya' out much."

Wyatt took a step forward. "No, Chance. I think I'll hold onto it."

John Doe cocked his pistol and aimed it at Wyatt. "I would highly recommend you keep your distance, Marshal. You don't want to see the Chief or the Mexican get hurt do you?"

Wyatt tilted his head, eyeing Felina and Cheyanne. Cheyanne lifted her head and shouted at Wyatt, "I told you, Wyatt! What took you so long to get here?"

"I'm sorry, Chief," said Wyatt as he shifted his gaze solely to Felina. "I guess I'm no good at showing up on time."

Felina's eyes were filled with sadness and joy and fear. She could hardly believe that Wyatt was truly standing in front of her, but she feared she'd only have a handful of moments to look at him.

Wyatt raised his pistol at John. "You must be the clerk," he said.

"Been a long time, Marshal."

"I hate to see you turn out this way. It's a shame you would turn your back on your duty, but if I were stuck in a steel box my entire life, I could see myself doing anything I could get out. But you know better than anyone, Clerk, that as a marshal I can't let you go free after what you've done. So you're first, and then you're next, Chance."

Chance began laughing hysterically, and he pulled Cheyanne closer to him. "Oh, this is the showdown I've been waiting for!"

Wyatt pulled back the hammer of his pistol. John moved his pistol away from Wyatt and pressed it up against Felina's temple.

BANG!

A shot fired out from behind John, and a bullet ripped through his hand, knocking his gun away. Juan, atop his horse, stormed into the tent from the back entrance. He galloped toward John and fired three more shots into his chest, then quickly holstered his pistol and extended his hand to Felina. She grabbed his forearm, and he lifted his sister onto the horse. Then they sped across the grounds toward Wyatt. The men with the native girls raised their guns at Juan, but Wyatt shot two of them before they could fire. The last two were holding the dancers, which caused Wyatt to hesitate, and both men fired shots at Juan and Felina.

Ashkii raced down from the top opening of the teepee, flying between Juan and the outlaws. He spread his feathered cowl and stared Juan in the eyes as the two bullets pierced his back. Ashkii crashed to the ground, then Juan fired at one of the men while Wyatt aimed at the other, taking them both out.

Juan hopped off his horse and turned Ashkii over in his arms. The feathers fell off his cowl, and his mask once again disappeared. Blood leaked out of his chest, and mixed together with the black paint smeared atop his skin. Juan looked up at Wyatt, who was already looking back at the boy. The Marshal turned away and started across the room toward Chance.

"Wyatt, what are you doing?" Juan shouted.

"Stay out of it, Juan." He strutted toward Chance, and a wave of wrath coursed through his heart. "Alright, Havoc! You've had your fun."

Chance reached behind his back and pulled out a pistol, then he pushed against Cheyanne's head. "No, Marshal. I don't think I have! Ya' see I set out on a mission to change this world we live in. And my fun will be over when you stand here and watch my dream come to fruition! Ya' see I've made the Western Heart a freer land by tearing it away from the tyranny of the Government and their petty marshals! And certainly by extinguishing these despotic natives. You marshals are supposed to stand for order? Well, order is crippling! All I want is for everyone to flourish."

"You're right... the order that the Apache abided by was harsh, and the same goes for the Comanche, and Sioux, and even the Government. But as a marshal I don't stand for any of their order, I stand for *my order*---an order that values the beauty of this world---but you don't value that, do you? You don't value anything at all."

Chance chuckled and gave Wyatt the most genuine of smiles. "Ya' really do get me, Marshal." He reached his other hand into his pocket and pulled out an old Government coin. "How about one final game to send us off? Let luck decide who's right? Fair and square. What do you say, Marshal?"

"Don't do it, Wyatt!" Felina shouted. "He is a cheat, he did the same thing to th-"

Wyatt raised his hand to stop Felina before she could finish. "Call it in the air?"

"You do the honors, Marshal. You call it right, I let the Chief go and you do what you must with me. You call it wrong and the bullet will already be out the other side of her skull."

Wyatt looked past Chance and saw a bald wrinkled head peeking through the back entrance of the teepee. Chance flicked his wrist and his thumb tossed the coin high into the air. "Call it, Marshal!"

Wyatt stared at the back entrance. "Hans," he said.

"Hans?" Chance repeated in puzzlement.

The little hunchback sped behind him and swung the blunt end of his tomahawk at the back of Chance's knee. Chance bellowed in pain, and his legs buckled beneath him. Cheyanne pushed herself away from him and kicked the gun out of his hand. As he knelt on the ground he watched the coin flip in front of his eyes and land in the dirt below him. He heard the clicking hammer of Wyatt's revolver. Lifting his head, he stared down the barrel of the Marshal's pistol.

"So long, Marshal," Chance sighed.

Without a moment's hesitation, Wyatt pulled the trigger…

BANG!

Chapter 16

OUR NEW HOME

"Are we close?" Hans asked.

"It's just up here," Juan replied. "Right, Doli?"

"That's right, we should be very close now." She held tightly onto Hans as he steered the small mule they rode atop. She pointed in front of him, "Just at the end of the horizon."

"This is close to where we first saw each other, isn't that right, Juan?" asked the red-haired girl, clinging tightly to Juan's waist.

"It was just a few miles south of here, Annie. Closer to my old home where we'll stop by next. After we take care of Ashkii." Juan reached back and patted his friend's body, which was wrapped up in blankets and slung over his horse.

After a couple hours of riding they made it to the Navajo camp and were greeted by Lady Kai. The sun was beginning to set, and the sky was painted in an orange and purple hue that reminded Juan of his father. Juan hopped off his horse then helped Annie down. He pulled Ashkii's body off the back of the horse and followed behind Kai. There was a large bonfire in the middle of the camp, with the entire Navajo tribe already gathered around it. Two medicine men approached Juan, and he handed them Ashkii's body.

"I'm sorry, Kai."

With a grimace, she laid her hand on Juan's shoulder. "Thank you for bringing him home. I always hoped that one day he would make it back. And I believe he is now worthy of this being his resting place."

The medicine men conducted the ceremony as they sent off Ashkii into the next life. Doli sat beside Kai, and they cried all through the night. When morning came, Juan, Hans, and Annie said goodbye to Doli and Kai before they departed.

"Where are you off to now, Coyote?" Kai asked.

"Back to the depot, to send off some friends," he said.

"You mean family," Hans corrected.

"Si, family!" He helped Annie onto their horse and hopped on after. Before taking off he turned back to Kai and said, "Gracias."

"Come back soon, Coyote."

He kicked the sides of his horse and they sped off toward the depot.

Wyatt and Richard hammered away at some lumber as they finished making a large wagon. They filled it with more wood and food from the depot. Meanwhile Felina was on the train with Misa and Dakota, brushing their hair and fitting them with new clothes she had made for them.

"Now, are you sure you don't want to come with us?" she asked.

"We're sure," Misa insisted, "we want to help Juan, and one day we can come see you."

Felina looked out the window and saw a cloud of dust moving closer. "They're back!" She hurried out of the train just in time to greet Juan and Hans as they came to a stop outside the depot.

"Juan!" Felina called. He jumped down from his horse and they embraced like they hadn't seen each other in years.

"We've only been gone for a day, Felina," Juan laughed.

"Oh, I wish you would change your mind and come with Wyatt and me."

"I'll make it out there someday, but someone must stay and fix the current state of the Heart. By the time Hans and I have things cleaned up, I'm sure you and Wyatt will have Paradise looking like a real home."

"That we will," said Wyatt. He walked up behind Juan and wrapped him in his arms. "Everything went well with the Navajo?"

"As well as they could for a funeral," Juan sighed.

"Well, he's home now." Wyatt looked over Juan's shoulder at Annie, who was still sitting on the horse. "How was your first trip with the gal?"

Juan blushed and punched Wyatt in the arm. "Not as exciting as the first couple of times we met, thank God."

"That's good. So, what's your plan then?"

"Well," Juan started, "the Apache are the closest. I think we'll go check them out first and see how the tribe is holding up. Kai and the Navajo offered to assist them, so hopefully they can come to an agreement about who'll run the land. Then we'll move east and make our way around until we have mended the Western Heart."

Wyatt's heart filled with pride as he listened to his young friend speak. He already seemed to be doing more than Wyatt had ever hoped to do as a marshal. Wyatt reached down and unpinned the star off his pocket. He flipped it around in his fingers for a minute, then handed it over to Juan. "Take it," he said, "it will help."

Juan grabbed the star and pinned it to his shawl just over his heart. Wyatt looked over at Hans, and he reached into his back pocket, pulling out another, dirtier star, and tossed it to the hunchback. "Don't end up like the last guy who wore that, ok?"

"I wouldn't dream of it!" Hans laughed. He hopped off his mule and walked over to the wagon where Richard continued to work. "How is it coming along?" he asked.

Richard wiped the beads of sweat off his brow and grinned through his thick beard. "Well, the Marshal isn't any help, that's for sure," Richard laughed.

"He is going to need the help trying to build a new home in a strange land," Hans said. "Luckily you have done that once before."

"Building a home in Paradise seems like the best way to spend the final stretch of my life. Are you sure you don't want to join us?"

Hans nodded his head. "If God wanted us to stay together for our entire lives, then he would have never sent us Juan. My place is with him, working to mend His garden."

"Very well," Richard sighed, impressed with Hans' drive, but saddened to know they would be apart.

"When we make it back to the village I'll be sure to tell the others of our adventure! And maybe bring them to Paradise to see you and the others," Hans exclaimed.

"That would be nice," Richard said. Then he dropped to his knees and hugged Hans tightly. "Be safe, my boy."

Hans returned his embrace and assured him he would be.

Juan couldn't help but tear up at the two's exchange. He turned to Wyatt and asked, "Are you sure this place exists?"

"I checked through the old history logs in the depot's computer. It's right by the new coast a ways west of here. It should take us a couple of weeks to make it, but it's there. I even have a route mapped out."

"I'll come see you there soon. Once things are made right here."

"Take your time, Coyote. We'll be there."

Wyatt finished loading up the wagon, and he hooked up Peaches and Richard's horse, then he helped Felina into the back. Richard started to climb up the side of the wagon, but was stopped by Juan, who was tugging on his coat.

"Richard, thank you," said Juan.

Richard paused and leaned down from the wagon. "No, Juan, thank you. You helped restore my faith, and for that I am eternally grateful."

Felina rushed to the side of the wagon and bent over the side, nearly falling out. She grabbed her brother and kissed him on the cheek. "Adiós, Juanito!"

"Adios, Felina," he held her tightly and kissed her on the forehead. "Adios, Wyatt!"

"Till next time, partner," Wyatt tipped his hat and whipped the reins. The horses and wagon trundled off toward the western horizon.

Annie walked up behind Juan and wrapped her hands around his waist. Hans stepped up beside him while Misa and Dakota followed. "Where are we off to next, Marshal?" Hans asked.

Juan turned to the others and adjusted the star that was pinned to his shawl. "We're off to make this our new home."

PARADISE

Wyatt sat with his feet in the cold glassy water of the lake outside his cabin. His fingers wiggled into the soft sand, and he spread the dirt around in his palms. "Beautiful day, don't you think, Deacon?" But the wooden cross he sat beside didn't respond. He heard some light splashes in the distance as a small boy ran along the shore in rolled-up slacks.

"Ricardo!" Felina shouted, "You're going to ruin your slacks!" Wyatt laughed and laid back in the dirt. Felina stood above him with her hands on her hips, looking oh so discontent. "And you think getting dirt all over your new poncho is funny?"

Wyatt raised his hands above his head and grabbed Felina's ankles. He tripped her, but he made sure to catch her before she hit the ground. "I think it's the funniest thing I have ever seen." He rolled on top of her, spreading dirt across her colorful dress. She couldn't help but laugh as they tumbled, and couldn't help but kiss him as they stared into each other's eyes.

"I always knew you would come back to me," she said. "But I never dreamed that we would actually find this place."

Wyatt looked around at the lush grassy lands. There were palms that stood tall around the edges of the lake, and they shaded their house and dropped sweet fruits from the tops of their trunks.

"At one point it was a dead sea, void of all life," Wyatt started. He watched with a smile as little Ricardo rushed toward them. "But not anymore. Now it's abundant with new life."

"Mama! Papa!" Ricardo laughed as he jumped on top of Wyatt and Felina.

"Hola, Ricardo," Felina chuckled.

The little boy pointed his finger out toward the horizon. "Who are they, Papa?"

Wyatt turned over and squinted his eyes. He saw two men on horseback riding toward them. One was small and wore a colorful shawl. The other wore a black leather hat, dark brown shawl, and a silver star pinned to his chest.

"Do you know them, Papa? Mama?"

Wyatt smiled and nodded his head. "Yes, son, we sure do."

THE END

Made in the USA
Middletown, DE
16 January 2023